DANGEROUS DECEPTION

Praise for the Beautiful Creatures series:

'Watch out *Twilight* and *The Hunger Games*' *Guardian*

'This novel has been creating *Twilight*-level buzz' *Teen Vogue*

'A headlong read from start to finish' *She*

'*Beautiful Creatures* is gorgeously crafted,
atmospheric and original. I devoured it'
Melissa Marr, *New York Times* bestselling author

'A lush Southern gothic whose memorable, eccentric
characters draw you into their captivating world'
Holly Black, *New York Times* bestselling author
of The Spiderwick Chronicles

'A hauntingly delicious dark fantasy, a cast of
fascinating characters, a rich Gothic setting'
Cassandra Clare, *New York Times* bestselling
author of The Mortal Instruments series

Kami Garcia and Margaret Stohl are longtime friends and co-authors of the #1 *New York Times* bestselling Beautiful Creatures series. The first book in the series, *Beautiful Creatures*, is now a major motion picture.

In addition to writing together, they have written solo series: The Legion series by Kami Garcia includes the instant *New York Times* bestsellers *Unbreakable* and *Unmarked;* and the Icons series by Margaret Stohl includes *Icons*, which is currently in development as a feature film, and *Idols*.

Kami and Margaret invite you to visit them online at www.kamigarcia.com and www.margaret-stohl.com.

Books by Kami Garcia and Margaret Stohl

The Beautiful Creatures series
Beautiful Creatures
Beautiful Darkness
Beautiful Chaos
Beautiful Redemption

Digital novellas
Dream Dark
Dangerous Dream

The Dangerous Creatures series
Dangerous Creatures
Dangerous Deception

BY

KAMI GARCIA &
MARGARET STOHL

PENGUIN BOOKS

PENGUIN BOOKS

UK | USA | Canada | Ireland | Australia
India | New Zealand | South Africa

Penguin Books is part of the Penguin Random House group of companies
whose addresses can be found at global.penguinrandomhouse.com.

penguin.com

First published in the USA by Little, Brown and Company,
a division of Hachette Book Group, Inc. 2015
Published simultaneously in Great Britain by Penguin Books 2015
001

Printed in Great Britain by Clays Ltd, St Ives plc

A CIP catalogue record for this book is available from the British Library

ISBN: 978-0-141-35412-5

For Nox & Floyd,
because it isn't easy loving someone
who doesn't belong to you.
And for our readers,
who love them all the same.

The depth of darkness to which
you can descend and still live is an exact measure
of the height to which you can aspire to reach.

—Pliny the Elder

BEFORE

Link

Love is ten kinds a crazy, right?

Especially when you meet the person you want to spend the rest of your life with when you're still in high school? The girl who is gonna elbow her way into more chapters of your autobiography than your folks, your car, and your best friend? The one who's got Satan on her speed dial, at least accordin' to all the parents in the Stonewall Jackson PTA.

Ridley Duchannes is every mother's nightmare—and a whole different kinda nightmare for their sons. Let me put it to you this way: If you can get away, run. Don't walk. Because once you're exposed, you'll never get a Siren outta your head.

If they ever make a vaccine for Ridley Duchannes, I'll be first in line.

But once you've been exposed, things get a lot more complicated. Rid's like those killer viruses they're always talkin' about on the Discovery Channel. She changes everything—including you.

What I'm tryin' to say is, it's too late for me. I'm headed down a one-way street, with no stoplights and no brakes. The craziest part is that I don't even *wanna* turn back, and you wouldn't, either. You don't need a Caster mood ring to tell you that.

Because there are three kinds of girls in the world.

Good girls.

Bad girls.

And Ridley Duchannes.

Rid's in a category all her own—and trust me, she's earned it. She'll let you peek in the window, right before she slams the door in your face. She does what she wants, says what she wants, and lovesick guys like me still write songs about her.

Sure, she scammed me into comin' to New York with her and joinin' a Dark Caster band. She even pretended we were goin' there to make all my dreams come true, instead a settling her debt with Lennox Gates. Not every girl bets her boyfriend's future in a Caster card game, that's for sure. Like I said, ten kinds a crazy.

And the part that's even crazier? How much your life feels like it's over when she's not around to wreck it anymore.

But I'm gettin' ahead of myself.

It all started with a fire.

CHAPTER 1: NOX

Ring of Fire

Nox woke up on the floor in the back of the SUV. The last thing he remembered was the car driving away from what was left of his club Sirene…before Silas' thugs started beating on him and he blacked out.

Not that it mattered.

Between all the smoke he'd inhaled inside the burning club and the two Dark Casters kicking the crap out of him, he wasn't sure how much more he could take. Mortals weren't the only ones who had their limits.

The car rolled to a stop, and a moment later, the sunlight blinded Nox as the driver opened the door.

Silas Ravenwood climbed out and stood over him, smoking a cigar. "I'd like to say it's been fun, kid. But mostly, you've been a huge waste of my time." He flicked his cigar at Nox, missing his face by just inches. “And a waste of a Caster. Not that I’d expect much more from the son of a whore.”

“Good one. Never heard that one before.”

Silas punched him in the face, sending a spray of blood across his cheekbone.

Nox clenched his fists, but he didn’t move. There was no point anymore. Ridley was safely gone, and he was going to take his beating like a man. He had known this would be coming when he set fire to Sirene instead of delivering Ridley and the quarter Incubus to Silas Ravenwood as promised.

But I’ll kill you one day, Silas. I swear to God. Then you can rot in the Otherworld with Abraham.

Silas stood in the shadow of the alley. “See you in the next life, kid. It’s sure as hell your last day in this one.” He slammed the door, and the driver pulled away from the curb.

Once Silas was gone, the real beatings started. Enough blows to the head, and Nox barely remembered his own name. Even worse, he had no idea where he was, or where they were taking him.

The river was his best guess. Maybe they’d toss him in like a sack of kittens.

I’d be lucky to get off that easy.

Then the SUV stopped at a red light.

Nox could see the cloud of smoke above the club in the distance. He was still staring at the smoke, dazed, when the side window next to him shattered.

A hand the size of a dinner plate plunged through the glass.

Sampson dragged one of Silas’ men out through the window and unlocked the door before the driver even realized what was happening. Instead of hitting the gas, the idiot came out and tried to take on close to seven feet of angry Darkborn.

Bad move, big guy.

Silas' other lackey was still in the back with Nox, and he jumped out to help. Sampson hurled him headfirst into a sign, leaving the guy's face almost as cut up as Sampson's hand. Nox crawled out of the car and stumbled to his feet, but the fight was already over. The driver and one of Silas' thugs were knocked out cold, and Sampson finished off the second guy, who was bleeding under the sign, with one hard stomp from his size fifteen Red Wings.

The Darkborn grabbed Nox by the arm and shoved him into the passenger seat of the SUV. "You're welcome. Now get your ass in the car."

"Sam, look at your hand." Nox could barely get the words out, but he pointed at the gashes slicing through his friend's skin and the blood running down his arm.

Sampson yanked his sleeveless T-shirt over his head and tugged down the ripped Sex Pistols one he was wearing underneath. "Wrap it around my fingers, but not too tight. I'll take care of it. After we get out of here."

"I owe you one," Nox said as he picked the slivers of glass out of Sampson's hand with a pair of tweezers. He had so much gauze stuffed up his bloody nose that he wasn't sure if Sampson could understand what he was saying.

After they'd ditched Silas' men, Nox had bought a first-aid kit from the nearest Duane Reade drugstore. Now they were parked in a seedy long-term lot near Penn Station, and it was the best Nox had felt all day. He could almost see out of one eye, and Silas' thugs hadn't knocked out any of his teeth.

It's the little things.

"One?" Sampson winced as Nox pulled out a big piece of glass. "You owe me three or four by now, boss," the huge Darkborn said.

"You don't have to call me that anymore. The club is gone, and opening another one would be like sending Silas an invitation to kill me."

"You mean *another* invitation?" Sampson didn't smile.

Nox ignored him, tossing a piece of glass on the dashboard. "So I hope you didn't risk your life for a job."

Sampson's jaw tightened. "There are other cities. And if you think I saved your ass and stole one of Silas Ravenwood's cars because of some crappy job, you don't know me very well."

Nox felt like a jerk. "Sorry, Sam."

"Forget it. You're just lucky those guys didn't kill you before I got there."

Nox knew Sampson was right, but he didn't feel lucky. Alive was different from lucky. A guy had to be pretty unlucky to lose the only girl he'd ever cared about.

Nox tipped the bottle of peroxide over Sampson's gnarled hand. "I think it's all out."

"Just wrap it up," Sampson said. "Darkborns heal pretty fast."

Nox wound a whole roll of gauze around his friend's hand until it looked like a prizefighter's.

Sampson pointed at his face. "You better clean out that cut on your cheek, stitch it up. Pretty boys don't look so pretty with scars."

"Yeah?" Nox flipped open the mirror on the visor and cringed. He looked like crap. Silas' punch had left a gash across his cheek. "I don't know, I think I look good. All things considered."

"Good for a hamburger, maybe. A rare one. Now sew that thing shut." Sampson screwed the top off a bottle of rubbing alcohol. "You're out of peroxide. Time to man up."

Nox found a needle in the first-aid kit and poured alcohol all over it. He was looking forward to the pain.

But the moment Sampson flicked on a lighter and Nox saw the flame, he felt something else. The alcohol stung Nox's skin, and the world faded away....

The sight of a flame triggered Nox's Sight, and the vision hit him all at once.

The fire...

Ridley's screams...

The fear.

This time he heard the impact.

Metal crushing.

Brakes squealing.

It was the last sound that hit him like a kick in the gut. A song—"Stairway to Heaven."

Nox had seen hints of this before in his visions, but the details had never been clear enough. It had always been a vague future. But it had become a reality.

This was the outcome he'd been desperate to avoid. If only he'd put the pieces together sooner.

So he hadn't saved Ridley from dying in a fire. He'd saved her from dying in one particular fire—the one at Sirene—only to let her die in another, the one at the car wreck. He'd done everything he could to keep her from meeting the fate he'd seen laid out for her in his dreams, and he had still failed.

I gave up too easily. I shouldn't have let her leave with that idiot hybrid. I should've asked her to choose me.

He'd sacrificed everything to protect Ridley—his club, his safety, even his heart. And it had been pointless. He hadn't protected her from anything.

Then I pushed her right into another guy's arms.

I thought he could protect her. I thought he was better for her. Safer.

Who's the idiot now?

"What's wrong, Nox?" Sampson asked.

"Everything." Nox could barely move his jaw, but he forced the words out somehow. "She's in trouble, Sam. We've gotta go. Now."

Finding the location of the crash was the easy part; in Nox's vision, the flames were already melting the road signs, which meant he'd gotten a good look at them in the process. "Hurry, Sam. We don't have much time."

What if we're already too late? Nox thought.

Nox stared out the window in a daze, trying to blot out the images of the fire and the sound of Ridley's screams. He pressed against his stitches, trying to feel the pain. At least his pain distracted him from hers.

She's not dead. I'd know. I would've felt it.

Right?

He pressed harder.

Sampson didn't say a word, but the speedometer inched up past ninety, and he covered a hundred miles in less than an hour.

By the time Nox spotted the cloud of black smoke, he was practically jumping out of his skin. The wind blew the dirty air through the SUV's broken window as they approached the flashing lights—two police cars, a fire engine, and an ambulance on the shoulder of the highway—behind a perimeter of orange cones and flares. One of the cops stood in the road, waving cars past the crash site. Traffic slowed as drivers rubbernecked while passing the wreckage.

Nox scanned the area for any sign of Ridley or a blue and white medical examiner's van.

It's not here. Not yet.

Sampson shook his head. "It looks bad."

Up close, it looked even worse. What was left of Link's piece-of-crap car was crushed like a tin can, and firefighters were hosing down the half-melted body of the Beater.

As Sampson guided the SUV toward the shoulder, Nox jumped out and bolted for the ambulance. He held his breath when he glanced at the wreckage. No bodies or body bags. Just a lot of charred and banged-up metal. Smoldering upholstery. Shattered glass.

Where is she?

Two paramedics were standing around behind the ambulance.

"Is she okay?" Nox asked, out of breath.

One of them looked up at him, confused. "Excuse me?"

"The girl in the car. Is she okay?" Nox repeated.

The paramedics exchanged a strange look. "There was no

one in the car when we got here. It was a hit-and-run. The police checked the area, but they couldn't find any sign of the driver. Do you know whose car this is?"

"Yeah. It belongs to this guy we know," Nox said as Sampson caught up with him.

One of the paramedics stepped back at the sight of the Darkborn. It was everyone's reaction to Sampson. At over six foot five, he looked like a linebacker.

"The police are trying to figure out what happened to the driver," the paramedic said. "They'll probably want to talk to you guys." He took a closer look at Nox. "What happened to your face?"

Nox stiffened. "I got in a fight."

The paramedic looked at him skeptically.

"More than one," Nox added. "What are you, my mother?"

The paramedic glanced over at the nearest police car. "Wait here."

The moment the guy turned his back on them, Sampson shoved Nox in the direction of the SUV. "We need to bail. As much as I don't like Mortals, I hate cops even more."

Nox agreed, and after seeing the wreckage, part of him was relieved Ridley wasn't there.

She's not dead. There would be a body.

But another part of him had a bad feeling.

Don't fool yourself. Nobody could walk away from an accident like that. The Beater looks like a burnt pretzel.

Lennox Gates' feelings were never simple when it came to Ridley Duchannes. There was no reason to expect them to be any less complex now. He climbed back into the car and slammed the door. "We need to figure out where she is. Fast."

"I'll work on that as soon as I get us out of here." Sampson threw the SUV into reverse, guided the car off the shoulder of the road, and flipped a U-turn. He waited until the flashing lights were out of sight before he hit the gas.

"Relax. It's not a high-speed chase." Nox grabbed the door.

The Darkborn glanced at the rearview mirror. "Not yet."

"We haven't done anything wrong," Nox said, though he didn't sound convinced.

"Yeah? That's not how it looks." Sampson kept his eyes on the road. "My hand is bleeding. The window is shattered. And you look like you lost a cage fight."

"Think it's possible she walked away from the crash?" Nox asked, hating how desperate he sounded. He didn't want to say the words out loud.

She's alive. She has to be.

"I don't know." Sampson seemed doubtful. "The back of the car was crushed." He glanced at Nox. "But yeah, anything's possible."

As Sampson turned back onto the highway, Nox noticed something on the side of the road. Something small, and furry, and out of place.

An animal.

A cat.

Lucille Ball. She was sitting on the shoulder, as if she was waiting for them.

"Pull over. That's Link's cat."

"I wonder how she got all the way out here." Sampson stopped the car a few feet away from Lucille.

The cat didn't move until they both got out. Then she trotted off into the trees.

Nox took off after her. "I think she wants us to follow her."

Sampson shook his head. "It looks more like she's running away from us."

"But toward what?" Nox asked. Ridley had told Nox a story about how Lucille had practically led Rid and her friends to her cousin Lena when she was missing once. He had no idea how much of it was true, but that cat was definitely different.

Lucille scampered ahead, stopping every now and then to make sure they were still behind her. Nox wasn't that interested in chasing mangy cats through the bushes, but he followed her anyway.

If that stupid cat was in the car with them... she could be leading us to Rid.

Nox wasn't so sure when the cat led them through a cluster of trees and he saw Link slumped against a trunk ahead of them. The ridiculous spiked blond hair and threadbare Black Sabbath T-shirt were unmistakable. Above Link, the branches were cracked and broken as if he'd hit every one of them before he finally made it to the ground.

Headfirst, knowing him.

"What are you doing out here, Link?" Sampson asked as they made their way through the brush.

Link barely moved. His skin was smudged with black smoke and ash, and one side of his shirt was singed above the burns running down his arm.

Nox leaned closer and grabbed a handful of Link's ripped shirt. "Hey. Wake up."

Confused didn't begin to describe the expression on Link's face. He opened and closed his eyes, shaking his head at the sight of Nox. "Aw, great. I'm in Hell. My mom was right."

"You're not in Hell. You're in New Jersey." Nox squatted in front of him. "Where's Ridley?"

Link jerked his head up at the mention of her name. "Wait. You don't know where she is, either?"

Nox stiffened. It was the million-dollar question, and Link didn't have the answer any more than he did.

"We were hoping you knew," Sampson said.

Link rubbed his eyes, wincing as he lifted his arm. "It all happened so fast. 'Stairway to Heaven' came on the radio. That's all I remember, until this black truck ran a red light and plowed right into the Beater." His face clouded over as he realized what he was saying. "Aw, man. The Beater."

"Mangled," Nox said, with a shred of satisfaction.

Sampson nodded. "You don't want to know."

Link pressed his hands against his temples. "The driver didn't even try to swerve out of the way. It was like he was headin' right for us." He rubbed his eyes like he was fighting the worst headache of his life. "The only thing I remember after that was the sound of metal crunchin' and Ridley screamin'. There was so much smoke I couldn't see her. I kept callin' her name, but she didn't answer. Then the Beater caught on fire."

Sampson examined Link's eyes. "Do you remember how you got here? You're pretty far from the crash site. I doubt you walked."

Link squinted, as if he was trying to piece everything together in his mind. "I didn't walk. I Ripped."

"And you didn't take Ridley with you?" Nox snapped. He didn't bother to hide the rage in his voice.

Why did she leave with this clown in the first place?

Link shook his head. "It wasn't like that. I reached out for her, but she wasn't in the passenger seat. The fire kept gettin' bigger, and then my shirt started burnin'. I don't know what happened. I wasn't tryin' to Rip, but the next thing I knew, I was out here."

Sampson glanced at Nox. "I bet it was some kind of defense mechanism. An Incubus fight or flight response."

"A cowardly one," Nox muttered. "All you had to do was get her out of here. You had her back for, what, two hours? And this was the best you could manage?"

"It's not like I had a choice." Link was trying to stay focused, but his vision was fuzzy. He fell back, pushing his hands against his temples.

Nox grabbed his arm and yanked hard. There it was. The Binding Ring—the one that should've been going off like a three-alarm fire.

It was completely dark now.

They all stared at it in horror. Even Link looked like he wanted to chuck it in the bushes.

"Maybe it's broken."

Nox's voice was hard. "Maybe you were just born an idiot."

Link rolled to one side. "I was right the first time. If I've gotta listen to you, Rich Boy, I might as well be in Hell." He winced, sounding more miserable than pained.

"This is real productive," Sampson said. Now everyone was annoyed.

Even though the hybrid had ruined everything, Nox knew it wasn't that simple.

Link didn't have a choice, but I did. I chose not to fight. I chose to give in—to give up everything so she'd have a better shot at being happy.

Or at least staying alive.

Nox sighed and bent down in front of Link. "Think. Do you remember anything else? Were there any other cars around, or people who might have witnessed the accident?"

Link shook his head. "No. The only car I saw was the truck that hit us. It wasn't a pickup like the junkers folks drive back home in Gatlin. It was one of those fancy black Raptors with the big tires and everything."

A black Raptor.

Sampson stared at Nox. "You know what that means, right?"

Nox nodded, not trusting himself to speak.

"What am I missin'?" Link asked, pushing himself off the ground.

Sampson grabbed his arm and pulled him up, so fast that Link's legs dangled above the ground for a second. "Do you remember if the truck had a huge bird on the hood?"

"Yeah," Link answered. "Full-on Big Bird sized. How'd you know?"

Sampson dropped him. Link stumbled, like his knees were going to buckle, and Nox grabbed him before he could fall.

"It's a raven." Nox tried not to think about all the things that might be happening to Ridley right now. "It was one of Silas Ravenwood's trucks."

CHAPTER 2: LINK

Don't Know What You Got (Till It's Gone)

Silas Ravenwood. The thought sent Link reeling. It was a punch to the gut multiplied by a hundred.

What if she didn't make it?

Don't do this to me, Rid. I just got you back.

"I'm the one they wanted. This is all my fault." Link couldn't bring himself to look at Sampson and Nox as they searched the area. Link hadn't been this banged up since he stopped being a hundred percent Mortal. But he felt even worse on the inside, like his heart was limping, too.

All he could think about was Ridley. He slipped his hand out of his pocket and stared at the lifeless ring on his finger.

Where are you, Rid?

"You're right. Your fault. No one's arguing with you," Nox said, walking ahead of them. He didn't bother to turn around.

Link ignored him. "She must've made it out of the car. Like I said, I reached for her and she wasn't there."

"Or whoever was driving Silas Ravenwood's truck grabbed her," Nox snapped. "Did you think of that?"

Link frowned. "Are you sure it was Silas' car?"

"Everyone knows that truck," Sampson said.

Link stopped walking. "I'm the one who killed Abraham Ravenwood, not Rid. His psychotic grandson shoulda taken me."

"Finally we agree on something," Nox said.

Link's expression hardened. "You can stop actin' like you're a big hero. The way I see it, we both let her down. At least I'm man enough to admit it."

Nox's eyes narrowed. "I wasn't the one behind the wheel."

Link stepped forward, moving closer to Nox. "You might as well have been."

Nox's hands curled into fists. "You have no idea how much I wish I was. Then I could've done something. Unlike some of us."

Sampson stepped between them. "You two can fight it out after we find her."

"After we find her, I'm taking her somewhere safe where you'll never see her again." Nox didn't take his eyes off Link.

Link barely kept himself from punching the guy in the face. "I'd like to see you try."

"And I'd like to beat the crap out of you both. Unfortunately, as Mick Jagger would say, you can't always get what you want." Sam shoved them both. "Now move."

Link didn't care if Lennox Gates had saved their lives at Sirene. As far as he was concerned, the guy was still a tool. Another piece of Underground club trash who was too rich and too slick for anybody's good. Not to mention the other thing.

A tool who spent the last few months tryin' to steal my girlfriend. Who only wants to find her so he can steal her again.

If she's even still alive.

Link tried not to think that way. Especially since now the three of them were holed up in a diner off the highway, doing their best to figure out a way to find Rid before they killed each other. Only exhaustion had prevented it from happening so far.

The three of them—four, if you counted Lucille—had searched the woods for hours, looking for any sign of Ridley, even though the odds seemed pretty high that Silas or one of his thugs had taken her.

Or her body.

That was the part no one said out loud.

The situation sucked.

I suck.

Link didn't have to say that out loud, either. He pushed the fries he'd never consider eating around on his plate. Mortal food tasted like cardboard, another downside of being a quarter Incubus. Not that he would've been able to eat at a time like this. "You really think Silas might have her?"

Nox didn't respond right away. Instead, he stared into the coffee cup in his hand.

A bad sign.

"If she's still alive," Nox said finally.

"Don't say that." Link started to lunge across the table, but Sampson caught him. "Don't ever say that again. She's alive. We just have to find her."

"Your ring—" Nox stared at it.

"Is busted." Link glared.

"Grow up," Nox shot back. "It's called reality. We let him take her."

Link lunged again, and Sampson picked him up by the scruff of his neck, as if the hulking hybrid was a harmless kitten.

"We don't know anything for sure yet." Sampson hauled Link back down to his seat. "And I'm not sure Ridley Duchannes ever *let* anyone do anything. So let's all relax. We're not gonna figure this out if we can't work together."

The bells on the door of the diner chimed and Necro and Floyd walked in, scanning the restaurant. Sampson had called them as soon as he'd sat down. The girls had been laying low in a crappy Motel 6 outside Brooklyn, waiting for Sam to rescue Nox from Silas' thugs so the band could head out to LA as planned. When Sam called to tell them about the accident, Link's bandmates hadn't wasted any time getting there.

Floyd's stringy blond hair swung over her shoulders as she searched for Link. When she saw him, her face broke into a thousand pieces, like she was about to start smiling or sobbing. Link couldn't tell which. She practically ran toward their booth, in her holey jeans and faded Pink Floyd *Dark Side of the Moon* concert tee, and caught Link around the neck in a huge hug. "You okay? We were so worried."

Link squeezed her tight. He knew Floyd still had a thing for him, but at that moment, he was so happy to see his friends that he didn't care. At least she didn't blame him for everything that had happened, like some people.

Myself included, he thought miserably.

Someone coughed, and Necro stood behind Floyd, flashing Link a pierced smile. Her short blue faux-hawk seemed bluer and her futuristic leather jacket looked even more Mad Max than usual. Maybe everything was a little sharper after you'd dodged death.

"Hey, man." Link reached to hug her, but she held up her fist instead.

"Pound it," she said, smiling.

Same old Nec. Thank god they're here.

Necro squeezed in next to Sampson, across from Link and Floyd. Nox was sitting on the other side of Sam, and the Darkborn took up more than his share of the booth.

"That was fast," Sampson said.

Necro nodded. "Hopped in the first cab we could find."

"A fifty-buck cab ride. Don't act like we don't love you." Floyd turned red as she stumbled over the words.

"And don't act like you actually paid the driver," Nox countered.

"So what happened?" Necro asked.

"Silas Ravenwood—or someone drivin' one of his trucks. That's what happened." Link shrugged. "The Beater took her last beatin', and Rid—" His voice faltered. He couldn't tell the story again.

Not without puking.

Floyd squeezed his shoulder. "Sampson gave us the highlights on the phone. He said Ridley's missing." Even though she had feelings for Link, she almost sounded sorry.

"We looked everywhere, and there was no sign of her," Nox said. "Our guess is Silas has her, but we don't know where he took her."

Sampson chugged what had to be his fifth glass of milk. The guy ate more than Link used to when he was still a Mortal. It was hard to know how things worked with Darkborns, since there had never been any until the Order of Things was broken last year. Everyone was still figuring it out, including Sampson. "Silas is the head of the Syndicate. He can't run an operation like that without a place to meet his scumbag associates. It's not like he can rent out office space."

"The Syndicate?" Link had never heard of it before. "As in a *crime* syndicate?"

"The Underground has even more organized crime than the Mortal world," Floyd said. "Gambling, drugs, power trafficking—you name it. And the Syndicate runs most of it."

"So you're sayin' Silas is the head a the Mob?" The thought made Link nervous. "You mean like Don Corleone, that fat guy from *The Godfather*?"

Sampson shoved the empty glass across the table. "The Syndicate makes the Mob look like a charity organization."

Link almost made a joke about his mom and her cutthroat Daughters of the American Revolution meetings; the DAR could give the Mob a run for its money, any day of the week. But then he remembered Rid wasn't there, which meant there was no one around to laugh at his Gatlin jokes.

Nothing's the same without her.

Then another thought crossed his mind.

The DAR. My mom.

Link bolted upright in his seat. "Holy crap. I've gotta call my mom."

"You didn't call her yet?" Sam shook his head. "The cops probably traced the license plates on the Beater by now. I bet they already called her."

Link dialed his home number as fast as he could. His mom

was going to kill him for not calling. The preacher and all her DAR friends were probably already at the house in one of their prayer circles.

His mom picked up on the first ring, and Link could tell from all the sniffling that she'd been crying.

"Ma? It's Link. I mean, Wesley—"

"Wesley!" He heard a muffled sound like she was covering the mouthpiece. "It's Wesley. The Good Lord Almighty answered our prayers."

Link could imagine the chorus of hallelujahs, in between big bites of *I Told You That Boy Was Trouble Casserole* and *Hope Your Son Doesn't Smoke Pot Pie.*

A moment later, his mom was back on the line. "What happened? The police called and told me they found your car totaled on the highway, but you were missing. *Up North.*" She said the words the way someone else would say "on the *Titanic*." Then she went on. "Are you all right? Do you have amnesia? Lord, please don't let him have amnesia."

"Calm down, Mom. If I had amnesia, I wouldn't have remembered our phone number. I'm okay. I wasn't even in the car." Link had only come up with that detail a moment ago, and he was pretty proud of himself. "It was a mix-up. Somebody stole the Beater, but I hadn't reported it yet, so when they got to the crash site, they thought I was the one drivin'."

"And you're just calling now?" The anger was already brewing in his mom's voice. "Do you have any conception of how worried I've been? I already called old Buck Petty and asked him to load up his hounds!"

Link sighed, rubbing his spiky hair.

"What were you gonna do? Drive down to Georgia Redeemer

with a truck fulla bloodhounds?" Link was proud of himself for remembering the name of the college he was supposed to be attending.

"That is what *good mothers* do when their sons are missing, Wesley Jefferson Lincoln! I have been absolutely *beside* myself. Did you forget how to call collect? We practiced before you left."

"I'm sorry, Mom. I just found out what happened a little while ago, and I can't talk 'cause the police need me to fill out a report." And his mom thought all those hours he'd spent watching *Matlock* were a waste of time.

"Why would someone steal a car from Georgia Redeemer and drive it all the way to the New Jersey Turnpike?"

"I don't know, but you'd better activate the phone tree and call everybody before the ladies in the DAR drive to Georgia and start nailin' my picture to telephone poles."

"You'd better call me back later, Wesley," Link's mother said under her breath. "This conversation isn't over."

"Okay, Mom. Gotta go. I'm losin' ya." Link crumpled a napkin into the speaker for good measure as he hung up.

Some things never changed, no matter how bad you wanted them to.

When he turned back to the table, everyone was trying not to smile—except the rich boy. "All right. All right. Show's over," Link said. "So where do we find Silas?"

"When Silas isn't throwing his weight around, he likes to lay low," Sampson said. "So he probably runs his operation from somewhere off the grid."

"That is about as low as things get," Necro said, turning to Nox. "You know Silas better than the rest of us. If he's got Ridley, where would he take her?"

"I don't know him as well as you think." Nox looked annoyed. "I'm not on his payroll. Silas comes around and causes trouble, then disappears. If he's using the Tunnels to get around, which I would, he could be anywhere." The Caster Tunnels ran below the Mortal world, and time and distance didn't follow the same rules down there.

Floyd looked at Nox. "And Abraham never mentioned anything back when"—she hesitated—"you knew him."

Nox rolled up the sleeves of what looked to Link like another one of his overpriced hipster shirts. "Like I said, I didn't spend a lot of time with him. Considering he pretty much kidnapped my mom. He only let me visit her a few times when I was young." Nox stopped talking and looked up at the ceiling. "The rest of the time he was in his labs."

I guess Fancy Pants has feelings, too, Link thought. Funny how it didn't make him want to punch the guy any less.

"Okay. At least that's something to go on. Did you ever hear him talk about the labs?" Sampson asked.

"Sure. Abraham was obsessed with them and his projects—that's what he called them. But he never invited me on a tour. They were somewhere behind his house."

"You know that for sure?" Link was suspicious.

"Like I said, I spent some time at his house. So did Silas. He even had his own room. I made the mistake of going in there by accident once." Nox shook his head, remembering. "I noticed this old record player in one of the bedrooms, and I wanted to see how the thing worked. Abraham was standing in the hall when I came back out. I'll never forget what he said. *I tolerate the way you sneak around my house, boy. But if Silas catches you near his room, he might think you're a thief and cut off your hand.*"

"Thanks for sharin' your creepy childhood memories," Link said. "That'll really help me sleep."

Nox frowned. "All I know is, Silas never stayed away from the labs for long, like his old man. If we find the labs, I bet we'll find him."

"So where's the house?" Sampson asked.

Nox shook his head. "I don't know. Abraham's men blindfolded me whenever they took me through the Tunnels to visit my mom. And the place is under some kind of Cloaking Cast, so Mortals can't see it."

Another dead end, Link thought. *Great.*

He considered calling Ethan, who was a thousand times smarter than him. But Ethan messing with Silas Ravenwood was a suicide mission. Link couldn't let anything happen to his best friend, not after Ethan had already died twice.

"There's gotta be someone who knows how to find those labs," Sampson said.

A thought formed in Link's mind slowly, like syrup pouring out of a bottle. "There is. The guy who grew up in them." He looked up. "John Breed."

"Who?" Sampson sounded suspicious, which seemed like part of his Darkborn nature.

"He's one a the good guys," Link said. "But he was a bad dude for a long time before that. So he's kind of my Dark Caster Wikipedia."

Nox crossed his arms. "I'm not sure a good guy is gonna cut it in this situation."

"He'll cut it and then some. Trust me."

Nox didn't respond.

"How can you be so sure?" Necro asked.

"Abraham Ravenwood engineered him in one of his creepy science labs." Link grinned. "And John's the one who helped me kill him."

"Are you saying one of Abraham's science experiments went rogue?" Sampson asked.

"We're talkin' Frankenstein meets RoboCop," Link said proudly.

Link skimmed over the details, like how John Breed was the hybrid Incubus who had bitten him, transforming him into the quarter Incubus he was today. It felt weird talking about it, like he was standing in front of everyone in his underwear. It was a hard thing to forgive, but it wasn't John's fault; Abraham had really screwed him up. Besides, John came through for him and his friends when it counted—and he and John killed Abraham together. It was the kind of bond you couldn't break.

Instead, Link told them how Abraham Ravenwood had handpicked John's parents, a Blood Incubus and an Evo—an Evo being a powerful Caster who can borrow the powers of any Caster they touch. Abraham used the two to create the perfect hybrid—with all the power of an Incubus and none of the weaknesses.

John could Travel and possessed the superstrength of a traditional Incubus, but he also had the powers of an Evo. And he could do the one thing no other Incubus could, except Link: John could walk in the sunlight.

If anyone could find the labs, it was John.

"So what are we waiting for?" Floyd asked. "Call him."

Link sighed. "He's not in Gatlin. He's at Oxford with his girlfriend, Liv."

"Again, it's called a phone." Floyd wasn't helping.

"You don't get it. Liv's this crazy genius who spends all her time in the library. She never carried a cell phone back in Gatlin, and John isn't any better now. I tried the number he gave me a buncha times, but it went straight to voice mail."

"Okay," Floyd said. "Then you'll have to Rip us all there."

"I don't fly." Sampson leaned back in the booth, arms crossed.

"Really?" Necro looked amused and nudged him playfully. "You?"

Sampson shoved his hands into his pockets, looking embarrassed.

"Rippin' isn't exactly the same as flyin'," Link said. "It feels more like gettin' sucked into a vacuum cleaner."

The Darkborn stared at him. "Even though you make it sound so appealing, I'll still pass."

"I hate to say it, but I'm with Sampson," Necro said. "Traveling in and out of my own body is bad enough."

Nox looked away. Necro had barely recovered from using her powers as a Necromancer to let Abraham take over her body and getting poisoned. Even now, Link noticed that the shadows under her eyes were darker than usual.

They've all been through enough, on account of Rid and me.

And Nox, too—he's caused his share of trouble.

But Floyd and Necro and Sampson? Think about how much easier their lives would be if Abraham and Silas had gotten what they wanted the first time around.

How can I ask them to sign up for round two of the Caster smackdown?

"I'll go," Floyd said right away.

Link was grateful, but he also felt guilty. "You don't have to do anything you don't wanna do." Like it or not, Link's heart had always belonged to one particular Siren, and he was going to find her, no matter what it took.

"Thanks for the clarification." Floyd smiled.

"I'm coming, too," Nox said from across the table.

"I don't think that's such a good idea," Link said. "John's kinda like Sammy Boy. It takes him a while to warm up to people. And you two don't have much in common."

"I'm going." Nox started to stand up, but Necro caught his arm.

"Let me put it another way," Link said. "You're not comin'. So unless you can Rip, you're outta luck. And if you really care about Ridley, you'll stop screwin' around and wastin' time."

The accusation seemed to hit a nerve, and Nox backed off.

"Don't worry, Nox." Floyd jumped in. "We'll find this John Breed guy."

Everyone followed Link outside. He led them behind the diner so he and Floyd could dematerialize without anyone noticing.

Link held out his hand. "Ready?"

Floyd nodded and took it.

Necro gave her a quick hug. "Good luck."

"We won't need it." By the time the words left Floyd's lips, they were gone.

CHAPTER 3: NOX

Street of Dreams

"Newark? As in New Jersey? I still don't get it. You know the Tri-State Area isn't our friend." Necro sounded annoyed as she followed Nox and Sam down the sidewalk. "Or am I the only one with the less-than-happy memories?"

"We'll be fine," Nox said. "Between the soccer moms and the Mortal Mafia, even Silas' thugs avoid the Garden State like the plague."

"Isn't it a little close to home, after the fire at Sirene?" Necro looked skeptical. "Because the place was swarming with Silas' men. I was there, in case you forgot."

"That's *why* Jersey's safe. The club is gone. Silas has bigger things to think about now."

Sampson stopped in front of a tacky condo complex made to look like a fake Tudor village. "The Essex House. This is April's place, or maybe June's. She's named after a month. That's about all I remember."

"Charming," Necro said. "It's nice to see how much your girlfriends mean to you."

"She wasn't my girlfriend," Sampson said, turning red. "Just someone I hooked up with once."

"As if that's better?" Necro raised an eyebrow.

"I don't care who she is as long as she left us the key," Nox said. After eavesdropping on Sampson's end of an awkward phone conversation, all he knew was that April or June—or whatever the girl's name was—seemed happy to let them hang out at her place in the hopes of reconnecting with Sampson.

Necro shook her head. "Have you ever had a relationship that lasted more than one night?" The Necromancer sounded like she was joking, but from the look on her face, she wasn't giving up until she got a real answer.

Sampson frowned. "Maybe I just haven't found the right girl."

"Keep telling yourself that," Nox said. "You still need to cover the other ten months in the year—why stop at April and June? There's September and October, November and December..."

"Enough." Sampson swiped the key from beneath a flowerpot on the stoop.

As soon as they got inside, Necro made herself at home and flopped down in a machine-distressed armchair. She picked up a decorative pillow covered with embroidered birds and a fat yellow sun and glanced at Sampson. "It's official. You win. You have the worst taste in girls."

Nox just stared at the pillow as if he'd seen a ghost. In a way, he felt like he had.

Is it possible? Could I really be that stupid?

The others hardly noticed.

"Fine. She wasn't a rocket scientist." Sampson sounded embarrassed as he opened the refrigerator, hiding behind the door. "At least I found us a place to stay. Nox can't go back to his apartment. And I can't go back to ours, not after I put my fist through the window of one of Silas' cars."

"And then stole it," Nox added. He glanced out the window, where the immense black car looked out of place in the condo lot full of silver minivans. Suddenly, he felt like he'd give anything to be out there, instead of stuck inside the cloying apartment.

He had to get his head straight and remember.

Sampson took out a loaf of bread and a mountain of sandwich ingredients, including a whole jar of pickles. "Artisanal mayonnaise? What's artisanal mayonnaise?" He popped open the jar with the hand-drawn label and smelled the mayo and made a face. "I'm pretty sure it's not food."

Nox grabbed his coat. "I'm gonna take a walk. I need some air."

I have to try to remember.

Necro propped her combat boots up on the arm of the chair and opened a coffee table book about coffee table books. "Don't do anything I wouldn't do."

As Nox closed the front door behind him, he knew what he needed to do. He'd barely reached the sidewalk before he drew the lighter out of his pocket. Then the world blurred and the vision hit him. . . .

Two men in a car, speeding down the highway with a trail of cigar smoke curling behind them.

"What do you want me to do with her?" the bigger of the two men asks.

"Depends." His voice... it's familiar.

Silas.

"Let's see how she reacts to the infusion. I have a good feeling about this one: lucky Number 13."

"Don't get your hopes up. You've been working on this for years, and it hasn't worked yet."

"Trial and error," Silas says. "That's the way science works. The doc thinks we've finally perfected the formula, and this girl isn't your average Caster. She comes from a strong bloodline."

"And if the infusion doesn't take?" the hulking man asks. He's so huge that he must be a Darkborn.

Silas flicks his ash out the window. "You can kill her like the rest of the failures, or keep her. Your choice."

"After all the trouble you went to to get her? Sure you don't want the leftovers?"

"I'm not interested in damaged goods," Silas says.

Nothing but miles of highway stretch in front of the car, until a green sign comes into view: NEW ORLEANS 42 MILES.

"If you pull this off, the Syndicate will be unstoppable," the Darkborn says.

Silas stops and turns to look at his associate. "No. I'll be *unstoppable."*

The edges of the world bled back into Nox's peripheral vision, and his heart thudded in his chest as he struggled to push the fog out of his mind.

Damaged goods.

Silas had to be talking about Ridley. He'd gone to enough trouble to take her. But if he was still talking about her now—

She's alive.

Nox forced himself to be logical, even as the adrenaline pounded in his veins.

Silas could've been referring to someone else. But I wouldn't have a vision about a random girl.

The second conclusion was the one that mattered.

He's got Ridley. Somewhere in New Orleans or close to it.

It means we still have some time.

Not much.

Nox let himself breathe again, but only for a minute. If he was right and Rid was still alive, the clock was ticking. He wasn't sure what kind of infusion Silas was talking about, but if it involved one of his experiments, it wasn't good.

At least I know where Silas has her.

If Silas was headed for New Orleans, it meant he was going to Ravenwood Oaks—Abraham's plantation. The place where Nox had visited his mom. That must be where the labs were, too.

I should tell Necro and Sam. But I can't.

They'd bought into Link's crazy plan to find this John person.

But come on. Who are they kidding?

No friend of Link's is going to be any help to us. The hybrid is a fool surrounded by fools.

Nox looked back up at the condo complex behind him, hands jammed in his pockets.

I can't take Necro and Sampson with me. I've hurt them enough. Especially Necro—she almost got killed because of me.

And Sam's taken a bullet for me more times than I can count. They'll only end up getting hurt.

Because the people he cared about always ended up getting hurt.

It was the most painful recognition of all.

I'm the real threat, but I've always known that.

Nox was better off on his own. Rid was the only person who understood how it felt to be the reason the people around you were always in pain—even if you didn't want them to be.

Wishing you could trade places with them.

It was selfish to put them in danger when Nox had collected more than enough talents, favors, and powers at the gambling tables in his clubs. Those TFPs would compensate for going in alone. Not to mention the fact that taking more people only increased the odds of getting caught.

I can get more done by myself. Without risking all of their lives again.

Nox knew where this was all headed—and what was about to happen.

Rid would tell me to do it. She'd understand.

She'd say, quit whining. Get off your butt and go.

Nox made his way down the sidewalk, still sensing Sampson's eyes on him from the window above. When he turned the corner, he picked up his pace and headed straight for the commuter train station. It also happened to be the location of the nearest Outer Door, one of the magical doorways that led from the Mortal world into the Caster Tunnels.

He wasn't waiting around for Link and Floyd to come back. Not now. If Ridley was still alive, she didn't have that kind of time, and he wasn't leaving her fate in the hands of her idiot boyfriend or John Breed, another hybrid Nox didn't know if he could trust.

Damaged goods.

His hands formed fists at the thought of Silas saying it.

And if she's gone when I get there—or if it isn't her and she's already dead—I'll make Silas pay.

Link was wrong about one thing: John Breed wasn't the only person who knew the location of Abraham's labs in New Orleans and the Syndicate.

Nox had known from the minute he first saw the stupid embroidered pillow in the Mortal girl's apartment—the one that looked like a giant yellow sun.

It had triggered the memory that told him where he needed to go and what he needed to do next.

He tried to silence the voice in his head, shouldering past the commuters on the platform waiting for the train, and slipped through an access door behind the elevators. The hallway was dark, the smell of mold clinging to the air. He passed abandoned electrical panels that hadn't been used since the city upgraded the station almost a decade ago. At the end of the hall, he spotted the Outer Door.

Nox bent down and touched the top of the manhole cover, whispering the Cast to access it. *"Aperi portam."*

In other words, open the damn door.

It slid aside easily, and he lowered himself toward what looked like a deadly drop. But Nox knew that the invisible steps were waiting below. Once his feet touched the first stair, he jumped the rest of them, leaving the Mortal world behind.

The predictability of the Caster world was comforting. The invisible stairs were always where the invisible stairs were supposed to be, and the Casts invariably opened the Caster doors.

Aside from the fact that time and distance operated differently in the Caster Tunnels, most of them weren't much different from the cities and streets in the Mortal world. Sure, some of them looked like you were walking through the pages of a history book—the Middle Ages, the Renaissance, Victorian London—while others reminded him of the fantasy novels he read as a kid.

This Tunnel wasn't one of them.

As his boots splashed through the rancid water, rats scurried through the watery sludge. Nox was grateful the Tunnel wasn't well lit. Though he didn't spend a lot of time hanging out in sewage tunnels, this probably wasn't far off—which was a depressing thought, considering that the place he was going was far worse.

CHAPTER 4: RIDLEY

Dreaming Neon Black

You remember every second of your death. At least, that was the way it was for Ridley.

If she was dead.

She wasn't sure. That part was a little foggy.

First came the guitar solo, crackling through the radio. Then sounds and images flooded her mind.

The black truck speeding toward the Beater—

The tires screeching and metal buckling—

Screams ringing in my ears. Link shouting my name—

And smoke, and heat, and flames—

Ridley opened her eyes slowly. She was lying on her back, and her head was fuzzy. Everything was coated in a hazy film like she was looking through a camera lens smeared with Vaseline. A terrifying thought ran through her mind.

Please don't let me be in a coffin. Seriously. I had epic plans for my funeral.

She blinked hard until she could make out what resembled a blurry bedroom ceiling above her.

Thank god.

She patted around her body and felt a stiff mattress beneath her.

Where am I? And how long have I been here?

And more importantly, where was Link?

She tried to remember the details of the crash, but after the flames and the smoke, there was nothing.

If he's dead...after all we've been through, I'll kill him myself.

That would be just my luck.

To finally lose my heart to a guy right before his stops beating.

She swiped at her face with her free hand, rubbing away a few stray tears. She hadn't even felt them coming, but the sudden movement sent a shock wave of pain tearing up her back. Her body felt like someone had taken a hammer to it. Her neck was so tender that it hurt every time she took a breath. Her arms were covered in yellowish-purple bruises, and if the way her shoulders and back felt was any indication, they probably were, too.

"Make sure you let me know when she wakes up," a man said from somewhere in the distance. "It should be soon."

Ridley turned her head to the side, wincing from the pain, as she struggled to fight her way out of the haze. She took in her surroundings in broad strokes. An ornate chandelier dripping with crystals provided the only light, and an expensive-looking

Persian kilim covered the concrete floor. The stone walls had been whitewashed a pale gray in an unsuccessful attempt to make the room look less like a prison, but the barred door ruined the effect.

I'm locked up in a cell someone decorated like a psychotic B and B. This is Silence of the Lambs *territory. Any minute now, some whack-job serial killer will be standing on the other side of those bars, deciding what kind of coat to make out of my skin.*

Another man's voice, harsher than the first, echoed beyond the bars. "You need to figure out where that hybrid went, or it's your ass. I'm not taking the blame for this. Are we clear?"

Hybrid.

They're talking about Link.

Maybe there's still a chance he's alive.

"You already lost one of them," the second voice continued. "A mistake he'll make us both pay for when this situation is under control. Find the hybrid, or I'm throwing you under a lot more than a bus. Understand?" The guy sounded Southern, like Link's neighbors in Gatlin.

The conversation dissolved into a string of mumbling as the fog wrapped itself around her once more.

Breathe. Close your eyes and focus. Even if it hurts.

It took a few moments before the muffled words began to make sense again.

"You really think the Siren will tell us anything?" the guy who'd taken a tongue-lashing asked.

The Southern guy laughed. "By the time he's finished with her, she'll tell him everything. That's when the real fun starts."

Ridley pressed the heels of her hands against her temples,

trying to clear her head. If their voices weren't echoing and vibrating like she was inside a carnival fun house, maybe she could figure out who she was dealing with.

What the hell did they give me?

Horse tranquilizers?

"So he juices her up. What then? Think he's gonna sell her?" the first guy asked. "I bet there are dozens of Casters in the Syndicate who'd love to have a hot little Siren like her."

Ridley's breath caught in her throat.

Sell me?

Who are these psychos? And how am I going to get out of here and find Link?

She didn't let herself consider the other possibility—the chance that there was no one left to find.

The guy in charge was silent for a moment, which didn't seem like a great sign. "He might keep this one for himself. He doesn't have a Siren, and the good ones are hard to find."

Who are they talking about?

Footfalls echoed against the concrete floor, growing quieter with every step. Ridley took a deep breath, hoping the two men were leaving.

As the echoes grew fainter, she heard the Southern guy one last time. "She'll make a perfect addition to the Menagerie."

Ridley had no idea what he was talking about, but she had the feeling it was a lot worse than being locked in a gilded birdcage. She'd been in enough trouble in her life to recognize the kind she was in right now.

It was the kind that started with being kidnapped and drugged by a man she didn't know and ended with her wishing she were dead.

"Hey? Are you okay in there, Pink?" A girl's voice pulled Ridley out of the fog she couldn't seem to fight her way through.

She had no idea how much time had passed, but someone had left a tray with a bowl of cloudy, pee-colored soup and a glass of water on top of the mirrored nightstand beside her bed.

How did someone come in here without me knowing?

Ridley tried to sit up, but she didn't have the strength. Her legs were cold, and she realized she was wearing what felt like a hospital gown—something as shapeless as a sack of rice, and about as rough and cheap. Nothing like the silk geisha robe she normally wore when she lounged in bed. And she wasn't about to touch her hair. She shuddered.

Excellent. Why didn't they just kill me and get it over with?

Ridley reached for the glass of water on the table beside her. She misjudged the distance, and it crashed to the floor.

Who am I kidding?

She had trouble moving, like she was trying to swim through a pool of Jell-O. A few hours ago, she probably wouldn't have heard it if a train had come through here. But now her head was clearing, and she shivered, realizing the person must have been right next to her bed if they'd left the tray there.

She reached out again, more carefully this time, and stuck her finger in the questionable bowl of soup on the tray. It was still warm.

Then she noticed the Binding Ring on her finger. It was lifeless, no color at all. As if the power was gone, along with whatever it was that had kept her Bound to her friends.

To Link.

She could feel the tears begin to well again.

"Hey, Pink? I just wanna know if you're all right." It was the same girl's voice, barely above a whisper. "They were kind of rough on you."

Ridley managed to push herself up and leaned against the headboard. Her arms were heavy, as if she was pulling them out of wet cement every time she moved. But that was nothing compared to the throbbing in her head.

They must have given me something stronger.

Do they make elephant tranquilizers?

Someone had drugged her for sure, and whatever they had given her was bad news. Sirens had a high tolerance for drugs and alcohol, and this was unlike anything Ridley had ever experienced.

Still, she managed to slide down from the bed and crawl across the floor, determined to find out who the voice belonged to, and if she could see where they were.

By the time Ridley made it over to the bars, she was feeling better and worse. Her thoughts were less jumbled, and her coordination was returning. But now waves of nausea racked her body with every breath.

Ridley laddered her hands up the bars until she was standing, even if her legs were shaking. "Who's there?" she whispered. "Get me out of here."

"I can't. I'm locked up, too." The voice sounded as low as she felt.

The words sent a jolt through Ridley; at that moment, her instinct for self-preservation was more powerful than any drug. "How long have you been here?" she asked.

"Months," the girl said. "I don't know anymore."

"Nine months," a second girl, with a German accent, muttered from somewhere in the hallway. It was so quiet Ridley had to strain to make out the words. "Drew's been here nine months. She came in after me. My name is Katarina."

This is a bad dream, Ridley thought. *Or a drug-induced hallucination.*

Either way, it's not real. It can't be.

"Who locked us up like this?" she asked. It wasn't her first time in a cage, but she'd never imagined it would happen again.

The luck of the Siren.

Footsteps echoed through the passageway. "Wake her up. She's been asleep long enough." Harsh voices. Men's voices. The kind that didn't care who heard them.

Ridley scrambled back to the bed, her vision blurry. A shadow moved in the hallway outside her cell.

A moment later, a hulking figure appeared on the other side of the bars.

"Sweet dreams, Siren? Hope you had a nice nap," an enormous guy said. Ridley recognized his Southern accent. He unlocked the cell and stepped inside, slamming the door behind him.

Ridley fought to keep her eyes fixed on him and summoned her Power of Persuasion.

You don't want to be here.

You want to turn around and leave.

Don't bother to close the door.

The guy pocketed the keys, moving closer. When he noticed Ridley staring at him intently, he laughed. "Don't strain yourself, Siren. Darkborns are immune to the Power of Persuasion."

Ridley let her vision blur again and slumped against the headboard. If she couldn't use her powers against her captor, how was she going to get out of there?

"What are you going to do with me?" she asked.

"Right now, I'm going to give you another shot of the good stuff." He slid a syringe from his pocket and uncapped it, tapping it with his finger. "On the house."

"Leave her alone. If you turn her brain to mush, your boss will be angry," Drew said from somewhere beyond the bars.

"Shut your mouth," the Darkborn wielding the needle snapped. "Or you'll be next up, Oatmeal Brain."

Ridley shrank away. "You don't have to do that. I'm not gonna scream or anything."

"Scream all you want, Siren. No one will hear you down here." He grinned, his teeth flashing in the darkness. "And I love screaming. I live for that crap. Ask your new friends." He raised his voice. "Am I right? You got anything to add now, Oatmeal?"

Ridley shivered, and no one said another word.

He reached for Ridley's wrist. She tried to fight him off, but the huge Darkborn was even bigger than Sampson.

This is one fight I'm not gonna win.

The needle slid into her arm, a thin, gray worm beneath her skin, and she winced, then involuntarily relaxed as a cold wave of chemical sleep rolled through her. She struggled to resist it, but her body floated away.

"Nice rock," the guy said, looking at her hand. "What's that, a present from your boyfriend?" He laughed, and she wanted to tell him where he could stick his stupid needle, but suddenly she couldn't even remember why.

No.

Fight.

If you lose control now, you'll lose everything.

Stay awake and find a way out.

Link will find you.

"What is this place?" she mumbled as the room pitched in and out of darkness. She had to know. She had to stay awake. She had to tell Link. . . .

She heard heavy footsteps; then the cell door closed.

"Welcome to the Menagerie."

CHAPTER 5: LINK

London Calling

Link and Floyd hurtled through the darkness, finally crashing into a heap. It hit Link right away: the familiar dizziness of Traveling—defying space, time, and the laws of physics as only an Incubus could.

It was exhilarating. And freeing. And—

"I think I'm gonna throw up," Floyd said from somewhere beneath him.

Nauseating.

Link rolled to the side and untangled his legs from hers. "Just stick your head between your knees. It works. Or you can hurl. That works, too."

Floyd took his advice, her long hair brushing the grass. "You really need to practice if you're gonna keep Traveling. You gotta stick the landing."

"Don't worry, I will." Link looked around. "On our way back."

"Promises, promises."

Link sat up, holding his hand high, and took a good look at his Binding Ring. It was glowing as red as fire. Knowing it still worked was bittersweet. It wasn't totally busted, only broken when it came to finding Rid.

"They gotta be here somewhere," he said. "John and Liv. My Caster mood ring is goin' nuts." He jammed his hand back into his pocket.

"You sure this is the right place?" Floyd sat up, rubbing the grass out of her hair.

Truthfully, Link wasn't exactly sure if he'd Ripped them to Oxford University or some other place with weird-looking buildings that reminded him of churches. Aside from a trip to Barbados through the Tunnels, he'd never been outside the United States—or outside the South—until this summer, when he and Rid had taken off to New York City.

And the day Rid and me spent in the South of France. She was wearin' her red bikini. But that was France, the place where the french fries sucked (go figure), and he'd wasted all day searching for the Colosseum (until Rid explained it was in Italy). How was he supposed to know what the UK looked like? Link racked his brain, trying to remember as much as he could from the *Harry Potter* movies. "Big red buses and phone booths, right? And guys in bow ties, and supersized beers?"

"What are you babbling about?" Floyd lifted her head up.

"The Unified Kingdom," Link said.

Floyd looked like she was trying not to laugh. "Yeah? Is that what it's called now?"

Link shrugged. "I'm not sure, but I hope we're in London."

She pulled her long hair out of her face and into a ponytail. "So let me get this straight? John's girlfriend, Liv, is a student at Oxford, so you took us to *London*?"

"You got a problem with that?"

"Yeah, genius. Because Oxford University is in *Oxford*. That's probably how they came up with the clever name."

Link looked around. They had landed in an open courtyard surrounded by gray stone buildings. He headed toward one of at least a dozen identical archways around them and hopped over some bushes and onto a covered walkway.

"Slow down," Floyd called from behind him.

"Sorry." He grabbed her and hoisted her over the bushes.

They followed the walkway through one of the buildings and onto a cobbled street right out of the movies. Students and grouchy-looking old men wearing tweed vests rushed past them.

Link glanced around. "How are we supposed to know if we're in the right place? Maybe we should ask someone." He stopped a scrawny guy with glasses in a Trinity College T-shirt. "Hey, dude, is this Oxford University? In the Unified Kingdom?"

The guy backed away and gave him a strange look. "Yes, I suppose it is. More or less." He started to turn away.

"Where's the library?" Link asked.

"Which one?"

Now it was Link's turn to give him a strange look. "There's more than one?"

Why?

The guy pushed his glasses back on the bridge of his nose and glanced at Floyd, which didn't seem to make him feel any better. "Of course. Which one are you looking for?"

Link frowned. There was only one logical place, considering it was Liv. "The biggest one."

Link stared at the enormous building, which looked about the size of a New York City block. It made Gatlin County Library back home look like an outhouse. He turned to Floyd.

"You really think that whole place is fulla books? Like the paper kind?"

She shrugged. "Only one way to find out."

They fell into line behind a group of girls who were probably students. They all had British accents, and Link wasn't sure what they were talking about. Even if it did seem like a scene right out of a movie or a TV show.

Link had spent enough time watching *Batman* to know the building was Gothic.

Like, Gotham City gothic. This place could be Wayne Manor.

With spires lining the roof that looked like serrated swords, it reminded him of a fancy church from the cover of one of those history textbooks he'd never bothered to open. But the building had the same intimidating and creepy presence as Ravenwood Manor, Ridley's uncle's plantation house in Gatlin.

They followed the students through the courtyard and into the main building. One by one, the students swiped what looked like ID cards to open the electronic turnstile. Link stopped when he reached it. "Crap. You need some kind of card thingy to get in. Never saw that at Hogwarts."

"Just hop over," Floyd said. "New York–style."

The turnstile was only waist-high, but there were lots of people around, and he and Floyd weren't exactly inconspicuous.

Someone cleared their throat behind them. "Excuse me," a guy said with an English accent, holding an ID card in his hand.

"Sorry," Link said, backing up. "We were just tryin' to get in."

The English guy gave them the once-over. "Only students have access to the library, unless you apply for a Reader's Card." He pointed behind them. "But you can buy tickets for the tour over there, next to the Great Gate."

"Thanks." Link tugged on Floyd's arm. "Let's get tickets. Then we'll ditch the tour once we get inside."

By the time they made it through the line and reached the ticket counter, Link was getting antsy. "Two tickets, please." He opened his wallet. "Ma'am."

"Seventeen pounds," the clerk said. "Sterling."

Link looked at the twenty-dollar bill in his hand. Everything was different over here, including the money.

He swallowed. "Yeah, okay, Mrs. Sterling, ma'am. Could you give me a minute? I gotta find some cash." He looked at Floyd, lowering his voice. "Jeez. How much cash weighs seventeen pounds? That's more than Lucille Ball."

"You're a regular poster boy for the Mortal school system, aren't you?"

Floyd rolled her eyes and plucked the bill out of his hand. As she slid it across the counter to the clerk, Link's twenty transformed into a weird-looking purple bill with the number twenty in the corner.

"Here you are," the woman said, pushing the tickets back toward them.

Link grinned as they walked away. Having an Illusionist around was pretty handy. He nudged Floyd with his shoulder. "Nice trick."

"What, that?" She tugged on the hem of her concert tee sheepishly. "Please. I was doing that in kindergarten. Wait until you see what I can do with a credit card."

"I'm thinkin' about what you coulda done with my report cards."

They joined the group of tourists gathered in front of a guide, who was just getting started. "With one hundred and twenty miles of occupied shelving and twenty-nine reading rooms, the Bodleian Library is the UK's second largest library. The largest is, of course, the British Library."

"Aren't they all British?" Link looked confused.

Floyd clapped a hand over his mouth. "Shut it."

The guide ushered everyone up a narrow flight of stairs that spilled into a long room, filled floor to ceiling with books.

Link stared up at the painted panels that ran the length of the room, with dark wood beams stretching horizontally below them. The bookcases were made from the same wood, with round pillars dividing them, like the fancy bookcases in Ridley's uncle's study.

Whole rooms just for old books.

It made no sense. You couldn't fill one room with Link's

favorite books, let alone a whole building. There weren't that many *Star Wars* novels in the world.

"This is Duke Humfrey's Library, the oldest reading room in the Bodleian," the tour guide said. "It houses maps, music, and rare books dating before 1641. You will notice that many of the volumes are chained to the shelves. Prior to the invention of the printing press, books were quite difficult to replace and were, therefore, extremely valuable. The chains are long enough to allow people to read the books, while assuring they remained in the library, where they belonged."

Link pointed at the chains. "They lock the books up like the leather jackets in the Summerville Mall. Think they've got *Harry Potter* in there?"

Floyd frowned and pushed her blond hair out of her eyes. "We need to figure out how we're gonna ditch this tour and find your friend."

The tour guide led the tourists down the hall, and Link grabbed Floyd's arm, stopping her.

"Let them get ahead of us," he whispered, nodding at a nearby staircase.

When the last person in the group reached the end of the hallway, Link grabbed Floyd's hand and pulled her up the steps. But he didn't take into account how much faster a quarter Incubus moved than a Caster, and when he rounded the corner three flights up, the momentum sent her flying into his chest.

She was staring up at Link, trying to catch her breath, when a guy walked by. The guy took one look at Floyd pressed up against him and gave Link a nod of approval.

Link felt his face getting hot.

Floyd stepped away from him, smoothing her T-shirt. "It's nice to see there are dirtbags in the *Unified* Kingdom, too."

Link gave her the smallest hint of a smile. "I guess when it comes to dirtbags, it really is a small world after all."

Link followed her through the doorway and into a huge library. Stacks of books towered above him, like the ones in the Caster Library, the *Lunae Libri*. Except these were even dustier. In the center of a large room, students were studying at long tables, while others read in carrels. He scanned the tables, searching for Liv's blond braids. There was no sign of her, but Link spotted someone who looked like John—if John had been a huge nerd.

A big guy with short black hair exactly like John's was sitting alone at one of the tables across the room. But instead of John's usual black T-shirt and leather motorcycle jacket, this guy was wearing a nerdy blue button-down beat-the-crap-outta-me shirt that John would never have been caught dead in.

That can't be him.

"Why are you staring? Is that him?" Floyd whispered.

"I'm not sure. But if it is, I think we're caught in the Matrix." Link walked over to the table and the nerdy guy who he wasn't sure was John—until the guy held up his hand and Link saw John's Binding Ring glowing brightly. Then the guy looked up, and Link saw his Caster green eyes and the embarrassed expression on his face.

"I knew it was you," Link said. "Holy crap." He grinned. "It's like *Invasion of the Body Snatchers*, except they only stole your clothes. I hope."

John grinned and pushed up the sleeves of his button-down,

like that would somehow make it look cooler. "It's for Liv. To help her fit in."

"Yeah? How's that workin' for you?" Link raised an eyebrow.

John shrugged, and Link messed up his hair. "Keep tellin' yourself that, man." Link cracked an imaginary whip in the air with one hand.

John shoved him away, studying Floyd. "Are you gonna introduce your friend?" He said it casually enough, but Link understood what he was really saying. At least, what he was asking.

"Yeah, sorry. This is Floyd."

"A Dark Caster?" John asked, as if he could see right through the colored contacts Floyd wore when she was around Mortals.

"Is that a problem?" she asked.

"Fine by me. I've seen Link with a Dark Caster girl before." John turned to Link and raised an eyebrow.

"She plays bass in my band," Link said, hoping the message was equally clear: *Dude, long story. Don't ask.*

"*Our* band," Floyd said, annoyed. "Which doesn't exist anymore."

"The infamous Sirensong?" John looked at Link. "Does that have anything to do with the reason you're here? Speaking of which, where's our favorite Siren?"

Link's expression darkened. "That's the thing. Rid's in trouble."

Or worse.

Link left out that part. He could barely stand to think about the possibility that Ridley was dead. There was no way he could say it to John.

John sighed and leaned back in his chair. "Is that supposed to surprise me?"

"It's not that kinda trouble. This is serious."

"It's always serious."

Floyd spoke up. "She's missing, and we think Silas Ravenwood might have her."

"What?" John froze at the mention of Silas' name. He had more history with the Ravenwoods than any of them. "How did she get mixed up with Silas?"

"He was lookin' for me. You and me, really. He wanted to avenge Abraham's death, and keep Rid in a cage, or somethin' like that. This tool Nox Gates sold us out," Link rambled on, barely taking a breath. "We almost got away, but they found us. There was a car crash, and the Beater caught on fire. I don't know what happened to Rid, but we're pretty sure Silas has her. He's the head of the Caster Mafia or somethin' like that. So I need you to help me find the labs."

"Slow down," John said. "I'm gonna need more than the CliffsNotes."

Floyd put her hand on Link's arm. "I've got this."

He nodded, and she filled in the missing pieces of the story for John. Link was only half-listening. Now that they'd found John, all he could think about was saving Ridley.

As soon as Floyd finished, Link jumped in again. "So will you help us find her?"

John unbuttoned his beat-the-crap-outta-me-and-shove-me-in-a-locker shirt and took it off. "Considering we're the ones Silas wants, it only seems right." He balled up the shirt and tossed it on the floor.

Link was relieved to see that John was wearing a black T-shirt underneath. Floyd looked disappointed he was wearing a shirt at all. Link had almost forgotten the effect John had on girls.

John picked up a backpack. "Meet me at the King's Arms pub in an hour. I can't take off without talking to Liv first."

"The King's Legs. Got it." Link held up a fist. "Thanks, man."

"I'd help you even if we weren't the reason Rid was mixed up with Silas. We're friends." John bumped his fist against Link's, which told Link the only thing he needed to know.

He's in.

Getting out of the Bodleian Library was a lot easier than getting in.

The pub John mentioned was right across the street, so Link and Floyd headed straight there. Even though Floyd was pretty skinny, she was always hungry, and Link didn't want to risk getting lost. Everything over here was sort of crazy; between the accents and the cars driving on the wrong side of the road, Oxford almost felt like somewhere out of the Caster world.

"It looks like a nice place," Floyd said as they approached a pinkish-peach-colored building with white windowpanes and black lanterns hanging on both sides of the door.

Link glanced down at his Black Sabbath T-shirt and jeans. "Hopefully not too nice." He sighed. "What are we doin' wastin' our time? We gotta go."

Floyd dropped a hand on his arm. It felt warm and full of life, like Floyd always did. "Chill out. Your buddy said an hour. We might as well eat."

Link made a face.

"Right." She shrugged. "I might as well eat."

Inside, the King's Arms was all dark paneling and vintage signs. A formal wooden bar dominated the main room, with liquor bottles stacked neatly on the shelves behind the bartender.

Floyd grabbed a table in the corner, next to the window, and dropped down into one of the plain ladder-back chairs. Link glanced at the menu on the table and scrunched up his nose. "Traditional ploughman's lunch and fish cakes? Scotch eggs? Mushy peas? What is this junk?"

Floyd studied the menu. "It looks like the traditional ploughman's is a plate of bread, pickle, apples, and cheese."

"Pickle, cheese, and bread?" Link shook his head and pulled a pen out of his pocket. "I'm glad I don't eat anymore."

She stood up with a menu in her hand. "Don't knock it till you've tried it. I'm going to order at the bar. I assume you don't want anything."

Link looked around at the other tables covered with plates of food. "Get me a Coke or somethin'. You know, so I don't look weird."

Floyd smiled. "The Coke won't help."

"Yeah? Just don't let anyone put an egg in my Scotch, and I'll be fine." Link watched her walk over to the bar like she was just another student.

Link grabbed a napkin and scrawled some lyrics across it. Ever since Sampson and Nox found him in the trees after the accident, song lyrics had been floating around in his head. The only problem was, they sucked—which was a new thing for him. He'd been writing songs for as long as he could remember, about everything from his lunch to all the times Ridley had broken his heart. Until now, he was pretty sure his lyrics had kicked ass.

He stared down at the black lines stretching across the napkin.

What if I can't write anymore?

There were probably a lot of things he wouldn't be able to do anymore without Ridley. She was more than just his girl—she was his muse. It felt like everything started and ended with her.

> Lose. Muse. Bruise.
> Why you gotta get me so confuse?
> Like I lost my favorite pair a shoes...

He dropped the pen.

I suck. I can't do this without Rid. I just gotta find her.

"What are you doing?" Floyd asked as she put his Coke down on the table. "Are you writing a song? Anything good?"

He crumpled up the napkin and shoved it in his pocket. "Naw. I haven't been able to write since I lost... her."

Floyd seemed to take the comment in stride and sat down. But if he'd learned one thing about girls in the past year, it was that they usually weren't thinking whatever you thought they were. Floyd had that weird look on her face again, the one where Link couldn't tell if she was going to laugh or cry.

Girls.

"Ridley's lucky," she said. "You stick with her no matter what she does, or how bad she screws up. I wish *someone* felt that way about me."

"Rid doesn't mean to mess up. At least, not most of the time," Link said.

Floyd rolled her eyes.

"Deep down, she's a good person," he said. "She just doesn't want anybody to know."

"That makes no sense."

"It does to me. She had it rough growing up."

"Everyone had it rough growing up," Floyd said.

"Yeah? After Rid turned Dark, her own mother wouldn't even take her in."

Floyd nodded as if she understood, but her expression said otherwise. "You don't have to tell me about having a crappy childhood. My dad is the head of a Dark Caster bike club in the Underground, remember?"

"I can't even get my head around that," Link said. "My mom wouldn't let me take off my trainin' wheels until I was ten, and my dad spent most of his free time at Civil War reenactments—mainly to avoid her." He shrugged. "I can't blame him. All that prayin' and fussin' gets on your nerves pretty fast, and if naggin' was an Olympic sport, my mom woulda won the gold medal for sure. Drape a flag over her housecoat and skip that woman straight to the victory lap now."

A waitress walked up to the table with an unappetizing plate of mismatched food on it, at least as far as Link was concerned. "One traditional ploughman's," she said. "Cheers."

Floyd popped a piece of cheese in her mouth. "It's actually good. Best traditional ploughman's I ever had."

"I'll take your word for it," he said. "But where's the plow?"

She stared at him. He shrugged. "Mortal food all tastes the same to me."

Floyd nodded and turned her attention to her food. It seemed like talking about her dad bothered her, so Link left it alone and went back to writing crappy songs on napkins.

By the time Link finished writing his fourth song and Floyd had moved on to mushy peas and french fries called chips—which made no sense to him—he was starting to worry that John wasn't going to show. He was about to bring it up to Floyd when the front door of the pub opened and he caught a glimpse of the familiar blond braids.

Liv, John's girlfriend and Link's friend before that, looked exactly the way he remembered her: blond and tall.

TDB. Third Degree Burns hot.

That was what Link had said the first time he saw her. It seemed weird now that he only thought of Liv as his friend and John's girl.

Even if she was John's hot *girlfriend.*

Liv was wearing the periodic table of elements T-shirt she'd had on when he met her. It only took her a moment to zero in on Link, and he could tell from the look on her face that she wasn't happy. She headed toward him, arms crossed and scowling, with John behind her.

Sorry, John mouthed.

"Wesley Lincoln."

The only person who ever called him that was his mom, and it was never a good sign. Liv followed with a tight hug that was equal parts intimidating and affectionate. Link backed out of it as quickly as he could.

He smelled danger.

Liv pulled out the chair across from Link and sat down, glancing at Floyd. "Olivia Durand. I apologize in advance for my foul mood. I'd like to think I'm normally rather personable." She turned to Link. "But I understand you want to take John with you to go after Silas Ravenwood."

"Aw, Liv," Link began. "It's just—"

She held up a hand. "Hence the mood."

John sat down next to her and put his hand on the back of her chair.

She pushed it off and glared at him, then turned her attention back to Link. "Correct me if I'm wrong, but Abraham Ravenwood almost killed both of you—all of us, really."

"Well, you're not *so* wrong—"

"And now you want to go after his great-great-grandson?" Liv asked. "What part of this seems like a sensible idea to you?"

Link tried again. "Not *exactly* sensible—"

"I told you, Ridley's in trouble," John said.

"I want to hear it from Link," she said without taking her eyes off Link. "What kind of trouble are we talking about, precisely?" She held up her ring. "And why did this only go off on your behalf, rather than Ridley's?"

Link sighed. There was no point trying to pull punches on Liv. She was too smart for her own good.

And mine.

He didn't really know where to begin, so he just plunged right in. "Silas Ravenwood knows that me and John killed his granddad, Abraham, and he wants us dead: me, John—and Lena and Rid for helping us. Maybe you and Ethan, too. I'm not sure. But he's the head of the Syndicate—it's like the Mob of the Underground."

"That's an understatement," Floyd added.

"Technically, it's a statement." Liv silenced her with one look. "And I've heard about the Syndicate from the Keepers training me."

"It's bad, Liv." Link let himself sound as miserable as he felt. "I wouldn't be here if it wasn't. He's got a thing for Sirens. And Rid's missin'. I don't know what he's gonna do to her if we don't find her."

Liv's expression softened. She glanced at the strange-looking device on her wrist. Link hadn't seen her selenometer in so long that he'd almost forgotten about it. It looked like a crazy black watch, but Link knew it measured all kinds of stuff, like the moon's gravitational pull.

She'd used it before, when things were almost this grim. The sight of it brought back all kinds of crazy, terrible memories.

He looked away.

"You and Ridley should never have gone to New York. I had a bad feeling about it from the beginning," Liv said. "I never should've helped you fake that acceptance letter." Liv had been a key part of Link's Escape from Gatlin plan, especially the part that involved a little forgery and the invention of a fictional Bible college named Georgia Redeemer.

Link turned red.

"Wait a minute," Floyd said. "What was Link supposed to do, just give up his dream? Ridley basically sold him in a card game, and Link didn't even know it. It's not like she's an angel. I watched it happen."

"Excuse me?" Liv stared at Floyd for a long moment, and

the Illusionist seemed to shrink back in her chair a little. "Who's the girl?"

It was the same question John had asked.

Two questions, really.

Who is this Dark Caster and why is she with you?

Link didn't answer, and Floyd tensed. "*The girl* has a name. Two, actually. If you want to get technical."

"Oh, I always want to get technical," Liv said.

Link put his hand on her arm. As much as he appreciated the concern, it wasn't helping. "Come on, Liv. Freakin' out on Floyd won't help us find Rid any faster. I need your A-game right now."

"I'm not *freaking out*. I'm just stating the facts." Liv looked like she was about to cry, which was when Link realized none of this emotion was about Floyd at all. Liv was worried about Ridley, too.

John slid his arm around her shoulder, giving her a sympathetic squeeze.

Link looked at Liv and John. "It's okay, you guys. Floyd is our friend from New York—Rid's and mine. She wants to help, and right now, we need all the help we can get."

Liv looked away.

Link tugged on Floyd's arm. "Give Liv a break. One of her best friends is missin'."

For a moment, neither of them moved. Then Floyd shrugged sheepishly. "I know. I mean, how you all feel. Ridley's a pain in the butt, but she's our pain in the butt, right?"

Link almost fell over. It was pretty much the nicest thing Floyd had ever said about Rid, and he knew what it cost her to say it.

"Well, she's certainly not anyone else's." Liv sighed.

Link smiled, in spite of everything. It already felt better, just knowing he had John and Liv back by his side.

"Are you guys positive Silas Ravenwood has her?" Liv asked him, getting back to business, the gears in her head already turning.

Link shook his head. "No. I mean, I didn't see him take her or anythin'. But one of his trucks hit the Beater, and now she's gone."

Liv frowned. "Do we know where Silas might be keeping her?"

"We're pretty sure he's running things from somewhere near the labs. That's why we need John's help."

John looked sick at the mention of the place where he grew up and Abraham experimented on him, but he just nodded.

Liv sighed and took out her little red journal. She began scribbling furiously, most likely writing down everything that had just happened, if only for the records the Keepers were responsible for maintaining. Who knew? Link could never track where her brain was headed next. When she finished, she closed the book. "We need to get going."

"What do you mean, *we*?" John looked at her, sounding shocked. "You have classes."

"I can email my professors and tell the Keepers overseeing my training that there's an emergency at home," she said. "Where you go, I go. That's the deal."

She held up her hand. Her ring was dead now, just like John's and Link's. The sight of the colorless rings made her point even clearer.

"Liv," John said quietly. "We're talking about Silas Ravenwood. It's too dangerous."

She pocketed her journal. "That's why you need me. And that's why I'm coming."

He shook his head. "Liv, please." The way John said her name, the way he looked at her—Link could hear it all in his voice. The crazy feelings John had for her. All the crazy fears about what could happen to her.

Been there, Link thought.

I'm still there. Still crazy. Still afraid.

It never gets any better. Not when you love someone so much it breaks you.

Liv stood up and tucked her pencil behind her ear. "We can argue about it on the way."

CHAPTER 6: NOX

South of Heaven

Less than an hour later, Nox stood in front of the Heavens. The name of the high-rise was a cruel joke on the Caster junkies squatting inside. Mortals might have invented street drugs, but Dark Casters had perfected them.

This was where the stitched yellow sun on the embroidered pillow had sent him.

Straight to the source of the Sunshine itself.

Sunshine was the Syndicate's latest achievement: a designer narcotic synthesized in Syndicate-run kitchens all over the Underground—a toxic combination of opiates and Dark magic. Casters who tried the stuff were hooked after one hit. It was the reason Nox had banned Sunshine from his clubs, Dark Casters and their demands notwithstanding. Sunshine led to trouble, and pain.

Nox had never been interested in drugs himself. His only

addictions were power and control, at least until he met Ridley. Whether or not there should be a twelve-step program for getting away from the pull of that particular Siren was another matter entirely.

The thought of what Silas might be doing to her, if she was still alive, sent him through the revolving metal door and into the building.

Get in and get out. For her.

The square atrium on the other side gave Nox a clear view of all eighteen floors above him. Each floor was identical. Numbered metal doors lined the walls behind the broken metal railings overlooking the atrium. In another life, the Heavens had been a low-rent tenement building, until the Syndicate took over.

Bodies slumped against the railings on every floor. He wondered how many of them were already dead. Given the road they were on, it was a technicality.

A filthy Dark Caster stumbled toward him, her golden eyes glazed, as if she was feverish. Other Casters wandered out of the stairwells with the same dazed expression on their faces, like zombies. None of them seemed to notice him—or anything else. He trudged up the stairs, dodging the junkies huddled in the corners smoking Sunshine from tinfoil pipes. When he reached the seventh floor, he spotted a dealer.

The Incubus stood in the corner, doling out cellophane bags filled with what looked like yellow rocks to the addicts shoving cash into his hands.

"I don't have any money," an emaciated girl said to him. "But I'll trade my powers."

The Incubus laughed, baring his canines, and shoved her

away. "You ran out of powers a long time ago. No money, no Shine."

The Shine—that was what they called the high that people got from Sunshine.

Nox felt sick just watching them, but he didn't have time to play hero. He elbowed his way to the front of the line, holding up a hundred-dollar bill between his fingers. "Then it looks like I came to the right place."

Come on, already.

The dealer raised an eyebrow and smiled. "You must be having a serious party. How much do you want?"

"I'm not looking to score any Sunshine," Nox said. "I want information."

He thought of the TFPs at his disposal. But this particular scumbag was too pathetic to waste one on. The pull of Shine to an addict was a power all its own—and one that required nothing more special than money.

And unlike TFPs, Nox had almost an infinite supply of that.

It was impossible to gauge an Incubus' emotions when the only thing you could see in their black eyes was your own reflection. "What kind of information?"

Nox pulled out another hundred. "I'm looking for a Caster who hangs out here. People call him the Chemist."

The Incubus laughed and snatched the hundreds. "Not anymore."

"Do you know where he is or not?"

The Incubus nodded toward the stairs. "Eighteenth floor. Apartment 13. Unless he jumped, he'll be inside." He saluted, pocketing the money.

Nox ignored him.

There was only one junkie who interested him. One he'd known a long time ago, before the guy was an addict—after his mom had been taken and his father was a broken man.

When Abraham Ravenwood governed everything about their lives and Nox's childhood was full of rules. But one rule was more important than all the others combined: *Never ask about Abraham's labs.*

Nox closed his eyes as the memories came flooding back. . . .

Mom was making tea when Abraham burst into the kitchen, looking more agitated than usual.

"Get your stuff." He snapped his fingers at Mom. "There's a problem that needs dealin' with."

She nodded. "Hurry up, Lennox. Get your things."

"The boy's stayin' here." Abraham's tone made it clear his decision wasn't up for discussion. "This is important business, and I'm no babysitter." He eyed me coldly. "Give the kid a pack a matches. Maybe if we're lucky, he'll set himself on fire."

Mom looked panicked, but she didn't argue. No one argued with the original Blood Incubus in the Ravenwood line.

"Go up to my room," Mom whispered. "Lock the door and stay there until I get back." I nodded. "I want to hear you promise me," she said, looking desperate.

"I—I promise," I stammered, terrified of saying anything to provoke Abraham's cruelty.

"Now go."

I bolted up the winding staircase in the foyer and watched him drag Mom out of the house. I kept my promise and stayed in her room—the one we shared when Abraham allowed me to visit her—for the first few hours. Then I realized this was my chance to see the labs Abraham was always disappearing to with his grandson, Silas. I wondered what a man like him was making in there. Surveillance equipment to spy on my mom and the other Supernaturals he forced to work for him?

Weapons or bombs?

Or the thing that terrified me almost as much as a threat to my family—the possibility that Abraham was testing the powers of the enslaved Casters on animals.

This was my chance to find out.

So I took it.

Sneaking out of the house was the easy part. Most of Abraham's thugs were stupid.

The labs were underground, but I knew the entrance was somewhere behind the plantation's original carriage house. What I didn't expect was how easy the heavy metal door was to find. It reminded me of a tornado shelter in the movies. Then again, when you were as feared as Abraham, you probably didn't have to worry about people breaking into your super-secret labs.

The door was so heavy that I almost gave up. But on the last try, it cracked open enough for me to wedge myself inside.

Whenever I imagined the labs, they always looked like the medieval alchemy labs from my favorite books. But there was nothing medieval about this place. Everything was shiny and state-of-the-art.

He was definitely making bombs.

I was surprised the hallway was empty. Maybe Abraham took his thugs with him and Mom. Or maybe they weren't allowed down here, either.

Farther down the hallway, I noticed a long window like the ones parents look through in hospitals to see their brand-new babies. I crawled below the window, and it took me a while to gather up the courage to peek inside. I didn't want to think about what Abraham would do to me if someone caught me down here.

When I finally peered through the glass, I saw that rows of hospital beds lined the walls, each one outfitted with medical equipment and glowing monitors.

Casters and Incubuses were lying, unmoving, in the beds. The only clue that they were still alive was the lines zigzagging across the monitors.

A boy was lying in the last bed. He was about my age, and unlike the others, he was awake. There was no mistaking the expression on his face as he twisted and writhed in the hospital bed. This kid was in serious pain.

"What the hell are you doing down here?" The voice came from behind me, and I almost jumped out of my skin. A skinny, nervous-looking Caster in a white lab coat stood behind me.

"I—I'm lost," I stammered, praying he'd believe me.

"This isn't a place you want to get lost. You need to get out of here before anyone else sees you, or you'll end up like him." He pointed at the boy twisting in the bed.

"What's wrong with him?" I asked.

"You're not too smart, are you? Unless you want him experimenting on you next, leave now."

The sound of footsteps echoed through the hall, and the doctor—or whatever he was—panicked. He opened a closet behind me and shoved me inside.

"There's someone out here," a harsh voice said from the other side of the door.

"Relax. It's just the Chemist," another man said.

"What are you doing outta the lab?" the harsh voice snapped.

"I—I needed a moment," the Chemist stammered.

The other man laughed. "Can't stomach your job?"

"I was told this was a genetics project. Putting a kill switch in a child and experimenting on Casters isn't what I signed on for," the Chemist responded.

"You signed on for whatever Abraham Ravenwood says you did. Now get back in there."

I waited for what felt like hours before I crawled out of the closet, and I promised myself I'd never go back there again.

Nox shook off the memory as he climbed the last flight of stairs.

I'll find you, Ridley. I promise. Just be alive when I get there.

The eighteenth floor was definitely no penthouse. With its broken railings and missing doors leading into uninhabitable apartments, it looked like the whole floor was in the process of being demolished. Only one door remained intact, with the number thirteen spray-painted across the front.

He paused at the door, praying the Chemist was alive inside. If the rest of the eighteenth floor was any indication, it was doubtful. He banged on the door and waited.

Nothing.

Screw this, Nox thought, turning the knob. It rattled a few times, and he gave the door a hard shove. The rotted wood gave way, and the stench hit his nostrils the moment the door opened—the smell of spoiled food and mold and rot.

The Chemist had to be dead. Nothing short of a decomposing corpse could smell this bad. But Nox had to know for sure. He crossed the threshold just as an old man in a filthy lab coat turned the corner.

Nox did a few mental calculations. The Chemist couldn't have been more than forty years old the first time Nox saw him, but the man standing before him now looked closer to seventy than fifty. His fingertips were burned, a result of smoking from one homemade aluminum pipe too many.

The man in the lab coat gave him the once-over. "I can cook up whatever you've got and double it, if you give me a taste." The man swayed on his feet and reached out for the wall to steady himself.

"I'm not interested in getting high," Nox said, disgusted. "I'm looking for the Chemist."

The man in the dingy lab coat backed away clumsily. "Sorry, don't know anyone by that name."

Nox pointed at his coat. "You sure about that?"

It took a moment for the junkie to realize he was wearing

his lab coat. "This thing? I found it down on the first floor." The Chemist's voice sounded much younger than his appearance suggested, and Nox had seen enough addicts to know how drugs aged a person. He also knew what made junkies talk. He held up another hundred-dollar bill.

The Chemist's eyes widened.

"I need some information, and I'm willing to pay for it." What was left of this guy wasn't worth wasting Nox's powers on.

The desperate man shoved his hands in his pockets, practically salivating. "What is it you need to know?"

Not so fast. I have to be sure.

Nox pulled his hand back, and the junkie's eyes followed the bill. "You can't help me," he said. "Only the Chemist can help me, and you're not him. Right?"

He could almost see the internal battle waging in the man's mind.

"What kind of information does this Chemist have that's so important?" the man asked.

"One thing. The location of the lab where he used to work."

"No." The man shook his head. "You should forget whatever you know about that place."

"Are you saying you know where it is?" Nox asked.

The Chemist's eyes darted to the doorway. He ran his hands through his hair, almost compulsively, like he was trying to pull it out. "We shouldn't be talking about this. If the wrong people heard you asking these kind of questions, they'd kill you—and me."

"You let me worry about that."

"No. That's how people die. That's how everyone dies." His eyes moved restlessly, avoiding Nox.

"If you're the person I think you are, it's a little late to develop a conscience."

The Chemist disappeared into what was left of a tiny galley kitchen. He rummaged through the empty drawers, desperately searching for something—most likely a fix.

Nox sighed, waving the money between his fingers. "You need this, don't you? Tell me what I want to know."

When the man realized there was nothing left in the kitchen except for a few balls of tinfoil and a half dozen plastic lighters, he began searching the cupboards, one at a time. "You don't know what you're talking about."

Nox moved toward the Chemist and slammed one of the cupboards shut just inches from the junkie's face. "I know what you were doing in Abraham's labs. Experimenting on Casters and Incubuses—and that kid."

The Chemist stood frozen, his hands gripping the counter in front of him. "What kid?"

"Don't bother lying. I know all about John."

The Chemist stumbled back as if Nox had pointed a gun at him.

Nox took a step closer. "John Breed. That was his name, right?"

"I didn't want to do it. Abraham Ravenwood forced me."

"He was just a kid." Nox shook his head.

"You don't know what he was like or what he would have done—" The Chemist examined Nox more closely, his whole body shaking. "Wait. You're the boy. John. You're finally here to kill me, aren't you?"

Progress.

Nox took advantage of the Chemist's fear. "I'm not John. But I know where he is."

It was sort of the truth.

And it could've been me.

"If you don't tell me where the labs are, I'll bring John here so he can thank you in person."

The Chemist started talking so fast Nox could barely understand him. "They're behind Abraham's house. You can't access them from here, but there's a door along the Mile that leads right into his house."

Of course.

"How do I find the door?"

"Get to the Mile just before the sun comes up. Ravenwood's cook will be there, unless the old Caster is dead by now. Follow her. But you won't find Abraham Ravenwood there. He's dead. People say your friend John killed him." The Chemist had a crazed look in his bloodshot eyes. "I'm probably next."

"If the labs aren't where you say they are, you will be." Nox tossed the hundred-dollar bill on the kitchen counter. The Mile wasn't a hard place to find.

The junkie's eyes flicked between Nox and the money, but fear was no match for the Shine. He lunged for it and scrambled past Nox.

By the time Nox reached the first floor again, the Chemist already had a plastic bag in his hand. He was killing himself, one tiny piece of Sunshine at a time.

As he made his way through the shadowy world of the Tunnels, Nox was haunted by his own demons. He'd spent most of his life trying to forget his past, and this was the reason. It opened a sea of darkness that threatened to drown him. No one was strong enough to hold off an entire sea, and he had never felt closer to going under.

He desperately wanted to think about anything other than his childhood—or Silas Ravenwood.

To be more specific, Silas Ravenwood and Ridley.

He tried to shake it off, but the more he tried *not* to think about it, the more clearly the images took shape in his mind.

What Silas might be doing to her right now—or making her do. What he could do to her, if he wanted to. Or if she was already gone.

Nox stopped and leaned against the side of the Tunnel wall, letting his head drop into his hands. The thought put him over the edge, and when he went that far over, he couldn't think straight. When he couldn't think straight, he made stupid mistakes. Stupid mistakes could end up getting Ridley hurt.

Stop.

Find something else to think about. Anything else. Just keep it together until you get to New Orleans.

He had to know if Silas Ravenwood had gotten his hands on Ridley.

Or her corpse.

Nox drew his lighter out of his pocket and held it up in front of him. He felt the familiar coiling in his stomach at the thought of the unshakable stone of whatever the future held.

Might as well strap the Wheel of Fate to my back right now.

But it didn't matter.

He didn't matter. This had stopped being about him the moment he'd seen the car crash, inside the lighter's flames the last time.

With a shaking hand, he struck the flint and looked into the flickering light....

At first there was nothing but fog, thicker and blacker than usual.

Nox made his way into the depths of it, just as he always did.

The smoke of time and memory and everything else that stood between the Dark Caster and his even darker visions.

Nox pushed through.

When the shadows began to clear and the vision began to take shape, Nox thought something was wrong.

I'm losing my Sight. I can't see anything.

Then he realized he *was* seeing something.

The smoke formed broad vertical lines, as if someone had spilled black ink over his head and now it was dripping in front of his eyes.

Like trees in a forest, flashing by a speeding car. Like a picket fence, only black, not white.

He almost smiled at the idea of one of his visions showing him something as happy and peaceful as a white picket fence. Then he stopped smiling, because the smoke began to focus itself into a more detailed shape, and Nox Gates realized exactly what he was looking at.

Bars.

Prison bars.

He forced himself to control the vision. Slowly, he pushed his way down the bars until he saw it . . . her face. Pale and unmoving. Scratched and bruised and covered with dry blood. Her lips were purplish blue.

Ridley—

Ridley, wake up. It's me. It's Nox.

It was no use. Her lips were parted but remained unmoving. He couldn't tell if she was breathing. He held on to the sight of her for as long as he could. He couldn't bear to let it slip away, because he didn't know if he'd ever see it again.

By the time the vision began to fade, his eyes were as blurry as the smoke.

She's alive. That's what the vision means.

It would take more than one Ravenwood to kill Ridley Duchannes. Maybe more than two. He couldn't let himself consider the alternative. He pushed himself off the wall and kept moving. Someone had to do the right thing. Someone had to show up for her, whether or not it was too late.

Not just anyone. Me.

Nox didn't trust anyone else. He was the only one who really knew, because he was the only one who had watched it all happen before.

I have to stop him. I have to find her.

Ridley.

He wouldn't let the Ravenwoods do this to another Siren he cared about. But it was more than that. Nox couldn't escape it, and he didn't want to. He'd never felt this way about anyone, and it terrified him.

Because he knew what happened to the people he cared about.

In the hands of a Dark Caster, love is a death sentence.

The thought—and the feeling—hit him hard, and Lennox Gates knew one thing for sure. He loved Ridley Duchannes.

CHAPTER 7: RIDLEY

Return of the Warlord

You have to stay awake.

Ridley struggled to keep her eyes open.

Fight it off. Stay in control.

If you stay awake, you can think. If you think, you can find a way out of here. A way back to Link.

But it was no use, and Ridley found herself drifting in and out of a restless sleep, filled with surreal dreams and hallucinations.

Not again. Don't close your eyes again.

Think of Lena and Link. Think of your friends.

Drugs. It had to be drugs.

Only now she couldn't remember them doing it.

Link. I can't. I'm so tired.

But then she felt her eyes closing again, and she almost didn't care anymore, because with sleep came dreams of Link.

"So where do you want to go? Sky's the limit, Babe." Link glanced at me from behind the wheel of the Beater. In front of us, there was nothing but highway, and above us, nothing but blue sky.

"Don't call me Babe," I said. But after everything that had happened, I was actually starting to like it. Not that I'd ever admit it to him. I propped my platforms up on the dashboard. "Definitely not the South. I think we should head west. LA, Vegas...somewhere we can hole up in a four-star hotel, order room service, basically the opposite of everything we were doing in New York."

Link grinned and turned up "Stairway to Heaven."

"Whatever you say, Sugarplum. But only because I'm crazy about you, and I've never been to the West Coast." He smiled at me again, looking happier than I've ever seen him.

Lucille meowed from the backseat and jumped between us. Today, even that fleabag couldn't ruin my mood.

The song was halfway over, and I realized I was holding my breath. It felt like something terrible was about to happen, and I was waiting for it.

Link sang along with Led Zeppelin, and I kept waiting.

And waiting.

The song ended, and I exhaled. Everything was okay. We were gonna make it. All the way to LA, or Vegas, or wherever the hell we wanted to go. And I was gonna charm our way into the nicest hotel I could find and keep Link as far from New York City as I could.

New York City.

A thought slipped through my mind, but I lost it. It had something to do with New York. Something I left behind.

Nox.

The thought slammed into me, and I saw the black truck speeding toward us, and "Stairway to Heaven" was playing all over again.

That's when the screaming started—

Link—

Ridley bolted upright, clawing at the sheets around her. The chandelier was switched on. But even in the dim light, her vision was still blurry.

Of course. They drugged me again.

She vaguely remembered the Darkborn entering her cell—her *room*. That was what he'd called it. But this wasn't a room any more than Ridley was a guest. She remembered bits and pieces of her conversation with other girls in the cells somewhere in the hallway.

I'm not the only prisoner. There were girls. They had names and faces.

I can't remember. Why can't I remember?

Menagerie.

The word lingered in her mind. Ridley had no intention of becoming a permanent part of the Menagerie, whatever the hell that meant.

Get up. You need to find a way out of here.

She took deep breaths, focusing her powers inward. She couldn't use the Power of Persuasion on herself, but trying pulled her out of the drug-induced haze faster. Anything to keep her mind sharp.

Another silver tray rested on the nightstand. Instead of soup, this time her captors had upped the ante and left a plate of filet mignon and baby carrots, as if the meal could fool her into believing they weren't going to do something terrible to her.

They probably put something in the food, too.

She stared at the meat as if it was a cherry lollipop. To Link, it would've been.

How did the words go? Little Fillet, I think of you most every day.

Her mind flooded with memories of stupid lyrics, until she almost smiled. With every word, the haze of the drugs lifted.

She looked down at her hands and realized she had scratched something into the side of the lacquered wood table next to her bed. One of her long pink nails was hanging off.

Rid traced the scratches with her finger.

A long line, and a shorter one—an L.

He was coming for her. She had to be ready.

Stay clear and get up.

As Ridley pushed herself up, she noticed that the dark purple bruises on her arms were gone. Come to think of it, her neck didn't hurt anymore, either. If it weren't for the drugs, she probably would've felt fine.

But I haven't been here long enough to heal, have I?

The familiar sound of footsteps in the hallway sent her flying back under the covers. She closed her eyes and pretended to be asleep.

Please don't come in here.

The sound of metal clinking and another girl's scream tore through the hallway.

"Come on out. We're taking a little trip." She recognized the Darkborn's Southern drawl.

"I don't want to go anywhere," the girl begged. Names started to come back to her. It wasn't Drew or Katarina. This girl had an Italian accent. "Please, just let me stay here."

"Now you want to stay?" the Darkborn asked. "After you've spent months begging to leave?"

Months. A knot formed in Ridley's stomach.

How long have I been here? She couldn't handle staying in this cell for weeks, let alone months.

Unless I already have.

"Don't worry," the Darkborn continued. "You're coming back."

Ridley heard shoes scraping against the concrete. He must've been dragging the poor girl.

"Where are we going?" The Italian girl sounded frantic.

"Men in the Syndicate are willing to pay a lot of money for an Empath's services. Depending on the services." He laughed cruelly.

Ridley opened her eyes and stared at the bars. She could tell from the sound of their footsteps that they were moving in the other direction.

Power trafficking. That's what these scumbags are doing.

She'd heard rumors about it in some of the darker Caster clubs, like Suffer. Casters being abducted and sold for their powers. Or in this case, rented. Either way, it was a dirty trade, something even Dark Casters looked down upon.

There's no way I'll let them drag me around like a dog and make me do tricks.

I'm not for sale.

I'm Ridley Duchannes.

Ridley waited until the footsteps were long gone, letting the anger churn inside her. She grabbed the plate from the nightstand and hurled it against the wall. The white bone china shattered across the rug.

She didn't like people messing with her, but using her was worse.

Just try me. Go ahead.

Treat me like a dog, and I'll bite you. But the anger only exhausted her. She was still so weak.

Ridley climbed off the bed and stumbled toward the bars, her legs unsteady beneath her. "Hey, Katarina? Drew?" she whispered. "Are you out there?"

For a moment, no one responded. Maybe the Darkborn had taken them all at the same time.

"Can you guys hear me?" she tried again.

"Shut up, Pink," Drew hissed from the darkness.

"He's already gone," Ridley said. "And my name is Ridley."

It took a moment for the German girl to answer. "Katarina—I'm here."

"What happened to that girl? Where was he taking her?"

"Her name is Lucia," Katarina said. "Silas rents out our powers to members of the Syndicate. He was taking her on a job."

"Shut up," Drew snapped. "Are you stupid? You don't want him coming back for you."

Silence fell over the cells, until Ridley spoke up again. "How many of us are here?"

Katarina finally answered. "Six, I think." Her voice was shaky.

"No. It's at least seven," a girl with a French accent whispered. "You're forgetting about Angelique."

"Idiots," Drew hissed.

"Who's Angelique? Did something happen to her?" Ridley gripped the bars, her knuckles turning white.

"Plenty of stuff happened to her, but she also escaped," Katarina said. "She didn't talk much to anyone, except Lucia. She went crazy every time they took Lucia."

Ridley sensed there was more to the story, but right now she needed to know something more important. "Are you all Casters?"

"I'm a Sybil," the French girl answered.

"Diviner," the German girl said.

"Thaumaturge." This girl sounded Spanish. "My name is Alicia. I'm the one they brought in to heal you."

Like Ryan. No wonder I don't feel like death warmed over anymore.

American. Italian. German. French. Spanish. Siren, Sybil, Diviner, Thaumaturge. Silas has his own little version of It's a Small World down here.

"Thanks for fixing me up." Ridley rubbed her hands over her arms where the bruises had been. At least that answered one of her questions. "Anyone else?" she asked. "Come on, we can help each other."

"An Illusionist and a Cypher were already here when they brought me in," the French girl said. "I don't know if they're still here."

"I'm here," a voice called out.

"Me, too." Another one.

"I'm a Siren," Ridley whispered. "Does anyone know what they're giving us? The drugs, I mean?"

Or am I the only one?

"You're pretty stupid, Pink," Drew said. "Sunshine is the only drug strong enough to knock some of us out. Including a Siren."

Ridley wondered who this girl was. She had backbone, which meant she was probably Ridley's best ally in the group.

Even if she is a pain in the ass.

"Sorry I'm not up to speed on all the drugs Casters are using these days. I'm not accustomed to anyone being able to knock me out under any circumstances." Ridley racked her brain, trying to figure out what kind of Caster would be as difficult to drug as a Siren. She needed to know more about this girl so she could find a way to bring her around. "Are you a Shifter?"

Drew laughed. "Please. An antihistamine could knock out a Shifter."

A light went on in Ridley's brain. *Of course. She's almost as defensive as Necro.*

"You're a Necromancer."

"Give the girl a prize." Drew sounded bored, or scared. It was hard to tell without looking at her.

"Is that why the Darkborn calls us the Menagerie? Because we're different kinds of Casters?" Rid asked.

Or is it because they treat us like animals?

For a moment, no one said a word.

"His boss *chooses* us because we're different types of Casters," the French girl said. "He'll keep doing it until he completes his collection."

The word *collection* sent a chill up Ridley's spine.

"Or until he needs a replacement," Drew said.

Ridley clung to the bars, her legs suddenly weaker. "Who's his boss?"

No one answered.

Footsteps echoed somewhere down the hallway.

"Shh," someone hissed.

A familiar scent floated through the passageway.

The stench of the Barbadian cigars Abraham favored when he was alive.

No.

Anyone but him.

But there was no denying it.

I'd know the smell of those smokes anywhere.

Up until that moment, Ridley had believed her life was in danger because she'd been kidnapped by a crazy Darkborn. Now she realized someone far more deranged and deadly was controlling her fate.

And he's standing in the hallway right now.

Ridley caught a glimpse of his expensive dress shirt with the sleeves rolled up carelessly, and his stupid wing tips.

Silas Ravenwood stopped in front of her cell, with a Barbadian cigar balanced between his fingers.

He smiled at her through the bars. "It's nice to see you again, Miss Duchannes. So pleased you could join us."

CHAPTER 8: LINK

Winds of Change

Link had more luck Ripping himself and Floyd to Oxford than he had Ripping them back. They ended up on top of a pile of garbage bags behind a Chinese restaurant.

At least they'd missed the Dumpster. Link tried to feel good about that. "Welcome to the good old US of A." He flopped back into the trash. "Home, stinky home."

"Thanks." Floyd pulled a handful of rotten lo mein out of her hair. "I was already trying not to puke. You suck at this."

Link grabbed a handful of noodles, eggs, and cabbage. "Maybe I felt like Chinese spaghetti."

"Yeah. And maybe I hitched a ride with the wrong hybrid."

"Whatever. Rippin' isn't as easy as it looks. At least we're not in China. I hope." He stared up at the Binding Ring on his hand. "This thing shoulda kept Liv and John close, but I don't see them. Do you?"

"All I know is, you were supposed to be aiming for New Jersey. That's what Necro said on the phone." Floyd was getting annoyed.

Laughter interrupted them. "Why didn't you wait for us to eat? You guys must've been really hungry." John grinned down at them.

Of course, John and Liv weren't covered in garbage.

"What took you so long?" John asked, pulling Link to his feet. "Still got your training wheels on?" Link punched John in the biceps and John punched him back, which turned into five more punches.

"Right. You're both wankers," Liv said.

"Losers," Floyd added. They finally agreed on something.

By the time Floyd was on her feet, she had already called Necro on her cell phone. "I've got the address. It isn't far. Some girl Sampson used to hook up with let them hang out at her place."

Link looked around. "Let's find somewhere with less people, and me and John will Rip us there."

Floyd cringed. "No thanks. I'm taking the train. I've had enough Traveling for a while."

"But—" Link began.

Floyd held up her hand. "I'm saying this as a friend. You *really* need more practice."

"The train's fine." Liv pulled out her phone. "It won't take long to get there. We're only a few stops away."

John noticed a snack truck parked by the curb. "Give me a minute. Link, front me some money, until I find somewhere to exchange ours."

Link took his wallet out of his back pocket, the silver

chain dangling from the end to where it attached at his belt loop. "What do you need money for?" he asked, handing John a five.

"Hold that thought." John jogged over to the truck and returned moments later with a huge bag of Doritos. "I seriously missed these."

Floyd gave him a strange look. "I thought hybrids don't eat."

John shoved a handful of chips in his mouth. "It's a personal choice, and personally, I like Doritos."

"Or anything made with disgustingly orange powdered cheese," Liv added.

"You know you love it," John said with his mouth full. He pulled her in for a kiss, and she jumped away with a yelp.

She wiped her cheek. "Not a chance."

Link tried to smile, but he couldn't. It was hard to watch John and Liv being John and Liv, when Ridley was gone. He noticed that Floyd was unusually quiet, too, as they walked through the station and boarded their train.

"What's up?" he asked as they sat down. "You haven't said anythin' since we came down here."

Floyd frowned and bit her lip. "Necro sounded weird on the phone."

"And now your Spidey sense is tinglin'?"

She nodded. "I think something's wrong."

"Of course it is." Liv adjusted the dials on her selenometer and looked up at John. "And you thought things would change while we were gone."

When they finally made it to the apartment complex, something was more than wrong. Link had barely made it through the introductions before Sam and Necro broke the news about Nox.

"What do you mean, he's gone?" Link was pacing in the middle of the living room, staring at Sampson, who looked even more out of place than usual on the floral couch. "And who was stupid enough to let him go?"

The Darkborn slid his thumb under the bike chain around his throat, fidgeting with the links. "Nox gave us the slip. He said he was going for a walk and never came back."

"We're pretty sure Nox went after Ridley on his own," Necro said. "We were about to go after him when Floyd called."

"Of course he did." Link was furious. "Because all Nox thinks about is himself. How he wants to get there first and be the big hero." Lucille threaded her way between Link's ankles, as if she knew he was upset.

"Calm down, Link." Liv picked up the cat and scratched behind her ears. "I thought the reason you needed John's help was because no one knew how to find the labs."

Necro ran her hands through her blue faux-hawk. "Either Nox lied to us, or he came up with some crazy idea to try to figure out where the house is himself. It's hard to know. He's not exactly predictable, and he isn't really into the whole trust thing." Nox and Necro had known each other longer than any of them.

"He's not exactly a whole lotta things," Link said.

Sampson stood up from his seat on the couch. "Enough with the chitchat. So where are these labs, and how do we get there?"

"Slow down, big guy. It's not that simple." John automatically squared his shoulders like he was trying to look bigger, but Sampson still towered over him, his huge arms making John's look scrawny—which wasn't an easy thing to do. Finally, John gave up and shoved his hands in his pockets. "I don't know how much Link told you, but I grew up in those labs. Abraham did things to my head. For a while, I couldn't even remember some of the things I did. The things he made me do."

Liv looped her arm through John's and leaned her head against his shoulder. "None of that was your fault."

"Maybe not," John said. Link could tell he was working the hard way around to bad news. "My point is, there are things I should know that I can't remember, like the location of the labs. Abraham created a lot of fail-safes when he screwed with my head. I think this is one of them."

Link felt like someone had hurled a rock at his head. He stared at John. "Wait. You don't know where to find them? Are you messin' with me?"

"Relax," John said. "*I* don't know the exact location, but I do know someone who does."

Necro turned to Link. "You know a guy who knows a guy? That's your *brilliant* idea?" She shook her head. "Why didn't I think of that? Oh, wait, because it's a *stupid* idea. In fact, it's not even an idea."

Floyd leaned against the wall, arms crossed, glaring at John. "You mean we went all the way to Oxford, and you don't even know where we're going? Didn't you think that was worth mentioning?"

Floyd took a step closer to John—and walked right into Liv,

who had her arms crossed in front of her. "Right. Let's all take a breather."

"Your boyfriend's lucky he's still breathing," Sam said, without a hint of a smile.

"It's not optimal. But considering you don't know where to go, I hardly think you're in any position to comment." Liv turned to Link. "Which makes me wonder if we shouldn't go after Ridley on our own. You and me and John. It's clear that not everyone here actually cares about her."

"Hold on. That's not true, Keeper," Necro said. "Ridley's my friend, and so is Nox. If he went after her like an idiot—which I'm sure he did, since he acts totally crazy when it comes to Ridley—we have to make sure nothing happens to him."

"And save Rid," Link added.

"That, too," Sampson agreed.

Floyd didn't say anything. Necro shoved her. "Oh, come on."

"Come on, what?" Floyd asked.

Necro wouldn't let it drop this time. "You may not like Ridley, but she's one of us. We're not going to let Silas Ravenwood have her. She's practically in the band."

Floyd sighed.

Link wanted to hug Necro, but he knew she'd rather have him slug her in the right eye. "Pound it," he said, grinning.

"Glad we ironed all that out," Sampson said. "You gonna make us hug now? Or can we go after Nox? Even though we don't actually know where we're going." John started to protest, but Sam waved him off. "Yeah, yeah. You know a guy. I heard." He eyed the flowered couch. "Anything has to be better than sitting around here."

John's eyes were on Link, and Link could feel the questions coming. *Who is this Nox guy and why does Rid make him act crazy? And what does the Illusionist chick have against Rid?*

Get in line, Link thought.

John took Liv's hand and nodded at Sampson. "The big guy has a point. Why don't we get out of here and stop wasting time?"

"After you, little guy." Sampson held the door as they all filed outside and locked it behind them.

"We need to find the closest Outer Door to the Tunnels," John said.

Sampson nodded up the street. "No problem. It's not far." He took off with Lucille trotting behind him. The cat had taken a liking to the big Darkborn. Link hoped it would give Sampson some cred with John and Liv.

Link and Floyd followed Lucille, while Necro fell into step next to John and Liv. "So who's this guy who knows where the labs are?"

"He's a musician," John said. "And he hates Abraham Ravenwood almost as much as I do."

Link stopped in his tracks. "Dude. I swear. I have no idea where the labs are."

John clapped his hand against Link's back. "And I swear he's not you."

Sampson turned down an alley, which looked like a dead end. By now, Link had seen enough Outer Doors to know better. Casters were experts at hiding the doors that led from the Mortal world into their own. It was one of the most annoying things about them, from a head-banging-into-a-hidden-doorframe perspective.

The wall in front of them was covered in Banksy-style graffiti. In the spray-painted mural, a girl in round glasses was taking a picture of a smartphone that was taking a picture of a smartphone that was taking a picture of a smartphone. It went on and on until you couldn't make out the images anymore.

"There it is." Sampson nodded at the mural.

"A palimpsest?" Liv touched the concrete wall.

"You mean, like Aunt Del?" Link asked.

Liv nodded. "In a way. A palimpsest is a picture within a thousand pictures that goes on endlessly. The way Aunt Del sees places at different points in time, all at once. It's actually sort of brilliant, for a Caster door."

Link tried not to think about what a dingbat Lena's Aunt Del was sometimes. "Hope it works better than Aunt Del's memory."

"Everything works better than Aunt Del's memory," Liv pointed out.

"Except maybe her watch," John said. Which was true; there was nothing like getting lost in time to make a person late for dinner.

Sampson reached out and traced the painted black outline around the largest smartphone in the mural. His fingers slid into the wall, revealing a hidden groove.

"*Aperi portam*," Sampson whispered. The image of the cell phone disappeared, and the wall slid back, exposing a narrow passageway. He held out his hand. "Ladies first."

Liv shoved her way between Link and Floyd. "Why is it that guys always say that when you're about to go somewhere fairly dreadful and potentially dangerous?"

Sampson smiled. "I was trying to be a gentleman."

Liv's eyes darted from the bike chain around his neck to his tattooed arms and leather pants before she slipped through the opening in the wall. Caster or not, Liv was still one of the bravest girls Link had ever met, right along with the one who went through next.

Atta girl, Lucille.

Floyd seemed unwilling to be shown up by a Mortal girl and a cat and strode forward, pulling Necro by the arm along with her.

Only the boys were left behind.

"Want to tell me where we're headed?" Sampson asked. "Or who this guy you know is?"

"I'm not sure you'd believe me if I told you," John said as the last sliver of the Mortal world disappeared.

"How far did you say it was?" Link looked back at John, almost bumping his head for what had to be the tenth time.

The ceiling in the narrow Caster Tunnel was so low that Link, Sampson, and John had to bend over as they walked. Even Liv had to slouch.

"I didn't," John said. "Stop complaining. It's not far."

Floyd shuffled along behind Necro. "How did you hit your head? You don't even have to duck."

"Link's stupid cat ran in front of me," Necro said.

"Her name's Lucille," Link said. "I wouldn't call her stupid. She probably understands what we're sayin'. She's ornery, just like the old ladies who gave her to me." Link heard Lucille's feet pattering across the dirt toward a circle of pale light in the distance ahead of them.

"And that is rather an understatement," Liv said.

"Please let there be a high ceiling in my future," Sampson said. The Darkborn was so tall that he was practically doubled over. His back had to be aching by now. Though Link still wasn't exactly sure how much pain Supernaturals like Sampson felt.

When Sampson stepped out of the passageway and stood up again, John let out a sigh of relief. "Thank god. I didn't know how much more of that I could take."

Link reached the opening right after Necro and Floyd, and he was so busy looking up that he plowed into them. Floyd swayed, and Link caught her arm. She glanced down at the spot where his fingers touched her skin, and Link felt a wave of guilt. Not because he had feelings for Floyd, but because he *didn't*. She was funny and pretty, in an indie rocker chick kind of way, and one of the best bass players Link had ever met. But no matter how cool Floyd was, there was one thing she'd never be.

More like, one person.

Where the hell are you, Babe?

Link was so miserable and so alone, it didn't matter how many of his friends were with him. All he could feel was the one person who wasn't.

"Check out the sky," John said.

Ribbons of pale green and lavender arched above them, the colors alternating in the same pattern as far as they could see. When Link looked carefully, he realized it wasn't a sky at all. Except for the carpet of grass beneath their feet, the rest of the tunnel was made of flowers and vines.

In spite of everything, it was sort of beautiful.

"I've never seen anything like this, not even down here." Necro stared up at the sea of lavender flowers. "It's miraculous."

Link understood what she was saying. Miracles were made of hope.

And hope was what they all needed most.

Liv drew a quick sketch in her little red journal. "Actually, it's a hedge tunnel."

"Buzzkill," Floyd said.

Liv ignored her. "We have some of the most famous ones back home, in the UK. But this looks exactly like the Wisteria Tree Tunnel in Japan."

Floyd gave Liv a strange look. "Who knows junk like that?"

"People who read." Liv walked past Floyd and Necro, heading deeper into the arched hedge. "You see, there are these remarkable things called books. They're full of pages and pages of words." She glanced back at Floyd. "Maybe you've heard of them. Or maybe not."

John stifled a smile and followed his girlfriend.

"Don't you get a headache from memorizing all that random stuff?" Floyd shot back.

Liv followed Lucille without bothering to turn around. "Not at all. What gives me a headache is explaining all that *random stuff* to other people."

The way Liv said *people* made it pretty clear that the only person she was talking about was Floyd.

"Sometimes I really don't understand your choice of friends," Floyd said, looking at Link.

"Liv's just givin' you a hard time," Link said. "She'll warm up to you, and then you two will get along great." He tried to sound more upbeat than he felt.

Floyd glared, and Necro raised an eyebrow. "Doubtful."

"Highly," Liv muttered.

The tunnel of flowers continued for at least a mile. Even Sampson seemed mesmerized, glancing up every few moments. But Link was having a hard time looking at them when he had no idea what Ridley was looking at right now.

With every step he only worried more.

What if she's all alone and hurt somewhere? What if she isn't *alone?*

Link clenched his jaw. He couldn't stand the thought of anyone hurting the only girl he'd ever loved. Because that was what it came down to, plain and simple. He loved Ridley, and it didn't have anything to do with her Siren powers. He would've fallen for her one way or another—Mortal or Caster, Light or Dark. He loved the sound of her voice, even when she was complaining, and the way she fit under his arm perfectly, even in her crazy high heels.

Ridley was all long legs, red lipstick, and pink-streaked hair on the outside; but on the inside, she wasn't a bad girl. She was a girl who never had a choice about being born into a family of cursed Supernaturals, or Darkness Claiming her on her sixteenth birthday, or her family turning their backs on her after it happened.

Inside, Ridley was all pain and heartbreak—just a regular girl who needed him.

Almost as bad as I need her.

CHAPTER 9: NOX

Gates of Tomorrow

Every Caster knew where to find the Mile, including Nox. It was hidden in the Tunnels beneath the French Quarter in New Orleans—a solid mile of identical Caster doors.

At night, drunk Casters and Incubuses would dare each other to open one of the doors, in the Caster version of Russian roulette. Without knowing what waited on the other side, you could find yourself in some fat guy's living room, watching him sleep in front of the television—or just as easily end up surrounded by Vexes and other deadly creatures.

Opening the door was the rush. The Wheel of Fate decided the rest—one way or another. It was a sucker's game. Nox would never take those odds.

Most other Casters and Incubuses must've wised up, because now the narrow alley lined with doors as far as the eye could see was deserted. Knowing Abraham Ravenwood, the Blood

Incubus' door would be protected by some sort of Cast. If Nox could open it at all, it would be a trap.

Yeah. A deathtrap.

Nox glanced down at his watch.

Any minute now.

He moved through the shadows, staying close to the doorways on one side, in case he needed to hide. If the Chemist was telling the truth, the door leading to Abraham's house was here somewhere, which wasn't much to go on.

Especially for a guy with no time to waste.

I'm coming, Ridley. Just be okay when I get there.

He fought the darker thoughts in the back of his mind. They were always with him, and he was afraid they always would be.

Ridley Duchannes doesn't love you. Don't be a fool.

She doesn't believe in you.

What do you believe in?

In yourself, and in how you feel about her? Even if she doesn't feel the same way about you?

He closed his eyes.

Shut up.

I believe in the way I feel.

I believe I can love her anyway.

Isn't that enough?

He leaned his head back against the wall of the dark passageway and wondered.

A few minutes later, he heard footsteps and looked at his watch again.

5:50 AM.

Right on time.

"Get to the Mile just before the sun comes up. Ravenwood's cook will be there." That's what the Chemist said.

Nox waited for a glimpse of Silas' cook. He probably should've asked the Chemist what kind of Caster she was, but it was too late now. He'd have to decide how to incapacitate her in the moment.

After she opens the door. His hands involuntarily rolled into fists.

Nox saw her shadow emerge from the street ahead of him, between two doors. *There she is. Just like he said.*

The woman wore a lightweight coat with the collar pulled up around her neck and the hem of her black uniform skirt peeking out from beneath it. Nox heard it rustle as she walked along the Mile.

A uniform. Of course.

Formal and pretentious. Like Abraham. And Silas.

Nox walked toward the woman, pretending to talk on his cell phone as if he was heading through one of those doors on his way to work, too.

She glanced in his direction, and Nox almost stopped walking. There was something about her—something familiar. She crossed the street in the Tunnel slowly, her crooked posture betraying her age. She was curled over, face to the ground, as if she was walking into a headwind determined to destroy her. This woman was bent by something more than just time.

Something more evil—and more powerful.

That was when he knew.

Silas hadn't just inherited Abraham's cook. He'd inherited the *same* cook who had worked in Abraham's house when Nox was a kid.

He'd inherited Mrs. Blackburn.

It all came rushing back. Even back then, Mrs. Blackburn's posture had been crooked when she leaned over the marble counter to knead dough or prepare tea service. By now she had to be at least sixty, by Nox's calculations. Was he really going to knock out an old lady?

Someone who Abraham Ravenwood already spent his life tormenting? Someone who made me cookies after he tormented me?

I have to, he told himself. *It's the only way to find Ridley.*

When Mrs. Blackburn reached the door, she rested her palm on the wood. Just as she began to whisper something, she noticed Nox and stopped.

He tried to act casual, as if he planned to walk right by her, but the old woman seemed to know better.

She looked him right in the eye and gasped. "You?"

Nox looked around, as though he thought she was talking about someone else. "Excuse me?"

Mrs. Blackburn shook her head. "I always knew you'd come back. But you're too late," she hissed.

Nox dropped the act. She obviously recognized him. "Too late for what?"

"You can't get what you came for. The old bastard is dead."

It took him a moment to realize she wasn't talking about Silas. "You mean Abraham?"

The old woman nodded, her Caster green eyes staring at him. He'd always wondered how Abraham had persuaded a Light Caster to work for him.

What was he threatening her with all these years?

Nox glanced at the door. "I'm not looking for Abraham."

She gave him a knowing look. "Silas?" Her voice rasped with age.

He nodded. "We have some unfinished business. You look like you might understand."

Mrs. Blackburn shrugged. "There's no other kind of business with Abraham and Silas Ravenwood."

He took a step closer. "Mrs. Blackburn, you were always kind to me. And I don't—I'd never want to hurt you. But I need to get inside."

The bent old woman shook her head. "Whatever trouble you're in, son, whatever you want with Silas, forget about it and get as far away from this place as you can."

"I can't."

"I've worked in that house since I was a child," she began.

"And I was a child," Nox added.

She nodded. "Abraham brought my mother there, just like yours. Those Ravenwoods have evil running through their veins—black and thick—where there oughta be blood."

"You don't have to tell me that."

"I know. But whether it's hate or vengeance or money—whatever's sending you back into that house isn't worth it. Nothing is."

Nox leaned against the doorjamb and looked down at her. "How about love?"

The word made her pause.

Then Mrs. Blackburn's ancient eyes softened. "You were always a sweet boy. I remember how Abraham treated your mother, and I know it must've killed you to stand by and watch. If anyone knows how you felt, it's me."

Nox tried to keep it together, but all he wanted to do was break something.

Do you? Do you know what it's like to hide, powerless, while the person you love most in the world begs for someone to kill her and put an end to the torture?

Mrs. Blackburn straightened the best she could. "But your mother's gone now. Yours, and mine. It's too late to save either one."

In that moment, Nox knew he could trust her.

Mrs. Blackburn, lowly cook of the Ravenwood kitchens. Servant of unpunished and unpardoned hearts.

You're fooling yourself if you think you're any freer than she is, Nox thought. *You're as bent under the weight of Abraham and Silas as the old woman.*

They were bound, the two of them, like survivors of the same plane crash.

Refugees from a shared war.

It's not over. It never will be.

"This isn't just about the past," Nox finally said. "Silas has someone else I care about, and he's going to do the same thing to her that Abraham did to my mom."

If Ridley's still alive.

The old woman nodded, as if she understood more than his words. She studied his face. "Nobody in their right mind would go back through this door if they didn't have to."

Nox shifted uncomfortably. "Like I said. I have to."

She frowned, skeptical. "And you know what he'll do to you?"

"I have it on good authority." Nox pointed to the misshapen

stitches along his cheekbone. "And we both know there's more where this came from."

Mrs. Blackburn sighed. Then she rested her palm on the door again, as if she'd made up her mind. "You must be the dumbest boy in the whole Underground. The dumbest, or the bravest."

He grinned. "Why choose just one?"

She frowned. "All right, then. You can follow me through. This Tunnel leads into the wine cellar inside the main house at Ravenwood Oaks. Silas is living there now, but aside from his flashy taste in decorating, I think you'll find the place hasn't changed much."

"Thank you, Mrs. Blackburn. I know what you're risking by helping me."

"Then keep quiet when we're in the Tunnel, and when I go up through the cellar, give me at least thirty minutes before you follow. If Silas finds out I helped you, it'll be the end of me." She hesitated for a moment, a sad expression passing across her face. "He'll be the end of me either way."

Nox nodded. "We all have to die sometime."

Mrs. Blackburn smiled almost wistfully at Nox. "After the things we've seen, maybe that would be for the best." She turned back to the door and pressed against the frame. *"Aperire domum tenebrarum."*

Open the House of Darkness.

"I'll come back for you," Nox said, his voice low.

"Don't," she whispered in return. "At least one of us should be free of this place for good."

The door opened by itself without a creak, and Nox slipped inside behind her.

It was a short walk through the Tunnel leading from the Mile to Silas' house—even if Nox was having a hard time thinking of it that way. He had too many memories of Abraham in that house, threatening him and tormenting his mom, to imagine it belonging to anyone other than the head of the House of Ravenwood.

Except for the sound of their footsteps, they moved in silence.

It didn't matter. Nox could still hear the ghosts following him as he walked. The chairs flying. The glass breaking. The screaming and the crying. *What are you looking at, boy? Who do you think you are?*

He prayed Silas wasn't doing the same thing to Ridley right now.

Please be there, Little Siren. Please be okay.

But if she was there, she wasn't okay. Nox knew that better than anyone.

I'm coming to get you. I swear. Even if no one came for us.

As they neared Silas' house, the passage turned and the Tunnel looked more like a hallway, with faded wallpaper peeling beneath paintings and black and white or sepia photographs of Ravenwoods who were probably long dead: Jessamine Ravenwood. Isaac Ravenwood. Mather Ravenwood.

Aside from Abraham, Nox didn't recognize any of them. But their dead black eyes marked them all as Incubuses.

Mrs. Blackburn caught him staring as they passed by. "You seeing ghosts, son?"

He looked away.

He was relieved when she hauled her ancient body up a

wooden staircase and mumbled the Doorwell Cast again. This time, it opened the cellar door. Walking down the Ravenwood memory lane hadn't done much to clear his head.

If anything, it had clouded it.

When they reached the top of the stairs and entered the narrow wine cellar lined with wine barrels, racks of vintage bottles, and shelves of humidors, Mrs. Blackburn turned to Nox and held a finger to her lips, signaling him to be quiet. She squeezed his arm, then scurried up another set of stairs that led to the kitchen.

And the face from his childhood was gone. The moment she disappeared, it was as if he'd imagined the whole thing. He wondered if he'd ever see her again.

Nox checked the time on his phone. Mrs. Blackburn had asked him to wait thirty minutes, but without knowing if Ridley was dead or alive, it felt like forever.

He tried to stop himself from thinking about it.

He had to be patient.

If Ridley's dead, then you'll know what forever feels like. And it will feel a thousand times worse than this.

Forever feels like forever.

Nox wanted to bolt. He wanted to ransack the place, scream her name, pound down every door. But he couldn't. He was trapped like a rat in one of Silas Ravenwood's walls.

He couldn't do anything to endanger the old woman.

Not after she risked her life to help me.

Nox studied the bottles; the Ravenwoods' cellar had everything from rare vintages to newer blends from their own vineyards. But it was the Barbadians that got to him—the stench of Abraham Ravenwood's signature cigar. The smell made Nox's stomach turn, and as a kid, it had always sent him flying in the opposite direction.

He didn't know how many times he checked his phone. But after what felt like the hundredth, thirty minutes had finally passed.

It's time. I'll be there soon, Little Siren.

Unless they catch me and kill me first.

Nox climbed the stairs and listened at the door. When he didn't hear anything, he took a chance and opened it. He remembered that the butler's pantry lay on the other side, just off the kitchen. What he couldn't remember was where the door opposite it led. He needed to get outside and around the back of the house. He only knew one way into the labs—the route he'd taken so many years ago as a child.

Nox had no choice; he was going to have to retrace his steps, relive some hide-and-seek that was almost too painful to remember. He opened the door slowly, and for once, luck was on his side.

The back of the estate stretched out before him, partially hidden by the shadows between what was left of the night and dawn. Weeping willows and old oaks dripping with Spanish moss guarded the property, along with more than a few enormous men. They had to be Darkborns—they were too unnaturally big to be Dark Casters, and with dawn breaking, Incubuses would have already fled inside to avoid the sunlight.

Unless Silas has more hybrids like Link and his friend John Breed.

Either way, this was a suicide mission, which wouldn't have mattered to Nox except for the fact that he was probably Ridley's only hope. Based on Link's track record of keeping Ridley safe, the chances of the hybrid finding his way here and getting her out were slim to none.

I won't fail you, Rid. No matter what.

Nox stole through the darkness like a shadow himself, staying close to the trees, working his way slowly toward the entrance to the labs, behind the carriage house. He crossed his fingers, hoping the door was still there.

As he edged his way around the side of the old building, he saw it.

The steel door that had reminded him of a tornado shelter when he was a kid lay a few feet away, unguarded. But Nox didn't let that lull him into a false sense of security. He remembered the Incubuses patrolling the labs the first time he'd snuck in.

When he opened the door, a chill ran up the back of his neck, as if Abraham Ravenwood himself was there, watching him.

Haunting him, the way he always had and always would.

After all the people I've hurt, maybe I deserve it. Maybe I'm no better than he is.

But there was no time to think about it now. Nox slipped inside and moved quietly through the passage that led to the main hallway. When the passage ended, he peered around the corner.

Finally.

He was startled to see how the labs had changed. When he was a kid, the labs had reminded him of a state-of-the-art military facility or futuristic hospital—with gleaming steel walls and glass observation windows.

The steel walls were still here, but the observation window was gone.

On the left side of the hallway, sheets of thick plastic hung from the ceiling in front of a sterile-looking white door marked AUTHORIZED PERSONNEL ONLY.

Nox almost expected to see people wearing biohazard suits coming out at any moment. He couldn't help but wonder if Abraham had continued his experiments—and if Silas was still conducting them now.

One look down the other side of the hallway made it clear that Silas was doing a lot more than that in the labs. Halfway down the hall, the steel walls ended abruptly, replaced by intricately carved mahogany paneling.

Strange.

The floor was covered in the hides of more animals than Nox could count; the crowning glory was the pelt of a huge Bengal tiger, complete with its head, paws, and tail.

What's this weird museum doing in the middle of the labs?

It was more than just the animal pelts and mounted heads.

Leather club chairs were arranged beneath them, in small clusters, like you'd find in an upper-crust men's club—and not at all the kind of club Nox himself had ever run. A huge marble fireplace added to the *Masterpiece Theatre* effect.

Nox looked away from the fireplace. Even though it wasn't lit, it was force of habit with him now.

Careful.

A portrait of a white-haired man in a Sunday suit hung above the mantel. Nox couldn't tell if it really was Abraham from where he was standing, but he was too fixated on what was hanging *around* the painting to care.

Animal heads—at least a dozen of them.

From a feral-looking wolverine and a black panther baring

its ivory teeth to a lion with a full mane, and a gray wolf, still snarling, the world's most dangerous predators surrounded the greatest predator of them all.

It's almost like Silas has a sense of humor. A deeply deranged sense of humor.

What could Silas possibly be doing with some kind of boys' club in the labs? When Nox was younger, Abraham never allowed visitors in the labs, and now it seemed as if Silas was entertaining in here.

What's he selling? Or dealing? And why here?

But then Nox heard voices on the other side of the biohazard door and quickly stepped back into the alcove, pressing himself against the wall.

"It's unrealistic. If production continues this way, we're gonna run out of space," a woman said. "We're already pushing maximum capacity as it is."

"If you want to be the one to tell him, feel free," a man said. "It'll be your blood spatter on the floor. But I'm not waiting around to mop it up. I'm going home."

Nox got a good look at the golden-eyed Dark Casters as they walked by in their pristine white lab coats. So the place was teeming with Ravenwood lab lackeys, just as it had been in Abraham's day.

At least one thing hasn't changed around here.

He waited a few minutes to make sure they were gone before he headed for the trophy room or whatever it was. To Nox, it was nothing more than a thousand disembodied skins and heads. But there was a door on the other side of the room, and his gut told him to start there.

As he slipped past the mantel, the eyes of dead animals stared at him from every side, some mounted on the walls like the ones above the fireplace, others frozen in lifelike positions on the floor. In one corner, the back of a full-sized mountain lion ready to pounce served as a side table, complete with a crystal ashtray.

I should get one of those for my apartment.

Across the room, a grizzly stood at least ten feet tall, its massive claws rendered less frightening by the silver tray of cigars it was holding.

That one's all Sampson.

Nox shook his head as he reached the door, remembering how much his own father had hated hunting. "Never take pleasure in killing anything, Nox," he'd said. "Even if you don't have a choice about doing it."

Which is why my dad's dead, Nox reminded himself, *and Silas Ravenwood isn't.*

But his father had been right about one thing: This whole place was disgusting.

The scarlet-carpeted hallway didn't have any alcoves, so he hoped for the best as he passed even more rooms.

He slid into the first open door and found himself in an office crammed with file cabinets and a huge computer monitor, facing a wall plastered entirely with photos of women. Green-eyed Light Casters, golden-eyed Dark Casters, and black-eyed Succubuses stared blankly back at him.

At least their eyes were open, which meant they were alive.

Then, Nox thought.

They were like an endless parade of victims at a crime scene—hundreds, maybe thousands.

Why only women? Are they all Sirens? After all these years, is that still all the Ravenwoods care about?

Nox looked more closely. Some of the photos were covered with huge black X's. His stomach twisted as he imagined what those X's might represent.

He tried not to think about it.

Nox scanned the wall, desperately praying Ridley's photo wasn't among them. But he wasn't used to having his prayers answered, and this time wasn't any different.

The picture was front and center, right near the top—a dazed-looking Ridley Duchannes. Even in the photo, she was as dead-eyed as every other face on the wall. But as with the others, her eyes were open.

For a second, Nox stopped breathing.

Because there wasn't an X across her face.

She's alive.

CHAPTER 10: RIDLEY

Shout at the Devil

Death would be better than this, Ridley thought as Silas unlocked her cell door.

She couldn't remember feeling more desperate. More destroyed.

All this could've ended at the club. Maybe it should have.

For the first time, she felt the total absence of hope.

Silas moved toward her, flanked by his thugs. The smoke from his Barbadian cigar reached her first.

I wish I'd never made it out of Sirene.

It was too late. Link wasn't coming. Neither was Lena or Ethan, Ridley or John. Not even Nox. A quick death would be the best outcome now.

Silas reached out and touched her cheek with the hand holding the cigar. Embers singed her skin, and she winced.

I wish I'd gone up in flames with the Beater.

Because Silas Ravenwood had a way of looking at you that made you want to die.

Predatory. Hungry. And desperate for my blood on his hands.

She could see it behind his eyes.

Ridley vowed right then never to let him see what was behind hers. Instead, she spat at his feet, her eyes blazing.

Silas Ravenwood only smiled.

"You've kept me waiting a long time, Miss Duchannes. And I'm not a patient man." The sadistic glimmer in his eye reminded her of Abraham Ravenwood, another man who had taken pleasure from other people's misery.

Ridley forced herself not to look away. "And all this time I thought you were just a bully and a scumbag." She sat up on the mattress, lifting her chin.

Come a little closer.

You want to come a little closer.

Silas did, but then he shoved her down, grabbing her wrist. "I'm both of those things." He smiled, leaning over her face until his eyes stared straight into hers. "And I'm about to become your worst nightmare."

Her hands curled into fists.

You don't want to hurt me.

You want to let me go.

Silas covered her mouth with his hand, his face hovering over hers. "Your turn, Siren. I'm going to let you go—"

Ridley felt a momentary surge of relief, but then Silas motioned to the guards behind him.

"—out of your room and straight into mine. Are you ready to find out what you're really made of? Because I am."

Ridley thrashed, angry at herself for believing Silas Ravenwood was stupid enough to leave himself open to a Siren's powers. He must've found a Cast or potion or Charm that could render him immune to her.

She dreaded to think how he was doing it.

"Now, now."

Ridley struggled to bite him, but the Incubus was squeezing her jawbones so hard it felt like he was crushing them.

When she tried to scream, the sound came out more like a whimper.

Silas licked his lips. "Caster got your tongue?" He snapped his fingers and his guards moved toward them. "Take her to the operating room."

A hood came down over her head and everything went black.

Ridley couldn't see much through the rough burlap hood, and every breath left her choking on dust. She was being dragged down some kind of hallway—bits of floor tile and the occasional doorway blurring past her.

Within minutes, the floor changed from tile to sterile white linoleum, and the scent of disinfectant made her gag. When they pushed her through a set of swinging doors and she heard the beeps and buzzing of machines, it seemed like they were in a hospital.

Why would Silas take her to a hospital?

He wouldn't.

He'd made their destination sound far more menacing.

The operating room. That's what he called it.

But everything around her reminded Ridley of a hospital—the fluorescent lights, the white floor, the stench of disinfectant.

The realization dawned on her slowly. If this wasn't a hospital, there was only one other possibility. . . .

Abraham's labs.

The place where he'd experimented on Casters and engineered John. The place she'd known she was headed to the moment she saw Silas in her cell—and the one thing she'd feared more than anything.

Her blood ran cold.

Not there. Anywhere but there.

No! No! No!

Ridley kicked and thrashed until someone pressed a cloth against the burlap over her mouth and nose. It smelled like bleach and dust and alcohol, all mixed together.

It only took a second for her knees to buckle. Then her thoughts flickered and she disappeared into the darkness.

Ridley opened her eyes.

Darkness.

Footsteps.

A word, here and there.

Dangerous.

Experimental.

Fatal.

Patient 13.

Ridley blinked. A single circle of light was aimed at her face. She could barely make out the bulb hanging from a long wire above her, like it was reaching down from the black shadows of the ceiling.

The harsh light burned her eyes, but she didn't look away. She didn't want to look at Silas as he emerged from the darkness beside her.

You bastard.

"No risk, no reward," Silas said, stepping closer to the table she was strapped to. "We're making history here, Doc."

"I understand, Mr. Ravenwood," another man answered, his voice shaky. "But there are limits."

"Not in my world." Silas laughed. "Relax, Doc. All in the name of science, right?"

Ridley struggled to stay calm.

You have to be smart if you want to get out of this mess alive.

She pulled against the restraints.

Shackles.

She ran her hands along the table. Smooth, hard, cool. Metal, most likely.

An operating table.

"Don't waste your energy." Silas bent over her and flipped what sounded like a switch under the table. "You're not going anywhere, *Siren.*" There was something strange about the way he said the word. "When I'm finished, you'll be so much more."

More? More of what?

Silas snapped his fingers at the man she couldn't see.

"Begin the infusion," he said, leaning closer to Ridley. "I'm afraid this is going to hurt. But not nearly as much as I'd like it to."

Ridley focused all her energy in the direction of the unseen man, somewhere in the darkness.

Don't begin the infusion.

Don't begin anything.

"I said, start things up," Silas barked over his shoulder.

Ridley didn't feel anything change, and she was so tired....

But she couldn't give up.

You don't want to hurt me, whoever you are.

You want to leave.

"Do I have to—?"

She heard the door close in the distance, footsteps in the hall beyond. Then she felt a slap sting her face.

"You have no idea who you're messing with."

Ridley stared back at him from beneath her tangled blond mane. Her signature waves had become something closer to dreadlocks.

"Yeah? Maybe I think *you* have no idea who *you're* messing with," she said through gritted teeth.

He grabbed Ridley's chin, forcing her to look at him. "Oh, I think I do."

She smiled, steeling herself. "Your grandfather said something like that. Right before my friends and I *killed* him."

Silas brought his fist down on a panel next to her, and an electric current shot through Ridley's body like her blood was on fire.

She screamed.

The fire burned its way from the entry point in her arm, pulsing up to her shoulders and head, then back down her spine to her legs. Her feet. Her toes. Like a second thunderous heartbeat.

With each pulse, Ridley's body writhed and spasmed. Her mind lost track of the fire and she focused on the sound of that other heartbeat.

The one far steadier than her own.

If she could hear the sound of that heartbeat, it meant she was still alive.

Didn't it?

As Ridley let go, she heard another sound from somewhere in the back of her mind.

A song.

The one Mamma used to sing.

"Mockingbird."

Maybe it meant she'd get to see Mamma again.

And Reece.

And Ryan.

And Lena.

She really wanted to see Lena.

Ridley smelled something burning far away.

Barbeque, maybe. A boy I once knew loved barbeque.

Link. I think his name was Link.

The thought made her smile.

Until she realized the burning smell was coming from her body.

And not just the smell.

The screaming, too.

After that, she surrendered to the pain and the fire, and listened to the voice singing "Mockingbird" in her head.

Only when the bird sang, it sang her to sleep with a boy's sweet, off-key voice.

That boy must really love me, she thought.

I only wish I could remember his name.

CHAPTER 11: LINK

Wasted Years

I think this is it," Sampson called out, pulling Link out of his thoughts.

When Link looked up, Sampson was standing in front of a wall of green hedge.

Another dead end.

Before Link had a chance to complain, Sampson reached into the hedge and pushed, and it opened up onto what looked like a small-town Southern street, back when Link's grandma was a kid and Gatlin only had one traffic light.

Another Caster door.

Figures.

As Link stepped through the Caster door and back into the Mortal world, he realized the door was cut into a huge Spanish moss–covered oak. On the other side, there was nothing around but more towering oaks and a broken-down house at the edge of a deserted intersection.

"Looks like we found it," John said.

"Where are we?" As far as Link could tell, there was nothing to find.

John pointed up at the white signs at the intersection that read 61 and 49, and Liv checked her selenometer as if they weren't standing in the middle of nowhere.

"Are those numbers supposed to mean something to us?" Floyd asked.

"We're at the intersection of Highways 61 and 49 in Clarksdale, Mississippi," John said.

Sampson shook his head. "I feel like an idiot. Any guitar player worth his strings knows about this place. It's where Robert Johnson made a deal with the Devil."

Floyd's eyes widened. "Seriously? We're at *the* crossroads?"

John nodded. "The one and only."

Liv glanced at John. "I'm assuming this is an American thing."

He put his arm around her. "Yeah, sorry. It's an old rock and roll myth—at least as far as Mortals are concerned. In the 1930s, a blues musician named Robert Johnson disappeared for a couple of weeks. According to the story, he brought his guitar right here to this crossroads—"

Link jumped in. "Then he traded his soul to become the most famous blues guitarist in history."

Sampson tugged on his leather pants, which weren't the best choice in the Mississippi heat. "Totally a fair trade, as far as I'm concerned."

"Thought the same thing myself," a man's voice called out from behind them.

Link wheeled around.

A young man wearing a wrinkled white shirt, a black jacket, and a Panama hat stood on the side of the road with a three-legged black Labrador. There was a weariness in the man's eyes of someone much older. A battered guitar hung from a strap slung around his back.

Lucille and the black Lab circled each other until the dog gave up and flopped down in the dust.

"Holy crap." It was the only thing Link could think of to say.

"I say that myself all the time, son," the young man said, which was weird since he didn't look that much older than the rest of them. He noticed John and tipped his hat to him. "Haven't seen you since you were a boy."

John shoved his hands in his pockets. "So you remember me, Mr. Johnson?"

"I think we've both seen enough to get past all that *Mr. Johnson* nonsense. Especially since I never did catch your name."

John held out his hand. "It's John Breed, sir."

The bluesman stared down at John's hand. "I don't shake hands anymore. Can't be too careful. But it's nice to meet you all the same, John."

Sampson inched forward. He actually looked nervous, which was completely out of character. "So the story's true, then?"

Johnson looked up at Sampson and whistled. "Kids sure have gotten taller since my day."

"Sampson's a bit . . . different," Liv said.

"You a Caster?" Johnson asked.

"You know about us?" Necro sounded shocked.

Johnson took a closer look at Necro's blue hair and piercings. "Of course I do." He glanced up at the midday Mississippi sun and walked toward a small house sitting alongside the road like a tornado had dropped it there. "Let's go inside. It's gettin' hot out here."

Link scanned the area, but there were no other homes anywhere in sight. The bluesman climbed the rickety porch steps and opened the screen door, the three-legged dog hobbling behind him. "Come on in. Make yourselves at home."

The house was small inside, but it was crammed full of stuff. The front door spilled them into a living room full of threadbare armchairs and mismatched picture frames on the walls. It reminded Link of the Sisters' house back in Gatlin. Ethan's three great-great-aunts had lived together for as long as he could remember with just about everything they'd ever owned—at least until Abraham Ravenwood burned the place down.

When Link and Ethan were young, they'd stop by the Sisters' after school and load up on sour lemon candies and buttercreams that were probably older than Ethan and Link combined. The Sisters' house looked like a museum, because the three old ladies never threw anything away. If they couldn't display it on the walls, they settled for any flat surface.

Johnson's place was no different. But instead of tiny spoon collections, broken china, and old photo albums, his place was decorated with blues relics and memorabilia—like a bowl of old harmonicas on the coffee table next to a collection of broken guitar strings in a jar. Link couldn't help but think about how disappointed the Sisters would be if Johnson invited them over without having a single dish of candy on the table.

Lucille slunk through the room, as if she felt right at home.

Sampson, Floyd, and Necro studied the yellowed newspaper

clippings framed on the walls alongside old photographs and the broken-off neck of a guitar.

Johnson sat down in a sagging upholstered armchair beside a whirling fan and set his guitar on the floor next to him. The Lab curled up at his feet. "Go ahead and sit down," he said. "I don't get many visitors."

Liv and John sat down on the sofa across from him. Link took a seat at an old pine table in the corner. He noticed a pencil sticking out of a mug, and without thinking, he pulled out the piece of paper he'd been writing songs on. He knew the lyrics sucked, but he couldn't seem to stop himself from writing ever since Rid disappeared.

The bluesman leaned forward in his chair and looked John in the eye. "Things must be pretty bad if you came lookin' for me."

"It has to do with Abraham Ravenwood."

"His grandson, Silas, actually," Liv added.

The moment John spoke Abraham's name, the bluesman stiffened, his hands gripping the arms of the chair so hard his knuckles turned white. "Haven't heard that name in a long time, and I would've been fine never hearin' it again."

Sampson, Necro, and Floyd tore their attention away from the walls.

"How do you know Abraham?" Sampson asked.

Johnson tilted his head, as if he wasn't sure if Sampson was serious. "Thought you said you knew the story?" He picked up his guitar, plucking at the strings absentmindedly.

Sampson glanced down at the floor. "People have written songs about it. Books, too."

The bluesman shrugged off his jacket and rolled up the sleeves. "So what are they singin' and writin' about me?"

Floyd walked over and stood next to Sampson, glancing at the bowl of harmonicas. "They say you were an amazing harmonica player."

Johnson laughed, slipping a hand-rolled cigarette out of his shirt pocket. "That's a real nice way of sayin' I was a bad guitar player."

Floyd blushed. "No—"

"It's all right." Johnson lit the cigarette. "I know I wasn't any good. Go on and finish."

"They say you came down here and disappeared," Floyd said. "And when you came back, you could play the guitar better than anyone."

Link jumped in. "Folks say you were the greatest blues guitarist in the history of blues guitarists. And probably the other kinds, too."

Johnson blew a few smoke rings and looked at Sampson. "And you know how they say I got that way, don't you?"

Sampson shoved his huge hands into the back pockets of his leather pants. Suddenly, he looked like a guy who was afraid to ask a girl to dance, instead of a powerful Darkborn and the lead guitarist in a Dark Caster band. "You made a deal with the Devil and traded your soul."

Johnson's eyes darted to John, then back to Sampson. He stubbed out the cigarette and let his fingers roam over the guitar frets for a moment, filling the room with an angry riff. "I guess that's what they have to say, isn't it? The only devil I made a deal with was Abraham Ravenwood. Then again, the man's no angel."

Link's head snapped up. "What? I mean, excuse me, sir?"

No one else said a word.

Sampson's mouth was hanging open, and Floyd and Necro looked almost as shocked. Liv was scribbling furiously in her journal. Only John took the comment in stride, as if he'd known all along.

"Met that bastard in a juke joint one night. We had a few drinks and talked about music. Lookin' back, I'm sure runnin' into him was no accident. He was lookin' for someone that night. Someone desperate."

"Incubuses can't grant wishes." Link looked at John, hopeful. "Can we?"

"You're right, son. Abraham brought a Caster to take care of that. A Siren. Said she belonged to him." Johnson played a few more chords. "But even she couldn't make me a better guitar player."

Sampson shook his head. "Let me guess. The Siren gave you a guitar."

The old man nodded. "Called it a lyre." He tapped on the bridge of the guitar. "She made it look just like mine, too."

Liv stopped writing. "I'm a little confused, Mr. Johnson. Abraham Ravenwood was capable of extraordinary things, but stealing a person's soul wasn't one of them. Unless there's something I don't know."

"Guess that part just made for a better story," Johnson said.

"Then what exactly did you trade, if you don't mind my asking?" Liv's pencil was poised over a fresh page.

John stood up and walked to the window, and the bluesman's eyes followed. There was something between the two of them—a secret, Link figured.

Johnson set the guitar down next to him again. "He needed me for experiments."

"But Abraham loathes Mortals. Why would he experiment on one?"

"Lots of talk about immortality. Abraham said if he could stop a Mortal from aging, he'd be one step closer to figuring out how to do the same thing with Supernaturals."

Liv gasped. "That's why you still look so young."

Link wasn't good at math, but he knew Johnson had to be around a hundred years old by now. But that wasn't the part that interested him. "And it's how you know about the labs."

Johnson frowned. "Question is, how do *you* know about the labs? Did your friend John here tell you?"

John walked back toward them. "It's the reason we're here, Mr. Johnson. We're pretty sure Abraham's great-grandson Silas is running the labs now, and we need to find him. But Abraham screwed with my head, and there are lots of things I don't remember. Like the location of the labs."

"You don't wanna go back there," Johnson warned.

John shrugged. "You're right. But I don't have a choice."

Link jumped out of his seat. "Silas might have my girl, sir. We think he's keepin' her in or near his creepy labs. I know you're probably gonna tell us it's dangerous and we shouldn't go and we're gonna die, and all that kinda stuff, but I'm still goin' either way. If there's any chance she's alive, I gotta find her. And if you help me, I'll give you anythin' you want."

Johnson rose from the chair and took out his wallet. He opened it and pulled out a faded photograph of a girl with a mane of wild blond hair. "I was in love with a Caster girl myself once. I should've stayed back home with her and settled for bein' a first-rate harmonica player and a second-rate guitarist. But things don't always turn out the way you plan." His eyes lingered on the photo for a moment before he glanced back at Link. "She probably thinks I'm dead."

"You never went back for her?" Necro asked.

The bluesman sighed. "After I paid my debt in the labs, Abraham sent me here. Another one of his Casters made sure I could never leave the crossroads. Guess the debt wasn't paid after all. But I've kept track of her."

"How?" The Keeper in Liv perked up.

Johnson bent down and scratched the dog's head. "Deuce here helps me."

The dog opened one eye lazily.

"He's a Caster dog?" Link asked. "Like Boo Radley." Ethan had told him all about the way Casters could see the world through the eyes of their Caster animals. Lena's Uncle Macon had used his wolf dog, Boo Radley, to spy on Lena all the time.

Liv inspected the Lab more closely. "But you're not a Caster. How is that possible?"

"It's one of those Caster spells," the bluesman answered. "The lady Caster who trapped me here said she was leavin' me a little gift. She didn't like Abraham much."

"It sucks you can't leave," Necro said sadly.

"Anything's better than bein' back in the labs," Johnson said.

Link cleared his throat. "Will you tell us how to find them, sir?"

Johnson shuddered. "I wouldn't wish that place on my worst enemy. I didn't make a deal with the Devil, but Abraham Ravenwood is as close as they come."

"Was," Link said. "He's dead. John and I killed him."

The bluesman walked over to Link and gestured at the sheet of paper Link had been writing on. "You a songwriter, son?"

Link shrugged. "I used to be. But I haven't been able to write since I lost Ridley. That's her name."

"Mind if I take a look?" the bluesman asked.

Link hesitated, then handed him the page reluctantly. He didn't like the idea of one of the greatest blues musicians in history reading his crappy songs.

But it's worth it if he helps us find Rid.

Johnson's eyes scanned the page.

"I told you the songs are real bad, sir." Link hung his head. "They don't even rhyme. Deep down, I always knew I wasn't the best songwriter, but I didn't think I sucked. Guess I was kiddin' myself."

John and Liv, and even Floyd and Necro, were in shock. It was more than they'd ever heard Link admit. From the moment he formed his first band, Who Shot Lincoln, and right on up to the Holy Rollers and Sirensong—Link had told everyone that he was destined to be a rock god. But he didn't care anymore about saving face—or about the band, or his career, or anything.

If I don't get Ridley back, none of it matters.

The bluesman looked up. "Songs aren't supposed to rhyme, son. They're supposed to make you feel. That's what music's about. All those words and notes are just a different way to tell someone you love them, or your heart's broken, or you're mad enough to kill somebody."

Link nodded, but he wasn't sure he understood.

"Isn't that how it feels when you sing it?" Johnson asked.

"I haven't actually gotten around to that part."

Johnson handed the paper back to him. "Then let's hear it."

It was one of those go-big-or-go-home moments, and as much as he didn't want to make a fool of himself, there was nothing Wesley Lincoln hated more than going home, and not just because of his mother.

I'm no quitter. If Robert Johnson wants to hear a song, I'll sing him one, even if it sucks worse than my mom's peach cobbler.

Like so many other times, Wesley Lincoln—tragically average Mortal basketball player, cheerleader kryptonite, and perpetual Pinewood Derby loser—had no choice but to man up.

Here goes nothin'. Link cleared his throat. *This is for you, Rid. All my songs are for you.*

He focused on the paper in his shaking hands and started to sing:

> *"Blond hair and mile-long legs,*
> *Bad attitude wearin' a borrowed smile.*
> *Never thought I had a chance with the Siren in you.*
>
> *"But you took my hand, listened to my songs,*
> *Hopped in my car and showed me the way outta here.*
> *Now you're gone and all I can think about is...*
>
> *"Half past the time I lost you*
> *And all the things I should've said.*
> *If I could just go back, I'd say it all,*
> *So you'll never forget you're mine.*
>
> *"Those nights we spent in my old car, lookin' at the stars,*
> *Holdin' hands, and makin' plans.*
> *Didn't know they'd be the last.*

"Just another Southern boy's first love,
Too many regrets and can't-forgets.
If I could just go back to...

"Half past the time I lost you
And all the things I should've said.
If I could just go back, I'd say it all,
So you won't forget you're mine."

Link stopped singing, but he couldn't look up. "That's all, I guess." He crumpled the paper in his hands. He sounded sad, like the words in his song.

Because it's how I feel. It's all true.

When he finally glanced up, his friends looked stunned, but Johnson smiled. "You got a real gift. Don't waste it."

No one had ever told Link he had a gift before, let alone a talent for something he actually cared about. He looked as shocked as his friends.

"Unless I find my girl, it doesn't matter." Link took a deep breath. "Help me find her, sir. Please."

"Wish I could, son." The bluesman shook his head sadly. "But I just can't remember."

John almost jumped out of his seat. "What are you talking about?"

"Your head wasn't the only one Abraham messed with." Johnson pointed at his temple. "There are things I can't remember. Things he didn't want me to remember."

Link dropped back down in his chair, shoulders sagging. "You don't know where the labs are," he mumbled. "You can't help us. We're screwed."

"Come on now, keep your head up, son." Johnson patted Link's shoulder. "Just because I can't help you doesn't mean I don't know somebody who can."

"Sir?"

"Are you willin' to make a trade?" Johnson asked.

Link swallowed hard. He didn't want to give the old man his soul, not that he figured it was worth much. And the stories had never exactly gone in favor of the guy making the trade—including Johnson's.

But I'll do it for Rid.

"I should probably tell you right up front that I'm a pretty big sinner," Link said. "At least, accordin' to my mom. And she practically lives at church. So you probably won't end up at the Pearly Gates with my soul."

The bluesman raised an eyebrow. "I'm not interested in your soul. I want that." He pointed at the sheet of paper in Link's hand.

"You want my song?" Link was shocked. "The one I wrote?"

"It was really good, Link," Necro said.

Johnson nodded. "Like I said, you've got a gift. And I've been lookin' for somethin' worth playin' for a long time. Gets lonely out here."

Link didn't hesitate. As far as he was concerned, the guy could have every song he'd ever written and every song he was ever going to write. "It's yours. Just tell me where to find this person who can help us."

Johnson tucked the page in his pocket and walked back to his armchair. "I can't make you any promises, but if anybody knows how to find those labs, it's the Girl with the Velvet Voice."

"Who?" Floyd and Liv asked at the same time.

"She's the Caster Archivist," he said matter-of-factly.

For a second, Liv didn't say a word. "You must be confused, Mr. Johnson. I've never heard of a Caster Archivist, and I'm studying under some of the most knowledgeable Keepers in history."

"Well, she's as real as you and me." Johnson ran his fingers across the frets of his guitar. "She monitors the whole New Order. All that crazy stuff, since the world got all shook up and back again."

At the mention of the New Order, Liv looked rattled.

The bluesman pointed at Link. "When you get to New Orleans, find Madame Blue's House of Voodoo. Ask for the Girl with the Velvet Voice, and tell her I sent you."

"You're sure about this, Mr. Johnson?" Link held his breath waiting for the answer.

Johnson put down the guitar and looked him in the eye. "I'd bet my soul on it."

CHAPTER 12: NOX

Every Rose Has Its Thorn

Nox stared at the picture so intently that the rest of the room began to blur around it.

She looks like a corpse.

In the photograph, Ridley's eyelids were heavy and she was leaning against the wall for support. It was unclear if she even had any idea her picture was being taken. But the way the photo was tacked over some of the others made it look like a recent addition.

He had to hurry. He snatched her picture off the wall.

I'm coming, Ridley.

He barely noticed the other rooms along the hallway as he rushed past them, stopping just long enough to be sure no one was inside. The only thing he could think about was finding her. Nox heard voices somewhere far behind him, maybe back in the trophy room, but he ignored them. He was almost at the end of the hallway now.

Just a little farther. Make it to the door.

When he reached the end of the hall, he saw an elevator on one side and a stairwell on the other. Both led in the same direction: down.

Good enough.

Just as he reached the first stair, he heard louder voices coming from below him. But he had an even bigger problem. The voices behind him were suddenly growing closer, and unless he continued down the stairs, whoever was coming would definitely see him.

At that moment, Nox wished he had the ability to Travel. Unfortunately, no Incubus had lost that ability to him in one of his high-stakes card games yet. What was in his arsenal of TFPs? Among all the talents, favors, and powers he'd won at his clubs, there had to be something.

Come on. Think.

Then it came to him.

The Evo.

He'd been saving this particular power in case he needed it to get Ridley out of the labs, but if he got caught before he found her, it would be worthless.

An Evo had lost his powers to Nox in the same winner-take-all series of Liar's Trade that Ridley had almost won. It had been a nasty game, but Nox remembered it fondly. It was that night that had first brought Ridley into his club.

Evos had the ability to Morph and make themselves look and sound like anyone they wanted—a power Nox could use right about now.

Nox pulled the queen of hearts out of his jacket pocket and whispered the words to make the power his. At least temporarily.

Quid opus est me.

Make me who I want to be.

Morphing into Silas was too risky, considering he could be somewhere in the labs right now. So Nox picked someone else.

Someone insignificant and unnoticeable. Someone who could move through the hallways without attracting any attention.

The tingle started in his toes and traveled up his legs and torso until it felt more like a sting, only one that radiated across his entire body. He glanced down at his arms, now hidden beneath a white lab coat, and flexed the fingers that looked nothing like his own.

It's done.

Nox caught a glimpse of the woman first, as she came up the stairs. She was abnormally tall—most likely a Darkborn.

The Incubus next to her looked like one of Silas' standard thugs. He glanced at Nox. "What are you doin' here, Doc? I thought you said you were leaving."

"I am," Nox said. "I was just finishing up a few things." Nox realized how lucky he was that he'd heard the guy in the lab coat talking in the hallway. Even an Evo couldn't impersonate someone else's voice unless they had actually heard it before.

The Darkborn hesitated for a moment and gave Nox a strange look.

Nox shrugged.

All he could think about was Sampson's crazy instincts. He had no idea how far they extended, or if they were unique to Sampson.

Please don't ask where I'm going, since I have no clue.

The Incubus hit the Darkborn on the shoulder lightly. "Let's go."

She nodded. "Take it easy, Doc."

A moment later, he heard the two of them talking to someone else. They must've caught up with whoever was coming.

Nox rushed down the stairs, careful to keep his footsteps silent. The tingling had turned back into a sting, and he didn't know how much longer this Evo power would last. That was the problem with borrowed powers; they were unstable by nature. And the more powerful the Caster they belonged to was, the longer they lasted. The guy who had lost his powers to Nox must have been pretty low on the food chain.

The sting of the power fading was worse than the one he'd felt when it took hold, and he had to stop at the bottom of the stairs to catch his breath. He stared down as the hairy, middle-aged hands transformed back into his own.

No. Not yet.

I still haven't done what I came here to do.

He pushed through the set of doors at the foot of the staircase and came face to face with a row of bars—

Behind it, a room full of cells—most of them occupied, though he couldn't make out the faces of the prisoners from here. Except for one in the very last cell—

Ridley Duchannes.

She gripped the bars as if they were the only things holding her up. Her pink-streaked blond hair snaked through them, curling off her shoulders in every direction.

Her hands were filthy, her fingernails black and ragged.

Nox approached the cell quietly so he wouldn't disturb the others. "Ridley? It's me. Nox."

"Nox?" Her voice trembled, but she didn't look up. She said it as if the word meant something more than just his name.

Relief flooded through him. "I thought I'd lost you."

He curled his hands around the bars between them. Even then, he still didn't dare touch her. She seemed so confused and scared, he wasn't sure she was entirely herself.

She looks fine, though. For someone who survived a traumatic accident.

He knelt down until his head was only inches from hers. "I would've ripped Silas apart if he'd touched a single hair on your head."

Her hands trembled, and she still wouldn't look at him.

Nox slid his fingers down the rough metal, closer to hers, and she held on tighter.

Slowly—gently—Nox let his fingers graze hers. "Shh. You don't have to say anything. I can't imagine what you've been through. But it's over now."

Her fingers relaxed into his.

They stayed like that for a moment, leaning in toward each other as if there were no bars between them.

Ridley reached out until her fingers curled under his jaw, barely grazing his neck. "Nox," she breathed.

This time, his name sounded different on her lips. Her voice sharpened it into something harder.

She was so close he could smell her hair. She smelled exactly the way he remembered—like cherry sugar and sunshine.

I found you.

He closed his eyes in relief.

In a flash, she lunged at him and her hand closed around his throat.

Her nails dug into his flesh. "I don't know who you are or how you got in here. But I won't let you hurt me."

"Rid, it's me. Nox," he said, choking. "I'd never hurt you."

"Liar!" she snapped, squeezing his throat tighter. "I won't let you near me, monster. I know what you do to little girls."

"What?" The words caught Nox off guard.

"I see your teeth. Your fangs."

"My what?" He was incredulous. "What are you talking about?"

"I know all about the black bones. You'll come when I'm not watching and rip my throat out in my sleep."

"You're hallucinating, Ridley. It's not real." Nox pried her hand off his neck. "The only thing I ever wanted to do was love you."

Ridley backed away, as if he had just threatened to kill her. "Stop it! Don't say that!" She covered her ears and slid to the floor. "Stop it stop it stop it stop it!"

She squeezed her eyes shut, cowering in the corner, her hands shaking. She rocked back and forth, singing a lullaby softly to herself.

Nox's heart pounded as he watched her, bile rising in his throat. He felt almost as hopeless as he had before he'd found her.

What the hell did Silas do to you?

His next thought was even more terrifying.

How am I going to undo it?

CHAPTER 13: RIDLEY

Mockingbird

Ridley was vaguely aware of her surroundings—the plush mattress beneath her, a sparkling crystal chandelier above, and brightly woven rugs overlapping on the floor. The rugs reminded her of Uncle Macon's study in Ravenwood Manor.

Maybe that was where she was?

Thoughts and memories tangled together like the yarn in her mamma's knitting basket.

Knit one. Purl two. Knit one. Purl two.

As a child, she'd watched Mamma knit for hours and hours. There was something soothing about the way the needles moved in and out—on and on forever—like they would never stop.

Mamma was sitting in Uncle Macon's favorite chair, knitting by the fire.

I ran toward her, my heart hammering in my chest.

"What's wrong, sweetheart?" Mamma asked, dropping the needles in the basket. She opened her arms and caught me as my seven-year-old frame scrambled into her lap.

"I saw her, Mamma." The words tumbled out so fast that I forgot to breathe. "I was all grown up, and she came looking for us. But she didn't take Lena. She took me."

Mamma held me by the shoulders, staring into my eyes like she could see my future as easily as her powers as a Palimpsest let her see everything that had ever happened—or would ever happen—in this room. "Who are you talking about, Sweet Girl?"

I swallowed hard. "Sarafine."

A strange expression passed across her face. "Where'd you hear that name?"

"Reece's friends were talking about her. They said she's the most dangerous Caster who ever lived, and she kidnaps bad little girls so they can come work for her. They said she rides on a cart made of black bones, pulled by giant rats with fangs so big they can kill you in your sleep. They'll rip your throat out first, and then your heart."

"Nonsense."

"I don't want to be a bad girl, Mamma. I don't want the rats to eat me."

Mamma tightened her arms around me. "Why would you think you're a bad girl?"

I nodded slowly, not wanting to admit the truth. "Why else would I keep dreaming about her?"

"What does she look like in your dreams?"

I didn't want to picture her again, but I tried. "Sort of like the Evil Fairy in Sleeping Beauty*."*

Mamma let out a deep breath, looking relieved. I wasn't sure why, because the Evil Fairy was the scariest person I'd ever seen. Nobody would want her to show up in their dreams. "It was just a nightmare," Mamma said, kissing my forehead. "No one's coming for you or taking you anywhere."

"No rats?"

"Not a single one."

I looked up at her, unsure. "Will you sing me the song? The one that chases the bad dreams away?"

She smiled, humming the lullaby she'd been singing to me for as long as I could remember. She taught me all the words so I could sing it to myself when she wasn't there.

"Mockingbird."

Ridley hugged her knees, rocking back and forth, singing the song that used to chase her bad dreams away. But this time, it wasn't working.

It didn't sound like her mamma, and it didn't sound like the sweet boy who had no name. It sounded like her voice, and she didn't like it.

Because it sounded like loneliness.

She kept her eyes squeezed shut, afraid that if she opened them, the rats would be there again. Images flashed in front of her without warning all the time now—the rats escaping from the cage. The rats racing toward the bed, climbing over one another. The Rat Man on the other side of the bars, calling her name. It all looked so real.

There were other flashes, too.

Ones even more terrifying than the rats. The bright light shining in her eyes. Fire blazing through her veins. Two men talking in the background as the heat pulsed through her body like a second heartbeat.

Patient 13.

And something about the powers of a Siren and an Illusionist.

The perfect combination to start with—wasn't that what one of the men said?

The memory slipped away, and Ridley rocked harder.

Just keep singing. The nightmares will go away if you just keep singing.

Things only change if you change them, Ridley, a voice said from somewhere in the back of her mind—a voice she recognized. ***Don't forget that. The Dark part of you will always protect you, just like the Darkness protected me when I was Claimed. But you have to control your power. Never let it control you.***

Ridley realized who it was. Auntie Sarafine. The only person who didn't turn her back on Ridley when she was Claimed.

I can't, Ridley answered silently. *I'm not strong enough. The rats will come back, and the nightmares.*

But she kept hearing Sarafine's voice: ***Things only change if you change them, Ridley.... Control your power. Never let it control you.***

Ridley didn't feel strong enough to control anything—not the rats or the blinding light or the fire or the pain. She focused on the pain and the memories, and realized there were other voices. Voices from the memory of the pain and the fire and the blinding light. So Ridley did the unimaginable and listened to those voices, too.

"Is the infusion ready?" a man asks. "Read me the specs."

"Patient 13. Siren. First Trial. Administering Power Infusion: Illusionist," another says.

"If this takes and she doesn't go crazy or die when the new power hits, we'll have made history. You know that, right?"

"Concentrate on giving her the infusion first."

A different kind of fire burned through Ridley—one she hadn't felt since they took her away.

Rage.

She couldn't remember who the two men were—the ones who referred to her as Patient 13—or who had locked her in this cage. So she played the song over and over in her mind, until the only voices she heard belonged to the black-boned rats, and she realized what she needed to do. It was her last thought before she drifted off again.

I'll make them pay.

Just like Auntie Sarafine taught me.

CHAPTER 14: LINK

Electric Funeral

The Girl with the Velvet Voice was a wild card, an unknown variable in an already complex situation—at least that was what Liv said. Still, John trusted Robert Johnson, and the whole Caster Archivist angle had Liv itching to find her.

"Why? Are you jealous?" Floyd looked amused every time Liv brought it up.

"Don't be ridiculous. I just think it's a bit odd, that's all. Keepers have been chronicling the Caster world for hundreds of years." Liv sniffed. "Why change the system now?"

"Things change. The Order of Things. Us. The universe. Change isn't always a bad thing." Floyd shrugged.

"It's not always good, either," Liv said.

John and Link knew better than to say a word.

As they made their way through the Tunnels, Sampson ducked into every Dark Caster club they passed, asking around to see if anyone knew the location of Ravenwood Oaks. Link didn't think anyone would be willing to talk, but Sam said he was wrong; plenty of scumbags offered him information. The trouble was, every one of them named a different place—from bartenders and doormen to dealers and thugs, he heard everything from Savannah to Saint Croix.

By the time they reached the French Quarter, Link was losing it.

"How come nobody knows where the hell that plantation is?" he asked, following Lucille down the dark sidewalk. "It's like we're tryin' to find Wonder Woman's invisible plane. Or maybe S.H.I.E.L.D.'s secret base, the one in the desert."

"None of the people Sam asked had ever been there," John pointed out. "My guess is it's some kind of Cast. Maybe you can't find Abraham's old place unless you've actually been there."

"Unless he messes with everyone's head so they can't remember," Link muttered, his mood getting worse by the minute.

"Cloaking Casts like the kind John is talking about relate to the location itself, in this case Ravenwood Oaks," Liv said. "You can't Cloak a place from people who've actually been there."

"Let's hope this Velvet Voice chick has." Link stopped at the corner and looked around. "How much farther is it to the House of Blues?"

Floyd looped her arm through his and pulled him down the street. "It's House of *Voodoo*, and we're almost there."

When they reached Madame Blue's House of Voodoo in the older section of the French Quarter, the shop was dark.

Link kicked an empty can against the side of the building. "Crap. It's already closed."

John cupped his hands and peered through the dirty front window. "Ring the bell anyway."

Link pressed the buzzer next to the front door, and within seconds, a light switched on somewhere in the back.

"Check out those voodoo dolls." Floyd elbowed Sampson and pointed at a row of goofy-looking stuffed dolls wearing top hats on the other side of the glass, thick pins sticking out of their chests.

"Looks like a typical souvenir shop in the Quarter." Necro gestured at decks of tarot cards and plastic bags full of coins and trinkets labeled LUCK BAGS in the window.

John hit the buzzer again. "It's still worth a shot."

The door opened, and a woman who looked a lot like a blond Tina Turner from one of Link's favorite movies, *Mad Max: Beyond Thunderdome*, stood on the other side.

"You only need to ring the bell once," she said.

"Sorry about that, ma'am," John said.

"The name's Magnolia Blue."

"Maybe you can help us, Ms. Blue," John continued. "We're looking for the Girl with the Velvet Voice."

The woman's eyes widened and she gasped, staring back at him from behind her wild mane. "Only one person has ever called me that. But there's no way—"

Link took another look at her hair, remembering the photo Robert Johnson had showed him of the Caster girl he'd left behind.

Could she be the same person?

"This might sound crazy, but Robert Johnson sent us, ma'am," Link said.

The woman brought a hand to her lips. "Is Bobby all right?"

Sampson shrugged. "Sure. For a guy who's trapped in a house by himself, in the middle of nowhere."

"I knew he wasn't dead," she whispered, her eyes welling.

Lucille circled Magnolia Blue's ankle, purring, which made Link feel better. Lucille was a pretty good judge of character.

A lot better than me, anyway.

Magnolia Blue bent down and scratched Lucille's ears. "Why did Bobby send you to see me?"

"He said you might be able to help us," Necro said.

She swallowed hard like it was difficult for her to talk about him. "If Bobby wants me to help you, I'll do whatever I can. Come on in."

Inside, the shop seemed even more like a tourist trap. Alligator-foot key chains and bottles of powder with labels like BAT WING and LOVE ROOT were lined up on the shelves above papier-mâché skeletons dressed in tuxes and top hats. Link wasn't sure why the skeletons were dressed like they were going to prom, but they looked about as authentic as Barbie dolls.

Necro eyed a taxidermy caiman and scrunched up her nose. "We're looking for Ravenwood Oaks, Abraham Ravenwood's plantation. Mr. Johnson told us you're the Caster Archivist, so you might know where to find it."

"I'm not sure how Bobby heard about that, but he shouldn't be telling people," Magnolia Blue said. "I can't do my job if everyone knows I'm the one doing it."

Liv cleared her throat. "Ms. Blue? I'm studying to be a Keeper, and I've never heard of a Caster Archivist. So I have to ask... what exactly *is* your job?"

"Relax. I'm not trying to steal yours, darling. When the Order of Things was broken, it caused unforeseen changes in both the Caster and Mortal worlds. It's my responsibility to identify and monitor those changes."

"I thought things settled down after the New Order replaced the old one," Liv said.

Magnolia Blue gave her a knowing look. "If you're talking about weather anomalies and insect infestations, then I suppose it would look that way. But the New Order gave us a lot more than a new breed of Supernaturals." She smiled at Sampson. "Like you, from the look of it."

He nodded, and she continued. "The New Order also upset the balance in every realm—Caster, Mortal, the Otherworld, even the Abyss."

The Abyss—the demon realm where terrifying creatures like Vexes were trapped until a nutbag like Abraham Ravenwood summoned them. It wasn't Link's favorite subject. He picked up an alligator-foot key chain and dangled it in the air. "What do these things have to do with the New Order?"

Magnolia Blue snapped her fingers, and the air shifted in front of the shelves like heat waves rising off hot asphalt. The tux-clad skeletons and potion bottles blurred, transforming into rows of books and unfamiliar objects—a glowing compass and a weird clock with pictures around the face like the images on a tarot deck.

Link pointed at it. "Hey, Liv, that thing looks like your crazy watch."

Liv turned to Magnolia Blue. "Is that a selenometer?"

The Caster Archivist noticed Liv's watch-that-wasn't-a-watch and smiled. "It measures the moon's gravitational pull."

Liv nodded, mesmerized. "It's a real beauty. Perhaps the finest I've ever seen."

Sampson walked over to a map on the wall. "Nice illusion."

The wild-haired Caster frowned. "I'm not an Illusionist."

Floyd frowned. "What do you mean? I haven't seen an illusion like that in years."

"While I appreciate the compliment"—Magnolia Blue fluttered her fingers at a jar of change next to the register, and it transformed into a margarita glass—"I don't disguise things. I change them." She took a sip of the drink.

"A *Shifter.* I should've known." Floyd said it the way the girls on the Cheer Squad in Gatlin said *Pep Squad.*

"Aren't Illusionists and Shifters kinda the same? You know, like lions and tigers?" Link asked, anxious to change the subject. The finer points didn't matter. Right now, he was more interested to know if Magnolia Blue's powers could do more than just tell them where to find the plantation.

Like save Rid.

Link was only half-listening when he realized Liv was answering his question. "Illusionists can alter the way a thing looks. Shifters change the object itself." Liv's eyes lingered over the collection of strange instruments on the shelves, until she finally turned back to Magnolia Blue. "I can't believe the Keepers don't know anything about all this, or about you."

"That's the reason for Madame Blue's House of Voodoo," the Caster Archivist said in a theatrical voice. "It gives me plenty of time to sell love potions and good-luck charms to Mortals who don't know the difference between the voodoo religion and Velveeta cheese, while still monitoring the disruptions in our worlds."

"What kind of disruptions?" Liv asked.

"It's a dangerous time. We've got Sheers crossing over from

the Otherworld in record numbers, Darkborns who are immune to Caster powers." She glanced at Sam.

Liv looked shocked. "I had no idea things were this bad."

Magnolia Blue sighed. "It gets worse. You said you were looking for Ravenwood Oaks, Abraham's old plantation?"

"Yeah. We need to find it." Link tried not to sound too eager.

"You might want to rethink those plans. I got a little visitor from there this morning. Looks like Silas moved on from dissecting frogs and pulling the wings off butterflies."

"He moved on from that a long time ago," John muttered under his breath.

"What are you talking about?" Link tried not to panic.

"Apparently, Silas is injecting Casters with new powers, and it's changing the nature of their abilities. Among other things."

Liv's eyes widened. "That's not possible."

A woman who didn't look much older than Link's cousin Louise—who got knocked up at twenty-five, right before her wedding last year—stepped out from behind a bookcase.

Link's first thought was *Third Degree Burns*, but a second later, he felt a little guilty for thinking it. The mystery woman wasn't as hot as Rid, but she'd definitely given a few guys whiplash. From the red waves framing her toffee-colored skin to the black leather pants she wore tucked into knee-high lace-up boots, and the tangle of necklaces hanging over her ripped T-shirt, everything about this woman screamed trouble—that and the golden Dark Caster eyes staring back at them.

Necro and Floyd gave her the once-over as Liv eyed her suspiciously.

"I find it hard to believe that Silas found a way to inject you with a foreign Caster power," Liv said. "Unless you wanted him to."

The redhead waved Liv off with a flick of her wrist. "I don't care what you believe, Mortal. What I can tell you is that you're standing on what used to be a Civil War burying ground." The woman turned in a slow circle, taking in the room around her. "One the Confederates never bothered to move. The building was a house of ill repute after that—and, from the looks of it, a popular one."

Link frowned, his eyes darting around the room. As far as he could tell, this place was still a cross between a library and a creepy apothecary.

Floyd crossed her arms. "So you're a Palimpsest? That doesn't prove anything."

"I used to be. Now I'm that and much more." The redhead smiled at Floyd, and at Liv and Necro, who looked equally skeptical. "I'm sensing you girls want proof. If you insist."

The mysterious Caster blew Link a kiss, and the front of his Led Zeppelin T-shirt caught fire.

The fire burned through his shirt, and he winced, patting down the tiny flames. He pulled at a charred hole in the fabric. "Come on. This was vintage Zeppelin, from the seventies."

But Link was worried about more than his shirt, even if he didn't want the redheaded firestarter to know it. He'd only seen one other Caster do anything like that before.

Sarafine Duchannes—Ridley's Dark Cataclyst aunt.

The Cataclyst flexed her fingers the way Link had seen Sarafine Duchannes do a dozen times. "I couldn't resist."

"So Silas Ravenwood is somehow combining Caster powers. Interesting." Liv took out her journal without missing a beat.

"Do you know how he's doing it? And extracting the other powers, while keeping them stable? Has he tried this on anyone else?"

"Slow down." John rested a hand on Liv's arm. "Give her a minute." He turned to the Cataclyst—or half-Cataclyst; Link wasn't too sure about the terminology in a situation like this. "Why don't we start with your name? I'm John, and this is Liv, Link, Floyd, Necro, and Sampson." He pointed at each of them.

The redhead flexed her fingers, as if she was still getting used to what they could do. "Angelique St. Vincent. My friends call me Gigi. But you can call me Angelique."

Link sighed.

Another Cataclyst with an attitude. Just what we need.

Angelique turned to Liv. "And to answer your questions: I have no idea how Silas is extracting the powers, but I *do* know that I'm not the first Caster he injected."

"How can you be so sure?" Necro asked.

Angelique extended her forearm toward them so they could see the tattoo on her skin: PATIENT 12. "After the kind of hangover I had, I'd hate to meet the first eleven."

Liv shook her head. "I'm sorry. I can't imagine what that must've been like."

Angelique shrugged and let her arm drop, along with her attitude. "He put me through worse. At least I was sedated during the injections."

"What else did he do to you?" Sampson studied the Cataclyst, sizing her up in a way Link didn't completely understand.

Angelique toyed with the chains around her neck. "He kept me locked up in a cell with the rest of the women in his little Menagerie—that's what the sick bastard called us. He left us caged like dogs until a Dark Caster or *Darkborn*"—she stared at Sampson when she said the word—"rented us out for the night to do their dirty work. I got off easier than most of the girls. Not many people want to pay for the services of a Palimpsest. My friend Lucia was an Empath. Silas' guys were always dragging her out in the middle of the night for jobs." Her face clouded over for a moment.

Then Angelique flexed her hands, stretching out her long fingers, as if the memory had passed. "Once I became a Cataclyst, the game changed, and I was the popular girl on the block. Everyone wants their own firestarter."

Link pushed his way in front of Sampson. "Did Silas have a Siren in his ménage-à-whatever? Long blond hair with a pink streak and stubborn as hell? She would've come in a couple days ago."

Say yes. Please tell me you've seen Rid and she's okay.

The Cataclyst shook her head. "I broke out a week ago, and the other girls in there were the least of my concerns. Every woman for herself. I got enough problems."

Magnolia Blue turned to Link and his friends. "Now do you understand why I said looking for Silas Ravenwood's place isn't a good idea?"

"I don't have a choice." Link went into panic mode and stepped closer to Magnolia Blue. "The Siren I asked about is my girlfriend, and we think Silas Ravenwood kidnapped her. What if he's rentin' her out like Angelique said? You gotta tell me where the plantation is, ma'am. We need to find her. Please."

The Archivist shook her head sadly. "I'm sorry, son. But I don't know."

Angelique scoffed. "Lucky for you, there's one person here who does."

Link turned toward her. He was ready to drop down on his hands and knees and beg if it got him closer to finding Ridley. "Will you tell us where it is?"

"Sure." Angelique examined her red nails. "The Outer Door is in the basement of the Gardette-LePretre House, not far from here."

That was easy.

Link almost couldn't believe how quickly she'd said it—the one thing no one had been able to tell them since the accident: where to find Silas Ravenwood.

"Isn't Gardette-LePretre the house people call the Sultan's Palace?" Liv asked. "I've read about it."

"Of course you have," Floyd muttered under her breath.

Liv shot her a look and turned back to the Cataclyst. "People say it's haunted. According to most of the stories, a wealthy Turk rented the house, and he was living there with a harem of stolen women. That is, until they were all murdered. It was the scene of one of the grisliest mass murders in New Orleans history."

"Imagine if people knew that all the women in his harem were Casters," Magnolia Blue said.

"A harem of Casters?" Liv asked. "I've never heard of anything like that. The Keepers certainly don't have any records of its existence. It must've been the only one."

"Not the only one," Magnolia Blue said. "Abraham Ravenwood had a Caster harem of his own, with girls to spare. Where do you think the sultan got the girls in his?"

The idea was sobering.

Link headed for the door. "We need to go."

"Even if you find the Outer Door, you still have to go through the plantation's main house and make it past Silas' Blood Incubus and Darkborn guards to get inside the labs," Angelique called after him. "I only found the way because some old lady carrying a tray of food led me to the Outer Door. What if you get lost? Who will save your Siren?"

Link stopped, then turned and walked back toward them.

"What you *need* is someone who's been there before," the Cataclyst teased.

"Are you offerin' to go with us?" he asked.

Floyd grabbed his arm. "Why would she go back there after everything Silas did to her? Think about it. She must have an end game."

"Of course I do." Angelique tossed her fiery hair over her shoulder. "No one does anything out of the goodness of their heart. I'm no different. I'm just willing to admit it."

"What could possibly be worth risking your freedom—and maybe your life?"

"Someone she loves," Necro said thoughtfully.

"Maybe a family member, or your Empath friend?" Floyd asked.

A flicker of sadness passed across the Cataclyst's face. "I would've taken her with me, but there was no way. . . ." Angelique shook off the emotion and forced a stiff laugh. "My motives aren't that sentimental. Just the opposite." She stretched out her fingers and flexed them again. "I want revenge. Silas Ravenwood locked me up like an animal and treated me like a slave. Then he used me as a lab rat. I want to kill him and burn down every inch of his precious labs."

"You get us inside, and Silas is all yours," Link said.

A vicious smile spread across Angelique's lips. "Do we have a deal?"

John stepped between Link and the Cataclyst. "Hold on. How do we know we can trust her?"

"This whole thing could be a setup," Necro added.

"It doesn't matter," Link said. "We can't turn back now." He looked at Magnolia Blue. "Mr. Johnson said we could trust you. So if you vouch for her, I'll take your word for it. Is she tellin' the truth, ma'am?"

"Link—" Floyd started, but Link held up his hand.

The older woman glanced at Angelique, who seemed amused by the dilemma.

Magnolia Blue shook her head sadly. "I wish I knew. But I can't predict what's going to happen. I can only change the way things appear here and now. If you want someone to tell you more than that, you need a Diviner or a—"

Link picked up a folded tarot card from the counter. "Or a Seer."

CHAPTER 15: NOX

No One Like You

Nox stepped away from the bars.

Ridley stared back at him from the corner of her cell, where she sat hugging her knees and singing "Mockingbird" to herself.

"What did Silas do to you?" he whispered.

"They took her away last night," a girl with a German accent said from somewhere behind him.

Nox spun around.

An emerald-eyed Light Caster with a braid of brown hair stood inside a cell across from Ridley's. Chills pricked the back of Nox's neck at the sight of yet another girl behind bars.

He stepped closer. "Who?"

He heard shuffling in the next cell over, and a golden-eyed blond with Dark Caster tattoos across her knuckles looked back at him. "Silas and his rejects. Who else?"

"Where did they take her?" he asked.

The Dark Caster shook her head almost sadly. "The labs. It's the only explanation for how crazy she's acting."

The German girl nodded in Ridley's direction. "She has been like that ever since they brought her back. One minute she's talking to herself, and the next she's screaming."

"Or singing that stupid song," the other girl said. "She's got it bad. Even worse than Angelique did."

"Shut up, Drew," the German girl snapped. "She can't help it."

Nox looked at the German girl. "What's your name?"

"Katarina."

"Katarina," Nox repeated. "Have they ever taken either of you to the labs?"

She shook her head, looking terrified. "No. Silas only takes me on jobs. Then they lock me right back up in here afterward."

Nox examined the girl more closely. She was probably seventeen or eighteen tops. It was hard to tell, because she had the tired expression of someone much older. "What kind of jobs?"

"He rents us out for our powers." She tugged on the end of her braid nervously. "It could be worse. He sells the girls who aren't part of the Menagerie."

Drew shook her head and leaned against the wall inside her cell. "Yeah, we're the *lucky* ones. We get to be part of Silas' little collection and hope he doesn't drag us off to the labs and lobotomize us next." She looked back at Ridley. "I wasn't talking about you. Sorry about that."

Nox turned back toward Ridley's cell. The Siren stopped singing and looked up, and for a moment, he thought she was looking at him. But her gaze stopped at the edge of the cell, just short of where he stood.

Ridley's eyes widened and she scrambled backward across the floor until she hit the wall. "Don't let them out of the cage!" she screamed.

"Rid, look at me," Nox called out. "You're okay. You're just seeing things."

She stared up at him without a hint of recognition, her eyes full of terror. Then she winced and pressed her hands against her temples like she was in pain.

"Ridley!"

She blinked over and over as if she couldn't get her eyes to focus—or maybe her thoughts.

"Shh. Be quiet, Rat Man. They'll hear you," she whispered.

Nox glanced around.

Nothing.

He gripped the bars and bent down so he was closer to her eye level. "Who will hear me, Rid?"

Her eyes were fixed on a random spot in front of him again, and she flattened herself against the wall. "The other rats."

Nox's heart sank.

She's still hallucinating.

He remembered the Chemist and wondered if Silas had drugged her. But Nox had seen plenty of high Casters, and none of them had acted like this.

Whatever Silas had done to her was something else, and he had no idea how to undo it.

What if I can't help her? And she stays like this?

Suddenly, Ridley screamed, pressing her hands against her temples again. Within seconds she was clawing at the wall like a cornered animal.

"Ridley, get on the bed!" Katarina shouted. "The rats can't get you if you're on the bed."

Ridley's eyes darted frantically toward the hallway, and she scrambled up onto the bed. She pushed herself into the corner and curled into a ball, her eyes still glued to the floor. "They're coming!" she screamed, covering her head.

"It's okay, Rid," Nox said. "I won't let them hurt you."

"You need to be more concerned about yourself, kid," a familiar voice said from behind him.

Silas.

Nox didn't even have to look to know it was him.

He didn't turn around. He couldn't tear his eyes away from Ridley. "You're gonna be okay," he repeated. It was a lic and Nox knew it, but he couldn't think of another way to protect her from invisible rats and whatever other tricks her mind was playing on her.

He felt the Darkborn's hands around his arms before he saw them. Nox remembered Silas' friend from the vision. His grip felt like a vise, at least twice as strong as any Incubus. The Darkborn jerked him away from the bars and turned Nox until he was face to face with Silas Ravenwood.

Guess I'm lucky he let me stay on my feet, Nox thought. But once again, he didn't feel particularly lucky. *Unless I compare my situation to Rid's.*

"What did you do to her?" Nox asked.

Silas rolled up the sleeves of his custom Italian shirt and lit a Barbadian. Nox kept his eyes away from the flame. The stench of the cigar made his stomach turn. Silas smiled. "I made a few improvements. What do you think?"

Nox tried to stay calm, even though he wanted to rip Silas' head off. But Nox knew he needed more information if he was going to help Ridley. "What the hell does that mean? Did you shoot her up with something?"

Silas laughed. "That was a few days ago. *This*"—he pointed in the direction of Ridley's cell with his cigar—"is something more permanent."

Ridley let out a bloodcurdling scream.

Nox tried to turn around, thrashing against the Darkborn, but he was too strong.

"Get them off! Get them off! Get them off!" Ridley shrieked.

Silas walked toward her cell, his expression a mixture of amusement and fascination. "And just think, I'm not even finished yet. My great-grandfather would've been proud." He tipped his head to one side, considering it. "Or jealous. The old man never was good at letting someone else be in the spotlight."

Nox's jaw clenched at the sound of Ridley's cries. "I swear, I'll tear your heart out for this, Silas."

The Incubus turned around slowly, his amused expression gone. He stepped toward Nox, holding the cigar between them. "When I finish with you, Lennox Gates, you're gonna wish I'd torn *your* heart out. You're also going to wish you had died in that little blaze back at Sirene. You've caused me enough problems. At least your Siren is repaying her debt."

"This is between you and me, Silas," Nox pleaded. "Do whatever you want to me. I won't even fight. Just leave her alone."

"Don't say that. It's more fun if you fight." Silas took another step closer, the burning glow of the cigar only inches from Nox's face. "And your girlfriend isn't getting off that easy, kid. She helped those hybrids kill my great-grandfather, and now she has a debt to pay."

Nox shrank away from the cigar. "I'll pay it. Whatever she owes—whatever you want—I'll pay it."

Silas took a long pull on the cigar, turning it between his fingers. "Don't worry. I've got plenty of beds in the labs and enough payback to go around." His expression darkened. "Do you think I've forgotten what you cost me? I'm taking every ounce of it out of *her* blood."

It's my fault. He hurt Ridley because of me.

"At least tell me what you did to her," Nox said, looking at Silas.

"Scientific improvements. Her body is having a hard time adjusting to the influx of new power. Give it some time, and maybe she'll snap out of it." Silas laughed. "Or maybe not."

Nox's thoughts were spinning.

Influx of new power? What kind of power? And where did Silas get it? He's bluffing. He has to be....

"Oh," Silas said as if he'd remembered something important. "And I think you mean what I am *doing* to her. Because I'm not done yet, kid."

"Listen to me, Rat Man," Nox said, angrier than he'd ever been in his entire life. "You're done. You just don't know it yet."

Without warning, Silas thrust the burning end of his cigar into Nox's neck, like a knife.

Nox could smell his flesh searing, but he barely felt the pain.

He was too busy listening to the screams of the girl he loved.

CHAPTER 16: RIDLEY

Silent Lucidity

Someone was talking to her from outside the bars of her cell.

Ridley pretended to listen, which was sort of like playing a game, even though it wasn't a very fun one. Still, it was the only game she could play in this box of a room.

It was the Rat Man. Talking. He sounded concerned. His voice moved up and down, like he was playing an instrument. Some of the sounds were loud and urgent, others were soft and comforting. It was funny because his mouth never stopped moving, and when she forgot he was talking, he looked like a sad little fish.

Not a rat.

But that was the tricky thing about rats. They almost never wanted you to see what they really were.

She tried to listen. It took her a long time to realize he was speaking to her, but it was still impossible to care.

"Nox," she repeated to him. "That's your name."

"That's right," Rat Man said.

"And you don't want to rip my throat out?" She leaned toward him, pulling on a bit of his long, dark fur.

He stared, opening and closing his mouth like he was talking.

"Link?"

He opened and closed his mouth again, and she tried to make out the words. But her mind kept drifting, and she only caught bits and pieces.

Did he say Lincoln?

Lincoln was the name of an American president. Why was Rat Man talking about a president? She leaned closer, resting her forehead against the steel.

Rat Man had a nice smell. Leather and sweat and sweetness. She resisted the urge to lick his face. She didn't want to let him get that close to her, because of his sharp teeth.

Ridley reached out her hand. "Do you mind if I pet you?"

His mouth opened again. She took that as a yes and moved her hand up and down the long brown fur on his head. He felt like a soft baby seal. She let her hand trail down to his face, where his cheek was warm and soft.

That was when she felt it—a burst of heat.

But it was the strangest sort of heat she'd ever felt. She couldn't tell if it was hot or cold, but either way, the heat made the hairs on her hand stand on end—burning and freezing to the same touch.

A chaotic tangle of feelings surged through her, stretching from the top of her head to the bottoms of her toes. She felt as if she were unfolding, doubling in size. Finally inhabiting the full space of her body.

"What was that?" she breathed.

Ridley reached out again, and the moment she touched his skin, she felt the electric shock of his power meeting hers. She craved it. She was starving for it.

Rat Man had the only thing she needed. More fire. More of the cold, cold burn. She would've told him if she could have found the words.

Instead, she drew herself into him, until her hands were wrapped around his head and her lips were pressed up against his jaw. She wanted to drink him in.

She moved her lips to his neck.

Who was the bone rat now?

Rat Man only stared.

No.

Not Rat Man.

She had to pay attention now.

She could tell this was important.

She could tell everything was about to change.

She closed her eyes and counted.

Three.

Two.

One.

When I open my eyes, I'll push my way through the haze. I'll make myself listen to the words. No more lullabies.

Time to grow up.

Time to listen to Auntie Sarafine.

Put away the bone rats.

Take your place.

You are a thing of power, Ridley Duchannes.
It's time to use it.

So she did.

And with the full force of the power exploding through her, Ridley drew this Nox to her lips and drank him in, until the universe spun around her and all the voices in her head finally stopped talking and *listened*.

CHAPTER 17: LINK

Wanted Dead or Alive

Link only needed to say one word—one *name*, actually—to break down his plan for John and Liv. It was a little harder to explain to Floyd, Necro, Sam, Magnolia Blue, and the Cataclyst in question.

Liv stared at him for a moment, speechless. "Have you completely lost your mind?"

John rubbed his temples. "I think it's pretty obvious he has."

"Where are we gonna find a better card reader?" Link asked. "Think about it. She'll know if we can trust Angelique or not."

"Does someone want to tell us who this Amma person is?" Necro asked.

Liv, John, and Link exchanged glances. Every time they heard that name, the pain of losing her returned.

Liv sighed. "She was a gifted Seer, born from a long line of Seers that went back generations. Her powers were legendary."

"Almost as legendary as her pie," Link added.

"Then what's the problem?" Necro asked. "She sounds perfect. I'll channel her, and we can get her to read the Cataclyst's cards."

Yeah, right, Link thought. *It won't be that easy*.

He tried again. "She's not like other people. You can't just pick up the phone and expect her to get on the line."

"Why not? I'm a Necromancer. My whole life is one giant phone call to the Otherworld."

It was pretty clear to him that Necro, Floyd, and Sampson didn't understand exactly what they were dealing with here. The idea of bringing the orneriest old lady he'd ever met back from the grave—and shoving her inside the body of a blue-haired Dark Caster—was scarier than walking through a swamp full of gators, carrying raw chicken. Not that Amma would've let him do anything that crazy.

She had raised Ethan, and Link had known her since he and Ethan became friends in kindergarten. Even though she couldn't have weighed more than a hundred pounds soaking wet, she was the only woman who scared Link more than his mom.

Now I just have to explain that without lookin' like a punk.

"We used to stay out of her way if she was doin' a crossword puzzle," he said. "She's not the kinda lady who's gonna be happy about bein' disturbed in the Otherworld."

Necro rolled her eyes. "Most people aren't."

"She'll get over it," Angelique said. "Are we really still talking about this?"

Liv paced, something Link couldn't ever remember her doing before.

A bad sign.

"I'm not sure Link is painting a clear enough picture," Liv said. "Amma Treadeau is very particular, and not the biggest fan of..."

"What?" Sampson asked.

"Dark Casters," John finished. "Actually, she's not a big fan of the Caster world in general."

Angelique burst out laughing. "Now *we're* the problem?"

"Of course not. At least, not the only problem." Liv eyed her coldly. "I'm just trying to think this through."

"Ethan's gonna kill me. He's gonna kill all of us," Link said to Liv.

"Does your girlfriend have time for that?" Magnolia Blue asked.

Link glanced at John, who shrugged. "It was your idea, man. You say the word, and we drop the whole thing."

Link took a long, hard look at his options—of which there were exactly none.

He shoved his hands in his pockets and shook his head. "If we're gonna do this, we're gonna need some pie."

Everyone sat on the floor and formed a circle while Liv lit four novena candles in the center and placed a pecan pie next to them. "It won't be anywhere near as good as one of yours, Amma," she said. "But it will have to do."

Magnolia Blue had used her powers as a Shifter to change a souvenir voodoo doll into the pie.

"Think it will taste the same?" Link was pretty sure it wouldn't.

"It's just an offering," Magnolia Blue said. "She won't actually eat it."

Good, Link thought. *Or she'll tan my hide.*

Necro took a deep breath. Even in the candlelight, she looked pale.

Sampson touched her arm. "Are you sure you're okay to do this?"

She nodded. "I'm not channeling Abraham Ravenwood. If Amma is the kind of woman they say she is, she won't hurt me."

The Darkborn glanced at Link.

Link shrugged. "Amma would never hurt anybody, unless you mess with someone she loves. So we're good."

Necro closed her eyes and spoke softly.

"Into my breath and body,
Flesh and bone,
I call the spirit of Amma Treadeau.
Let my voice guide you back
From the unknown."

*"In spiritum et corpum meum
Carnem et ossam
Voco animum Amma Treadeau.
Vox mea te reducat
Ab incognota."*

Link held his breath, but after a minute or so, he felt like he was going to pass out.

It's not gonna work. What the hell was I thinking?

He should've known no one was strong enough to summon

Amma. She never did anything she didn't want to do back when she was alive.

Please, Amma. I'm in trouble.

Necro inhaled sharply, and her chest expanded as if her body was filling up with something—or *someone*.

The blue-haired bass player still looked like herself, until she sat up straighter than his mom's uppity friends in the DAR and stood up with both hands on her hips.

She gave Link the Look.

He'd seen that look in Amma's eyes a hundred times before, mostly when he screwed up, and there was no mistaking the way she was looking at him now.

"Wesley Jefferson Lincoln. You'd best hope the Good Lord Almighty himself told you to call me back from the other side." Amma's eyes settled on Liv and John. "I'm surprised to see you here, Olivia. And John. You both should know better." Amma glanced around at the others and crossed her arms, unimpressed, before turning back to Link. "Dark Casters? That's what you called me here for, Wesley Lincoln? They'd better be threatenin' your life, or I will."

"A-Amma, I can explain," Link stammered. "I'm real sorry, but this is a life-or-death situation, and you're the only person who can help me."

Her eyes narrowed. "Help you do *what*, exactly?"

This was the part he was dreading—the part where he had to explain exactly what he wanted Amma to do, knowing there was no way in hell she'd want to do it. "Silas Ravenwood's alive, and he's got Ridley. He's gonna kill her or use her as a slave or somethin' even creepier if we don't save her, and I can't do that without you." Link swallowed hard. "Ma'am."

He swore he could see Amma's dark eyes staring back from behind Necro's gold ones. "Ridley Duchannes? That's why you called me back from the best hand a gin rummy I've had in twenty years?" She eyed the pecan pie on the ground. "And this is what you bring me? That's the sorriest-looking pie I've ever seen, Wesley Lincoln. You should know I don't eat anybody's pie except my own. Why don't you just toss one a those Oreos at me and spit in my face while you're at it?"

"Well, your loss. I'm *starving*." Angelique reached for the pie, and Amma gave her more than the Look. Angelique frowned and put her hand back in her lap. Even the Cataclyst sensed she shouldn't mess with Amma.

"I'm sorry, Amma," Link said, his stomach twisting in knots.

Amma held up a hand, silencing him. "Explain to me why I should care about any a this. These are Dark Caster problems you're talkin' about, and I don't want any part a them. If Silas Ravenwood is involved, you'd best steer clear a him. I'm sure Ridley can get herself outta whatever trouble she's gotten herself into this time."

Sampson stood up tentatively, as if he sensed Amma wasn't the kind of lady you wanted to tangle with. "Excuse me, ma'am." He tried to make his Yankee accent sound a little more Southern. "My name is Sampson, and I'm a friend of Link's and Ridley's. I can tell you're not fond of Dark Casters, but my friends aren't like the ones you've probably met, and they definitely don't hurt people, the way a Blood Incubus like Silas Ravenwood does." The Darkborn slouched, but he was still a good two feet taller than Amma.

"And from everything I've heard about Ridley from Link, it sounds like Rid's done some good things, too. If there's any way you'd consider helping us, I'd be in your debt, ma'am."

Amma snorted. "I spend my days in the Otherworld sittin' on the porch, drinkin' sweet tea and playin' cards with my Uncle Abner, Aunt Delilah, Ridley's Aunt Twyla, and an ornery old Mortal lady. What makes you think I want anythin' from you?"

Link was pretty sure the Mortal lady Amma mentioned was Ethan's Aunt Prue. He couldn't imagine an ornerier Mortal old lady in the Otherworld.

Amma took a step closer to Sampson. "And I know you're not a Caster or an Incubus, so why don't you tell me what you are?"

"I'm a Darkborn. I'm not sure if we were around before you crossed over, but we were born from the Dark Fire after the Order of Things broke."

"So your heart's as black as the rest a them," she said without missing a beat. "I'm not interested in a boy like you owin' me any kinda debt, and I'm done with Dark Casters and all their business."

Link knew the situation was going from bad to worse, and fast. Begging had never done him much good when Amma was alive—in fact, begging and bragging were the twin sons of the Devil, according to her—but it was all he had left. "I know how you feel about Rid, Amma, and I know she's done a lot a bad things. But she helped save Lena, and she saved Ethan's life out in the woods when Hunting Ravenwood's Blood Pack attacked us. She also helped us get Ethan back after he...you know."

Died.

Link still couldn't say it—not on a good day, and definitely not to the woman who loved Ethan most. "Ridley's not all bad, and good or bad, Light or Dark, I'm in love with her. So if you don't wanna do it for her, or Lena and Ethan, then I'm down on my knees beggin' you to do it for me."

Amma raised an eyebrow. "Doesn't look that way to me."

Link dropped down on his knees.

She sniffed. "That's more like it."

The Seer patted her sides where the pockets of her apron would've been if she were alive and wearing it, which meant she was either searching for the One-Eyed Menace—the wooden spoon she wielded like a weapon—or a handkerchief. With Amma, it was hard to tell until it was too late.

She shook her head. "I'll consider helpin' you, Wesley Lincoln. On one condition, and one condition only."

Link stood up and stumbled toward Amma, almost knocking over the candles, and stopped just short of throwing his arms around her. "Anythin'. You name it."

Necro pointed at him, and Link could practically see Amma's bony finger. "You don't involve my boy Ethan in whatever mess it is you've gotten yourself into. You clean it up *without* him. He's had enough heartache in the last year for two lifetimes. He doesn't need you draggin' him down the dirty side a the drain with you. Those are my terms."

"You have my word," Link said. "I won't tell Ethan anythin'. I don't want him to get hurt, either. That's why I haven't called him about this."

She crossed her arms. "Then what is it you want from me?"

Liv spoke up. "We think Silas has Ridley somewhere in the labs, behind Abraham Ravenwood's old house. But we have no idea how to get there."

"But I do." Angelique waved her fingers at Amma from where she was leaning, lounging in her spot around the circle.

Amma stared at Angelique for a long moment. "You remind me of someone."

"Oh?" Angelique looked bored.

"Someone I didn't like," Amma added.

"Angelique says she'll show us the way to the labs," Link said. "But we don't know if we can trust her."

Amma gave him the Look again. "I'm waitin' for the part that involves me."

"Link wants you to read her cards." John pointed at the tarot deck on the floor.

"Of course he does." Amma eyed the deck disapprovingly and turned back to Link. "I don't like readin' from somebody else's deck. It's almost as bad as bakin' from another person's recipe."

"Are you going to read my cards or what?" Angelique asked. "I have places to burn down."

Amma pointed at the candles. "Move those things outta the way so I have somewhere to lay out the spread." She watched as Floyd and Sampson rushed to move them, then looked at Magnolia Blue. "I reckon I'm gonna need that deck."

Magnolia Blue pushed the tarot deck across the floor in front of her and nodded respectfully.

Link rushed forward to hug the old lady he loved more than his own grandmother. "Thanks, Amma."

Amma stopped him just shy of reaching her. "Don't thank me yet. The cards reveal what they want to tell us, not necessarily what we want them to." She sat down cross-legged in the center of the circle and wagged a finger at Angelique. "Come on over here."

The Cataclyst scooted forward until she was sitting in front of Amma. "This should be fun. The fortune-tellers at the carnival were always my favorite."

Liv sucked in a sharp breath, as if she knew what was coming. Calling a Seer a fortune-teller was like calling a lawyer an ambulance chaser.

"I. Am. Not. A. Fortune-teller." Amma enunciated each word like she wanted to bite Angelique's head off with every one. "Now shuffle."

Angelique seemed amused, but within seconds, the cards were flying between her hands like she was a Vegas blackjack dealer. Everyone watched in silence as Amma fanned out the deck and the Cataclyst chose her cards. Then Amma flipped them over one by one, her eyes widening. "The Tower, the Devil, the Hermit, the Moon—"

The Seer glanced at Magnolia Blue, who looked equally shocked, and continued. When she turned the final card, Link recognized it—the Death card.

"Does that mean she's gonna die, or she's gonna kill us?" Link asked.

Amma sniffed. "Neither. Death card's about transformation, a new cycle."

"That's good, right?" Sampson asked.

"Depends on the position in the spread." Amma shook her head. "But this spread doesn't make any sense."

"Do tell." Angelique perked up, suddenly interested. "I love a good mystery."

Amma studied the images staring back from the floor—a horned beast, a gray tower, a knight riding a white horse—then turned her gaze back to the Cataclyst. "There's somethin' familiar about you and this spread."

"Oh?" Angelique asked, the smile never leaving her lips.

"What is it?" Magnolia Blue asked.

For a moment, Amma was silent. Then she reached down and scattered the cards.

"What's wrong?" Link asked, because he'd known Amma long enough to recognize when something had her rattled.

"What did you see?" Liv asked, looking almost as worried as the Seer.

Amma pointed at Angelique. "This one's trouble, sure as the day is long and I'm livin' in the Otherworld."

John put his arm around Liv. "So we can't trust her?"

"She'll take you to the Ravenwood labs like she told you," Amma said. "But I can't see what'll happen after that."

"Did you see Rid?" Link couldn't stop himself from asking.

"Do I look like your personal crystal ball, Wesley Lincoln?"

He swallowed hard. "Sorry, ma'am. I had to ask."

Liv pulled at the strings tied around her wrist like bracelets. "And there was nothing else?"

Amma sighed. "Like I told you before, the cards don't always tell you what you want to know. The rest is up to you to figure out." She straightened the bottom of Necro's leather skirt like it was one of her good church dresses. "Now I have a glass a sweet tea and a game a gin rummy to get back to. You take care, Wesley. And don't forget what you promised me."

Link shook his head. "I won't, ma'am."

"Then I'll be seein' you. And if you disappoint me, I'll be payin' you a visit or two down here. So don't." Amma closed her eyes, and a second later, Necro drew in another sharp breath, followed by one of the worst coughing fits Link had ever seen—not that he was surprised. Channeling someone like Amma couldn't be easy.

Sampson rushed to Necro's side and rubbed her back.

"I'm okay," she choked.

"You don't look like it," Sampson said.

Floyd handed her friend a bottle of water, and Necro took a huge swig. "Better?"

"Yeah, thanks." Necro slumped against the wall, looking exhausted. "Are you sure that old lady wasn't a Caster?" she asked Link.

"A hundred percent," Link said. "Maybe two hundred. Amma was more Mortal than I am." He couldn't stop staring at Necro. Now that Amma was gone, he felt the sadness of losing her all over again.

Ethan's gonna kill me if he ever finds out about this.

"What did she say?" Necro asked, closing her eyes.

Angelique stood up and strode over to a carved table that was probably Magnolia Blue's desk. The Cataclyst hopped up and sat on the ancient wood like it was the hood of a car. "Big picture: The Seer said you can trust me to take you to the labs."

Necro seemed to sense there was more to the story and looked up at Sampson. "And after that?"

The Darkborn frowned. "She wasn't sure."

"Oh, please," Angelique said. "Let's not get bogged down on the details, here."

It didn't matter to Link. If Angelique knew how to get to the labs, he was going with her. He approached the Cataclyst slowly, trying to get a read on her—as if he had any chance of seeing something Amma couldn't. "Tell me the truth, Angelique. Can we trust you *after* we get to the labs?"

A mischievous smile tugged at the corners of her mouth like she was thinking about something funny. "Of course you can't.

But that's why I'll be the one to do what needs to be done once we get there."

Link was afraid to ask the next question, but someone had to. "What is that, exactly?"

Angelique looked him dead in the eye, and a vicious smile spread across her lips. "Kill them all."

CHAPTER 18: NOX

What Is and What Should Never Be

Nox broke off the kiss and pushed her back, out of breath.

But the moment they weren't touching, an inexplicable sadness washed over him. He stared through the bars at the girl he'd risked his life to save.

The girl he loved.

Ridley.

The girl watching him wasn't the Ridley Duchannes he met in that game of Liar's Trade a few months ago—and years before that on a beach in Barbados when they were kids. This girl was a different kind of predator. She tracked his every movement—stalking him the way he had watched her the first time he laid eyes on her.

What did Silas do to you, Rid?

Do you even know?

Nox had to find a way to reach the girl he fell in love with, even if it meant losing her. "Rid, you're talking crazy. You're with Link." He hesitated, dreading the next part. "You love him."

It was about the third time he'd tried to say it, but it didn't seem to be sinking in. Part of him wanted to shut the hell up and pull her mouth back against his.

The rest of him knew the truth.

Not like this.

I don't want her this way.

Ridley said nothing. She moved closer to the bars again, never taking her eyes off him. The way she was looking at him—biting her lip, with those sleepy eyes beckoning him.

Every cell in his body told him it was real—

She isn't thinking about Link, you idiot. She wants you.

She closed her eyes.

"Three."

She slid one arm around Nox's neck.

"Two."

She found her way through the bars with her other hand.

"One."

She opened her eyes, pulling him close, until her lips hovered next to his. . . .

Nox pushed her away, though it was the last thing he felt like doing. "You don't know what you're saying."

"I know what I'm saying. I'm saying Mortal boys can't give me what I need. They don't feel like this." She reached her hand inside the collar of Nox's shirt. "Don't you feel it?"

"Feel what?"

"All of it," she said. "Everything that matters. The burning cold. The electricity. The chaos when we touch. The power surge."

As she spoke, Nox realized it was true. There was something different about her touch now. She'd always driven him wild—even the thought of her, the one person he couldn't have—but now even the brush of her skin against his sent him over the edge.

"That's not true," he said, though he didn't know why he said it. Every cell in his body was telling him to shut up, to kiss her back, to never let go.

She laughed in his face.

"This isn't you," he faltered, trying again.

She snuck her arm back around his neck as a black snake slithered out from under the bed. It wound itself around Ridley's bare leg and twisted its way up her torso, looping itself around her neck. She didn't seem to notice at all.

"The snake," Nox pointed. "Around your neck."

She glanced down and ran her fingers over the delicate skin below her chin until she reached her collarbone. Her fingers slipped right through the serpent's body, as if she'd touched a hologram.

It's an illusion, Nox thought. *Of course.*

He'd seen Floyd manifest illusions often enough. He should have recognized this one. He'd probably won a handful of Illusionist powers in TFPs, too. Liar's Trade seemed to draw Illusionists to the game tables.

But she wasn't finished.

The cell darkened around her, like a wave of black clouds was rolling in. A flash of lightning cut across the space above her head, which suddenly looked exactly like a real sky.

Nox looked up at the darkness that used to be the ceiling. "Is that you, Ridley?" He'd never seen her do anything like this before.

"How long have you been projecting illusions, Rid? Do you remember what Silas did to you?" He hated asking but couldn't figure out how to undo it unless he knew.

Maybe I don't want to undo it. She wants me.

What's my problem? I just need to shut up.

We could finally be together, if we can get out of this place.

Rid licked her lips and tilted her head to the side. "He made me more powerful. More of what I was destined to be." She paused. "More of everything, *Nox*."

The way she said his name made him shiver. Her powers were stronger now. He could feel the pull—tugging at him.

"I feel it even more when I touch you." Ridley raised her arms over her head, exposing the Dark Caster tattoo that encircled her navel. "Don't get me wrong. I'm still going to kill Silas. No one does anything to me without my permission. Even if it does feel absolutely decadent."

"You might not get the chance to kill anyone," Nox said, trying to emphasize the gravity of the situation. "There's no way out of here."

The dark clouds around her disappeared. Only the snake remained, coiling through her pink-streaked hair.

"There's always a way, Nox." She kept saying his name, making him forget everything but her. "If you want something bad enough."

Ridley slid her hands down the bars, and Nox could almost feel her touching his skin. She lowered her voice. "Do you want me bad enough? Do you want *us*?"

The intensity in her eyes—

The need in her voice—

Nox's head swam.

"More than I've ever wanted anything," he said.

I want you, Rid. More than you'll ever understand.

He tried to pull his eyes away from the Siren standing in front of him.

I want to kiss you and hold you and run my fingers through that wild hair.

He tried not to think about it, about her, about the way she said *us*.

I want to protect you and make sure no one ever hurts you again.

He knew what he wanted. Maybe he had always known.

I want you to let me love you. Finally.

But first he had to find the girl he loved.

Is she still the same girl?

This girl wanted *him*, so could it really be her?

He knew they belonged together the first night he met her at the card table—maybe even before that, on the beach in Barbados—and he also knew that if Link wasn't part of the equation, Ridley would've acted on her feelings. He was sure of it.

Was it so wrong if he let her love him now?

You don't even know if her feelings for you are real.

She probably doesn't even know.

Still…

The sound of boot steps echoed through the passageway, and Ridley turned toward the noise. The snake around her neck vanished, replaced by the stench of a Barbadian wafting through the air.

A moment later, Silas Ravenwood's wing tips followed. He ignored Nox and walked straight to Ridley's cell. "How is the most powerful Siren in history feeling today?" He smiled at her like a proud father.

Nox's stomach twisted.

Ridley tossed her blond locks over her shoulder. "I'd be doing a lot better if I was sleeping on silk sheets in a real bedroom."

"There will be plenty of time for that if you behave yourself."

"I always behave myself," she purred.

Silas took a pull on the cigar, studying her. "But you've got a lot of power pumping through your system, my dear."

"That's how I like it." She pouted.

"We have to make sure you're stable."

"Why? That never stopped me before, and I'm pretty sure it never stopped you, either." She leaned toward Silas. "We're not stable. We're Dark."

Nox couldn't stand to watch any more of this. He could see it now. Ridley had become another person entirely.

"Tell me what you did to her, Silas. Or I'll make you suffer when I figure out how to get out of this cell. And I *will* find a way out."

Silas turned toward Nox and flicked his ash into Nox's cell. "Sorry, kid. You won't get the chance. Today is the day you're going to die."

CHAPTER 19: RIDLEY

Eyes of a Stranger

None of it was real—not the snakes or the rats.

Ridley understood that now.

After they dragged the Rat Man away, she'd had plenty of time to think about it, and the realization had settled over her slowly. She realized the ceiling wasn't *actually* rolling with storm clouds. Her arms weren't crawling with snakes, and her cell wasn't teeming with giant rats. The storm was *inside* her—something Ridley had always known. But it was comforting to finally have confirmation.

It also meant she was done cowering in the corner of her cell.

I just have to practice controlling this new power. No one else is going to help me.

Ridley couldn't count on anyone except herself—something else she had always known.

It had been that way since the night her powers were Claimed for the Dark at sixteen.

Why should things be any different now?

Her memories were coming back, too. Silas threatening her. Those idiot doctors discussing her infusion. The Rat Man—Nox's—face.

Nox.

The idea that he might have been there with her, and not just an illusion, seemed even stranger. How did he survive the fire at Sirene? Why would he risk his life to come here, after he'd escaped Silas?

For me... he came for me.

That thought—and the hope that came with it—was the anchor keeping her from drifting back to the crazy place. The place Silas left her after he pumped her veins full of a power that might have killed her.

How did Silas do it? Infusing one Caster with another's powers wasn't like mixing a martini. It must've required research, maybe years' worth.

Who cares? You're even stronger than you were before. A Siren with Illusionist powers—you'll be unstoppable. You just have to figure out how to control the powers. Don't let them control you.

It was easier said than done.

The illusions came and went without warning, and they always caught her off guard, with heat searing its way through her veins and her vision blurring until the flashes started.

The cell door opening on its own.

Snakes twisting around the bars.

Her senses were in some kind of supernatural overdrive, and it was still hard to differentiate reality from illusion.

When Ridley heard Silas' Darkborns in the passageway, she pretended to be asleep. If they were really out there, maybe they'd leave her alone. If they were another illusion, she could practice ignoring it.

"Did you clear all the other girls out?" one of the Darkborns asked. "Silas doesn't want anyone down here except for the two of them."

"Yeah. Moved 'em all earlier," the other guy said. "What do you think Silas is gonna do with him?"

"Kill him. What else?"

"Or experiment on him, which is probably worse."

Ridley tensed as the rage burned inside her again.

I'm not your victim. But eventually, you'll be mine. Right after Silas gets what he deserves.

"Then kill me already," someone groaned.

Rid recognized his voice.

Nox.

He had survived whatever Silas had done to him. He was really here.

The images came back to her slowly. Nox standing outside her cell, talking to her. The sound of her own screams. Silas grabbing Nox and dragging him away.

She'd begun to think he was just another illusion for sure. Something she conjured to feel better. Something to give her hope.

Was that it?

The Darkborns had dragged his beaten body down the dim

passage to the cell next to hers and slammed the door. Nox lay on the floor, blood smeared across his cheek, as if Silas wanted to be sure she saw him.

Heat burned through Ridley's body at the sight of him—the *feel* of him. She could sense his power. It tugged at her like a magnet, the cold heat returning to her.

We're the same.

Dark. Irresistible. Strong.

Power meeting power.

Electricity.

Ridley walked to the door of her own cell, her fingers curling around the bars between her and Nox. She could hear his heartbeat from across his cell—thudding softly. Calling out to her.

We're the same.

Nox moaned and rolled over, his eyelids fluttering.

Open your eyes. Look at me.

He blinked as if he wasn't sure she was standing there staring at him.

"Rid?"

The sound of his voice made her blood burn. Something about it.

Something about him.

There was so much power inside her now, and it seemed drawn to only one thing.

More power.

"Looks like they gave you a serious beating," she said, her tone more flirtatious than concerned.

Nox pushed himself to his feet. "You're okay. Before... you were—"

"I was having a hard time *adjusting*." She waved off his shock. "But I'm good as new, now. Better, actually." It was true. She was doing better by the hour. She remembered her old life now, and her old friends.

Even though it felt like that life had happened to someone else.

Nox rested his forehead against the bars. "I thought..." He stopped himself.

Ridley bit her bottom lip, her eyes cast toward the floor. She didn't want to look at him, not with all these feelings swirling around inside her. Not when the sound of his voice made her pulse race.

"What were you going to say?" she asked. Part of her just wanted to hear his voice.

"I thought I lost you," he said softly. "Not that you're mine."

"I don't belong to anyone, Nox."

"I just meant that I know the way we left things. You're with Link, and I have to live with that."

Link.

She'd almost forgotten about him. Not him exactly, but the reason she'd cared about a former Mortal like him in the first place. There had to have been something.

But not this. Nothing that felt like this.

We never felt like this. We were never the same.

Powerless, she thought. *The quarter Incubus. That's all he is, isn't he?*

As much as the idea of being with someone so limited baffled her now, the possibility of being with someone powerful attracted her even more.

Nox was brimming with it—whether or not he'd stolen or

won or borrowed it, he had access to the abilities of dozens of different Casters.

Now that she could sense the power within him, she realized he was capable of so much more than he'd ever let on.

"You're really ready to accept me being with someone else?" she asked.

He didn't look at her.

"What if I don't want you to have to live with it?" she asked, feeling Nox's eyes on her. Heat and a sweetness she could almost taste.

"Don't play games, Rid. Not about this." Nox sighed. "I can't take it."

Another snake emerged from the shadows and she watched it slither across the floor.

It's an illusion, she told herself. *Try to control it*.

Ridley focused on the black serpent, willing it to disappear. Instead, it wound itself around thc bars below Nox's hands. She closed her eyes, listening to his breathing—ragged and uneven, like someone who had been running for too long.

Stop running, Nox.

"There's something between us, Nox. I know you can feel it, too." She breathed the words, her head swimming with the sound of his heart hammering in his chest. "We're the same."

Nox was silent for a moment. "You know how I feel about you, Rid."

"Maybe I want to hear it again." It wasn't a question.

"Ridley, look at me," he whispered, and the distance between them seemed to disappear.

She finally raised her eyes to meet his, and he sucked in a sharp breath.

"Your eyes. They aren't gold anymore, Rid."

"What color are they?"

He stared at her as if he was hypnotized. "Violet." An eye color that doesn't exist in the Caster world.

Until now.

CHAPTER 20: LINK

Tornado of Souls

So we're really gonna break in?" Necro asked, her electric blue Doc Martens shining in the darkness.

"Did you think the tour company was going to leave us a key?" Angelique asked in a condescending tone.

It was the middle of the night, and Link, Sampson, John, Liv, Floyd, Necro, and Angelique stood on the sidewalk staring up at the Gardette-LePretre House, in the French Quarter. The streetlights near 716 Dauphine Street bathed the Greek Revival house in soft light.

"So that's the Sultan's Palace?" John asked. "It's pink."

Sampson nodded. "And then some."

Link realized he and John were probably thinking the same thing. With its green shuttered windows and delicate black lattice balconies wrapping around the third floor and the roof, it was hard to imagine the pink house as the scene of a mass murder. Still, knowing this place was on the top ten list of the "Most Haunted Houses in America" (a fact he'd looked up on his phone) and the location of what lots of people considered the grisliest murders in New Orleans history (a fact Liv knew without looking it up) gave him the creeps.

He sighed and folded up the scrap of paper he'd been writing on. The songs kept coming to him, driving him sort of crazy until he wrote them down.

Liv scribbled something in her journal before tucking it back in her pocket. "Let's take a moment and think this through—"

Floyd sighed. "Let me guess? Breaking and entering is too lowbrow for your fancy Oxford sensibilities."

John raised an eyebrow and looked away like he didn't want to witness the verbal beatdown Floyd had coming her way, as Liv tucked her pencil behind her ear.

"What I was about to say, before I was so rudely interrupted," Liv said, stepping closer to Floyd, "was that if we're going to break into one of the most infamous houses in a city that never sleeps, we should use the back door. And you don't need to be worried about my Oxford sensibilities. In the last year, I've faced Vexes; a pack of Blood Incubuses; Sarafine Duchannes, the most powerful Cataclyst in recorded history; the End of Days; a corrupt Council from the Far Keep; and the wrath of Abraham Ravenwood. If you think I'm worried about getting in trouble, think again."

Angelique nodded at Liv. "Sarafine Duchannes? I'm impressed."

"We killed her twice," Link said proudly. "Once here and once in the Otherworld."

"We?" John looked at Link pointedly.

"Well, our boy Ethan handled it the second time. But that's a long story, seein' as he had sorta kicked the bucket, too."

"You done?" Floyd tugged on the bottom of her *Dark Side of the Moon* T-shirt, shifting uncomfortably. "We know you've seen your share of action, and you're a real badass, Oxford. But the Sultan's Palace isn't just any house. It's haunted, and we all know how brave you Mortals are when it comes to Sheers."

Goose bumps pricked Link's arms at the mention of the Caster term for what he considered plain old ghosts. But he wasn't about to act like a big chicken in front of his friends. "Let's not go throwin' names around. I'm still half Mortal. Or is it three-quarters?" He tried to do the math in his head. "If John was half, and I got half a his half—"

John grinned. "Some days you really make me proud I bit you."

"I try." Link held his fist up in front of John. "Pound it."

Sampson was still watching the house. Even in his leather lead-singer pants, ripped T-shirt, and bike-chain collar, he reminded Link of a wolf watching the woods. It was almost as if Sampson knew there was something in there. It wouldn't have spooked Link half as much if Lucille wasn't standing right next to him with her ears perked up and her tail waving back and forth like a snake about to strike.

"What's the deal, Sammy Boy? Do those Darkborn eyes a yours see somethin' we don't?" Link asked. "Somethin' we probably don't wanna know about?"

Sam kept his gaze fixed on the house. "It's not what I can see. It's what I can *sense*."

Link should've taken the hint and stopped asking questions, but Rid's life was on the line. If there was anything inside the

Sultan's Palace that might keep them from getting to the door in the basement that led to the labs, he needed to know. Plus, all that talk about Sarafine reminded him that no matter what was goin' on in this Sheer Shack, he'd seen worse. "What's your Darkborn radar pickin' up? Lay it on us." He sucked in a breath, ready for anything.

"Something bad happened in there, that's for sure," Sampson said.

Necro walked up beside Sampson. "I feel it, too. It's like one big after-party for the dead in there."

"A graveyard rave? Great." Floyd shook her head.

"Yeah. I never really wanted to party in a graveyard." Link was less excited.

Angelique sauntered past them. "Just the spirits of more than a dozen murdered girls and a Turk who was buried alive. I've already been through here once, when I broke out of the labs."

"So there are definitely ghosts in there?" Link asked, wishing she hadn't told him. In his experience, knowing nothing was a hundred times better than knowing the wrong thing.

Necro flinched, as if something had startled her. "That's an understatement."

I knew this was gonna suck.

Link took a deep breath. "Ghosts or no ghosts, I'm still goin' in."

"Of course you are. We all are." Liv checked her selenometer, then glanced at Floyd. "Unless any of *us* are having second thoughts."

Floyd stepped off the curb. "Nice try. I've never met a Mortal girl who didn't freak out at the sight of a Sheer."

Liv headed toward the back of the house. "Well, you have

now. Like I said before, I've gone head to head with Vexes." She waited for John to catch up as Sampson and Necro followed Angelique to the gate ahead of them.

Lucille trotted along next to Sampson like she was his personal Seeing Eye cat.

When they reached the back of the property, they saw that the iron gate was secured by a padlock. They probably weren't the first people who had tried to break in. Partying in haunted houses was practically a rite of passage in a city like New Orleans.

Link peered through the gate and into the overgrown courtyard. Magnolia trees lined the walkway, with a huge stone fountain in the center. Tangles of sweet jasmine and bougainvillea snaked their way through the garden and up the back porch. *Just like every other courtyard in New Orleans*, Link thought. *Ghosts included.*

Necro yanked on the padlock and glanced at Link and John. "Are you two gonna Rip us inside?"

John laughed and walked over to the gate. "That would be a waste of a trip." He closed his hand around the lock and pulled, breaking it off effortlessly.

"Nice one, dude." Link held up his fist and John bumped it.

Necro looked impressed. Not to be outdone, Sampson grabbed one of the gates and jerked his arm up. The heavy hinges ripped right off and clattered onto the sidewalk. He stood there for a moment, holding the gate in the air.

"Shh," Necro whispered. "You want to wake up every Sheer in there?"

"Seriously, Sampson," Floyd said. "Put that thing down."

Angelique patted his arm as she strode by. "We could've just climbed over the gate like I did last time."

Sam looked embarrassed and propped the gate against the side of the house. "Just trying to help," he said sheepishly.

"Show-off." John winked as he walked past Sampson.

Liv and Floyd exchanged one of those weird girl looks that always went right over Link's head.

Girls. They're like aliens.

When they crossed the threshold and stepped into the paved courtyard, Necro stopped and inhaled sharply.

"What is it?" Sampson sounded concerned.

"Just what I said before. Some real bad stuff went down here."

Link swallowed. "Like, how bad? Slasher movie bad?"

"The dials on my selenometer are going crazy," Liv said, studying her weird watch.

"If I can go through the house a second time, the rest of you will survive," Angelique said impatiently.

"Will the ghosts give us any trouble?" Link asked, shoving his hands in his pockets.

Angelique waved a dismissive hand. "They'll stay out of your way if you stay out of theirs."

"That's kinda hard to do if we can't *see* them," Link said.

Necro looked at Angelique. "The Sheers didn't bother *you* because you aren't a Necromancer. They can sense when one of us is around. It wakes them, for lack of a better word."

Sampson stepped in front of her. "Then you shouldn't go in."

Necro seemed confused for a moment. "Are you trying to get rid of me?"

"Or save your life," Sampson said. "Depending on how you look at it."

"He's just watching out for you, Nec." Floyd put her hand on Necro's arm gently.

Necro's expression softened. "Sorry, Sam."

Sampson gave her a rare smile. "It's all good."

"But I'm still going inside," Necro said, taking another step into the courtyard. "Stay together and don't touch anything." She paused in front of Link. "Got that?"

"Yes, ma'am. I won't touch a thing." Link raised his hands and clasped them behind his head.

The last thing I wanna do is piss off a whole buncha ghosts.

As they followed Angelique, moving into the center of the courtyard, Sampson sniffed the air. "Smell that?"

Necro nodded. "Yeah. It's strong."

Link inhaled deeply and snorted a few times for good measure. "What? I don't smell anythin'."

"Then you're lucky." Sampson took another step and winced, like he couldn't bear the stench. "This whole place reeks of blood."

John bent down next to where Necro was standing and inspected the ground.

Suddenly, Link felt like the emperor in his new clothes. "Dude, can you sense it, too?"

John shook his head. "No. I just wanted to see if I could pick up anything. Sampson's and Necro's powers are a lot stronger than mine when it comes to this kind of thing."

Necro stopped a few feet shy of the back porch. Her eyes traced a path up the steps to the back door. "The blood is coming from underneath the door."

Link craned his neck to get a better look. He'd never seen ghost blood before—not that he could really see it now. But he didn't like the idea of it either way.

"I don't mean to be morbid, but is the blood hazy or opaque?" Liv asked, flipping open her journal.

Floyd shot her a disgusted look. "You aren't seriously asking her that."

"This isn't a diary." Liv tapped a pen on a fresh page. "I'm a Keeper-in-Training, and it's my responsibility to record anything of note. As far as I'm concerned, this is scientific data. The average Necromancer can't see apparitional residue." Liv scribbled something in the little book. "This is quite remarkable."

Angelique leaned against the door that led into the house. "Are you guys always this much fun, or did I just catch you on a bad day?"

Floyd ignored her and grabbed Necro's arm, pulling her away from Liv and the blood no one else could see. But within the space of a few feet, Necro froze, the color draining from her face.

Lucille leaped onto the edge of the fountain with her ears pulled back and hissed like she was ready to tear someone—or *something*—to shreds.

Link caught up to the girls. "Why are you stoppin'?"

Necro's eyes widened, and she stumbled back a few steps, reaching for something to grab on to. "The bodies," she whispered. "I can see them."

A chill ran up the back of Link's neck as he looked around, but he didn't see anything.

Sampson, John, Liv, and Floyd glanced around the courtyard, too.

"How many bodies are we talkin' about?" Link asked, feeling jumpy.

"Dozens," Necro said, growing paler.

The air shifted subtly, like waves of heat coming off hot

asphalt. At first, Link thought his eyes were playing tricks on him in the dark.

Until the bodies began to materialize.

One by one—bare feet peeking out from beneath billowing silk harem pants; thin arms covered in gold bracelets from wrist to elbow; long, dark hair. They were hazy, but Link and the others could still see the blood all over them. These were the girls Liv told them about—the ones who were slaughtered along with the Turk who kept them locked up. Even though the murdered girls' Sheers were still a little hazy, they looked terrified.

Liv gasped and clamped her hand over her mouth.

John pushed her behind him, and the pencil tucked behind Liv's ear dropped in a puddle of blood at their feet.

Don't freak out. They're just ghosts, Link reminded himself.

Which only seemed about half true when the ghostly bodies began to rise.

Floyd shoved Necro toward the porch. "Keep moving. Don't look at them."

Link tried to follow Floyd's advice, even though he knew it wasn't meant for him. He jumped the stairs two at a time.

Sampson took Necro's elbow and steered her toward the steps. "Come on, let's get out of here."

Link tried the door, but it was locked.

"I locked it on my way out," Angelique said. "In case someone was following me."

"At least we know Nox hasn't been here," Floyd said, coming up next to him.

"What do you mean?" Link asked.

She gestured at the door. "It's still locked. Nox isn't an Incubus. He would've had to break in."

Link knew it was stupid, but secretly, he was glad Nox hadn't made it here first. That guy had caused enough problems between Ridley and him. Link didn't need Nox getting in the way of his big rescue.

This time, Link was the one who pulled the door off the hinges. Though it did take him a little more effort than the gate had taken Sampson.

Whatever. I'm only a quarter Incubus, not a seven-foot Caster version of Hellboy.

As they stepped into a gleaming foyer, Necro coughed and buried her nose in the crook of her elbow, as if the stench had gotten worse. She crossed the foyer, making a wide circle to avoid something on the floor that no one else could see.

"More blood?" John asked.

Necro averted her eyes. "It's everywhere. There was a huge pool of it just inside the door."

Link checked the bottoms of his shoes. Even if it was invisible ghost blood, he didn't want it on him.

Liv followed Angelique, staying close to the peeling wallpaper covering the walls at the perimeter of the room, which led into a huge parlor. An enormous crystal chandelier hung above the threadbare velvet couches and floor pillows scattered around the room.

Link walked up to what looked like a long-necked glass vase with a weird pipe thingy attached to it. "What the hell is that?"

"A hookah," Liv said. "People fill it with leaves called shisha, like a pipe. But a hundred and fifty years ago, they probably weren't smoking anything nearly as tame."

"Huh?" As usual, Link felt like he was failing a test he didn't even know he was taking until a second ago.

"Opium," she explained. "At least, that's what people generally smoked in hookahs back then."

Sampson and Lucille rushed ahead, following Angelique and dodging the ropes that sectioned off the house like an exhibition in the Fallen Soldiers Museum back home.

Angelique gestured down the hall. "The Outer Door is in the basement."

"Let's get it open," Sam said.

"John, look at the dials." Liv tapped her selenometer. "This is not good."

Link rushed over in time to see the hands on the dials spinning in opposite directions. "What does it mean?" he asked. Liv was always worried about the *why*, but all Link cared about was the *what*. If some kind of supernatural hurricane was about to hit this place, Link didn't want to be the last to know.

Liv shook her head. "Honestly, I have no idea."

"I think I do," Floyd said.

The air shifted again, the same way it had in the courtyard.

Within seconds, the bodies began to appear—girls, around his age if Link had to guess. Most of them had dark hair and golden skin, and they were all dressed in flowing silk and gold jewelry like the ones in the courtyard. Except their beautiful faces were covered in blood. A few of them had knife wounds or jagged lacerations that turned Link's stomach.

"Down here," Sampson called from somewhere far away, most likely the basement.

"Let's get out of here." John moved in front of Necro and Floyd.

Necro didn't respond. Floyd gave her a gentle push, and Necro shuffled forward, almost as if she was in a trance.

Link reached the front of the parlor and saw the long hallway leading to the open basement door. Lucille sat in the doorway, as if she was waiting for them. Link grabbed Necro's hand, practically dragging her. One of the harem girls rushed toward them, and Link yanked Necro's arm harder, but it was too late.

The hazy harem girl stepped right into the Necromancer's body.

Necro's body jerked back so hard that she took Link along with her.

It felt like someone hit Fast-Forward. . . .

Necro's body slammed against the wall—

Her hand slipped from Link's—

Floyd called out to her—

Necro's mouth opened in a scream that never came—

She scrambled away from Link, her posture more formal than he'd ever seen it. As Necro's eyes darted between her friends, it was clear she didn't recognize any of them. "You have to help me," Necro said in a frantic voice, softer and more innocent than her own. She rushed toward Liv, clutching at her arm. "There are men upstairs, and they are hacking everyone to pieces."

Before Liv had a chance to respond—or anyone could explain that the men weren't there anymore and the Sheer was just remembering the crime—the Sheer turned toward the doorway as if she heard a noise. Link knew the sound had to be in her head, because he didn't hear anything.

Necro's eyes widened, and she dropped Liv's arm and bolted toward the back door—and away from whoever she'd seen in the doorway.

But someone else appeared under the archway.

Sampson.

"What's wrong?" he called out, looking panicked.

Necro turned when she heard his voice and let out a blood-curdling scream.

The harem girl's Sheer stepped out of Necro's body and took off running again. The girl's form faded just before she crossed the threshold to the courtyard.

Necro swayed, looking dizzy and confused.

Floyd caught her arm for only a second before the Sheer of another harem girl appeared. The Sheer ran toward Necro, glancing behind her as if she was being chased, and Necro jerked back the moment the injured girl stepped inside her body. Just like the first time, Necro looked confused for a second, then terrified, as she took on the expression and even the crooked posture of the dead girl.

She turned and tried to run for the back door, just like the first girl had, but her injured leg slowed her down long enough for Sampson to catch up with her. He grabbed Necro by the shoulders and shook—not too hard but hard enough. "Get the hell out of her!"

"No! Please!" Necro covered her eyes, screaming.

Sampson scooped her up, tucking one arm under her legs. Necro cowered, her screams growing more intense.

"We have to get her out of here," Sampson said.

"The Outer Door is at the bottom of the stairs," Angelique called out, pointing.

Sam turned to Link. "Rip her out of here. We'll meet you on the other side."

John charged forward and took Necro's quivering body from Sampson. "I've got her. I've been Traveling a lot longer than

Link has." John turned to Liv. "Stay with Link. I'll meet you there."

She nodded, and Link waited for John to dematerialize.

But a moment later, he was still standing in the exact same spot with Necro screaming in his arms. John looked confused and closed his eyes like he was concentrating. The air around him shifted, and light pricked through his form as if he was beginning to disappear... but he was still standing there.

"It's not working," John said. "It must have something to do with the Sheer. I can't Rip with the Sheer inside Necro."

"How do we get it out of her?" Floyd asked.

John looked down at Necro, who was hysterical now, and shook his head. "I don't know."

Necro's head snapped to attention, her eyes darting wildly around the room as if she'd heard another sound no one else had.

John turned toward the arched doorway, following her gaze, and Necro wiggled out of his grasp.

"No!" Sampson shouted.

Necro took off toward the back door, dragging her injured leg behind her. The Darkborn ran after her, but even if she could have outrun him, it wouldn't have mattered. The moment she reached the door, the Sheer stepped out of Necro's body and kept running down the porch steps and into the courtyard.

Another Sheer—a man wielding a curved sword—darted out of the bushes. He swung the weapon and caught her in the back, slicing right through her body. The Sheer let out a raspy cry as she vanished into thin air.

The murderous Sheer rested the bloody knife against his shoulder, already scanning the area for another victim.

Sampson caught Necro just as she collapsed and, carrying

her, bolted out of the room and toward the basement. Link was right behind him. Even though the Incubus in Link was fast, the Darkborn was faster, not to mention the fact that it took Link three strides to match every one of Sampson's.

"Follow Link," John called out.

The basement door was open, and Lucille stood in the glow of the doorway. When she saw Sampson coming at her, she pulled her ears back and hissed.

It only took Link a second to realize that Sampson wasn't the one she was hissing at.

Another harem girl turned the corner and collided with Sam. He pivoted like a linebacker, trying to throw her off, but the Sheer glided right through him and into Necro.

The Necromancer inhaled sharply, like a drowning person who had finally come up for air. She stared past Sampson's shoulder and pointed a trembling finger. "They're coming."

Sampson ignored her and bounded down the stairs.

Link slipped and slid down the first few on his butt. And for once, no one had time to make fun of him. As he reached the bottom of the stairs, he saw Angelique standing in front of the Outer Door—and it was already open.

"Take your time," Angelique said. "It's not like I have places to go or people to kill."

Sampson ignored her and skidded to a halt when he reached the door. The Darkborn shifted his weight, like he was trying to decide whether or not to take the next step. He turned to face the others. "What should I do? Can I take her out of the house?"

Link looked to Liv automatically, realizing everyone else was looking at her, too.

Necro lifted her chin, raising her eyes to the top of the stairs. "No!" she shrieked, trying to claw her way out of Sampson's arms.

Liv flipped through the pages of her journal frantically.

"There's no time." Sampson looked panicked.

John squeezed Liv's arm. "Trust your instincts."

She nodded and turned to Sampson. "Take her through."

"But the Sheer's still inside her. What if she gets hurt?"

Liv swallowed hard. "The Sheers are anchored to the house. When you cross the threshold, I think it will force the Sheer out of Necro's body."

"You *think*?" Floyd asked, sounding frightened.

Liv squared her shoulders. "It's science. Spirits are energy. This house is functioning like a black hole trapping that energy within it. Take her across."

Lucille ran into the Tunnel and waited.

Sampson glanced at Necro, unsure.

Come on, Wheel a Fate. Give us a break for once, Link thought.

Link couldn't remember Liv being wrong before, but as Sampson lifted his foot to cross the threshold, dread twisted in Link's insides.

There's a first time for everything. Especially the bad things.

Necro let out a bloodcurdling wail, but Sampson kept moving.

The moment Necro's body reached the boundary between the basement of the Sultan's Palace and the Caster Tunnel, her shoulders jerked and the harem girl's Sheer lurched forward—out of Necro's body—as if someone had thrown her. It was like the Sheer had hit a force field from a sci-fi movie. The

Sheer's bare feet hit the ground, and she bent down in a crouch, as if she was just as shocked as Link. Then she rushed back up the stairs.

When Link turned back to the Tunnel, Sampson was already standing on the other side next to Lucille. He was still carrying Necro, her limp body leaning against his massive chest.

Floyd ran toward them. "Is she okay? Why isn't she moving?"

Link swallowed hard.

Come on, Nec. You gotta be okay.

"She's breathing, and her pulse is strong." Sampson looked down at her. "Beyond that, I don't know."

Necro stirred, and she pushed closer to Sampson, like someone having a nightmare.

Liv touched Necro's wrist and counted softly, checking her pulse. "Sam's right. Her pulse is a little fast, but it's strong. She's probably just weak. I can't imagine it's easy to have spirits stepping in and out of your body that way."

Sampson took a deep breath, looking relieved.

"That certainly was dramatic, and a little anticlimactic," Angelique said, glancing at Necro before she headed down the Tunnel.

"You should shut your mouth," Sam called after her. "Before someone does it for you."

The Cataclyst winked at him. "Aw. Say it like you mean it."

"Let's go," John said. "We can't afford to lose her until she gets us to the labs."

Sampson nodded and pulled Necro closer to him, following Angelique, while Lucille trotted next to the Darkborn.

The Tunnel resembled a storage cellar in an old bar. Boxes filled with cartons of Lucky Strike and Pall Mall cigarettes were stacked next to crates with the word COFFEE stamped on the outside.

John reached inside one of the crates and pulled out a bottle of whiskey. "These have probably been down here since Prohibition." He checked the date on the bottle. "Bootleggers smuggled liquor in coffee and tobacco crates all the time."

Liv pushed up on her toes and peered inside another crate. She pulled out an unmarked bottle of clear liquid. "Gin, maybe. I'm surprised Abraham left these down here."

"Maybe it's part of the décor," Floyd said, following Sampson farther into the Tunnel. "When you have as much money as the Ravenwoods, I bet cases of old cigarettes and liquor aren't big concerns."

"Not if you're selling harems of Caster women and girls," Liv said.

"I'm gonna kill that bastard Silas when I see him," Sampson said as he stormed behind Angelique.

"Get in line," Link said. "If that son of a bitch did anythin' to Rid..." He couldn't finish. The possibility that Silas might have already done something terrible to Ridley was too much. Deep down, Link knew things could be even worse—that he might get to the labs and find out Ridley was dead.

She's okay.

He had to believe it. It was the only thing he had left to hang on to.

Angelique slowed down. "Now, boys, let's not get carried away. Silas is *mine*."

"What happened?" Necro mumbled, her hand sliding around the back of Sampson's neck.

Sampson froze, as though he wasn't sure if Necro was really

talking or if he was imagining it—at least, that was the way it looked to Link.

If anyone knows what that feels like, it's me.

How many times had he found Ridley or one of his friends hurt and wondered if they were gonna be okay?

At least I knew if they were alive or not.

"You're awake." Floyd rushed to her friend's side and wrapped her arms around Necro.

Liv and John rushed over, too.

Necro rubbed her eyes and stretched slowly. "I feel like I was run over by a bus."

"Do you remember anything?" Liv asked tentatively.

Necro nodded, wincing. "Some of it. I saw the Sheer of one of the harem girls coming at me, and I felt it when she stepped inside me. But after that, it's all pretty hazy. But I'm guessing from the looks on your faces it was worse than that."

Angelique waved a hand in the air. "Lots of blood, some severed limbs, a man wielding a machete. That sort of thing."

Floyd glared at the Cataclyst before turning back to Necro. "There was more than one Sheer. It was like you were a magnet. They just kept coming at you, and there was nothing we could do."

Necro closed her eyes and nodded. "I get it. This isn't my first rodeo."

When she opened her eyes again, she glanced down at Sampson's arms wrapped around her. She raised her chin and looked up at him. Link couldn't swear to it, but it looked like Sam was blushing a little. "I'm guessing you're my knight in shining bike chain," she said, smiling. "Did you swoop in and save me or something?"

Sampson shrugged. "Liv's the one who figured out the Sheers couldn't cross the threshold into the Tunnel."

Necro looked at Liv with an expression of gratitude.

Liv waved off Sampson's compliment. "It was nothing, really. Just the principles of physics and a lucky guess. Sampson's the real hero here." Liv gave Sampson one of those looks that seemed to have a secret message hidden inside it.

"I think I can walk, Sam," Necro said, pulling her arm from around his neck as if she'd suddenly realized it was there.

"Yeah, I mean, sure." Sampson lowered her to the ground carefully, keeping one hand behind her back for support. Necro swayed, and he pulled her close. "If you don't feel okay, I can carry you. It's not like you're heavy or anything," he added.

"Good to know." She smiled. "But I think I need to walk it off."

Sampson stayed glued to Necro's side, but it was a short walk. Within minutes, they reached the end of the Tunnel.

"So what's the plan?" Link asked. "Are we just gonna bust in and save Rid?"

Floyd elbowed him. "That sounds like the opposite of a plan."

"One of you geniuses should assess the situation, so we know exactly how many men Silas has out there," Angelique said. "I'm sure he added guards after my escape."

Floyd nodded, her stringy blond hair falling over her shoulder. "I'm the Illusionist; I'll go."

Link put his arm out in front of her. "Hold on. I'm the Incubus. I can Rip out there and see what's happenin'."

"That's a brilliant idea." The sarcasm in Liv's tone made it clear she thought Link's idea was anything but brilliant. "While you're at it, why don't you take John with you? I'm sure Silas' men would be thrilled to get their hands on the Incubuses responsible for killing Abraham."

Link scratched his head. "You think they have our pictures or somethin'?"

Liv sighed. "You definitely should *not* be the one to go."

Floyd pushed her way in front of Link. "I don't know why we're still talking about this. I said I'd go."

"Why is it any safer for you?" Link asked. "Can you make yourself invisible or somethin' all of a sudden?"

Floyd rolled her eyes. "Now that you're a Supernatural, you really need to brush up on Caster powers. I'm sure there's a Wikipedia page."

"You shouldn't believe everything you read online," Link said, feeling clever. "Isn't that right, Liv?"

Angelique stared at them in disbelief. "Is this an actual conversation or are you two staging it for my benefit?"

"I'm all done talking." Floyd took off her jacket and handed it to Link. "And to answer your question, I don't have the power of invisibility. But I can make myself look like all kinds of things, temporarily."

Link knew it was true. Ridley's brother, Larkin, was an Illusionist, and Link had seen his powers in action.

Even if he was a tool when he was alive.

Sampson closed his eyes. "I'm not picking up on anything." When he opened them again, he seemed satisfied that no one was waiting to grab Floyd on the other side, and he stepped away from the door. "It seems clear, but I wouldn't go far. If this really does lead into the labs or anywhere near them, Silas will have his thugs around somewhere."

"I've got this." Angelique pushed past him and rested her

hand on the door, whispering the words to open it. The seal broke on the Caster door, and it opened just enough for Floyd to squeeze her skinny body through without opening it any wider.

Sampson closed it behind her just enough to fool a casual observer, but Link kept his hand wedged in the top of the doorjamb just in case.

It felt like an hour passed before Floyd finally returned, even though Liv had been keeping track of the time and it had only been seven minutes.

With his supersonic hearing that trumped even an Incubus', Sampson was the one who heard Floyd on the other side of the door. When the Darkborn opened it, Link grabbed Floyd's arm and pulled her inside.

"Ow!" she said. "Take it easy."

"You were gone long enough," Link said, scowling.

"What's wrong?" Floyd shrugged. "Did you miss me?"

Liv cleared her throat loudly. "Did you actually see anything?"

"Yeah. I saw plenty." Floyd crossed her arms, suddenly all business. "There are a bunch of trees and a big building on the other side. I'm guessing it's the labs, because this place is crawling with Incubuses and Darkborns."

"How many?" Sampson asked.

"I'm not sure," Floyd said. "I saw at least three Incubuses and another two or three Darkborns. Oh, and one of the Darkborns looked like she was the one in charge."

"Wait. *She?*" Sampson raked his hands through his hair. "Did she have blond hair?"

Floyd gave him a strange look. "Yeah, platinum. It was practically white. How'd you know?"

"We're screwed," he said. "That's Chloe Boucher. She's

the most dangerous Darkborn in the Underground. She's an assassin."

Link raised an eyebrow. "But you can take her, right?"

"Chloe Boucher has been around longer than I have, which makes her stronger. No one even knows where she came from. She just showed up on the scene with a buck knife and a name for killing."

"*Chloe Boucher* doesn't sound that intimidating," Liv said.

"It's the last name. She started using it because she thought it was funny," Sampson said, looking pale. "*Boucher* is French. It means 'butcher.' "

CHAPTER 21: NOX

Witching Hour

As Nox stared at the iron bars in front of him, he was at a crossroads. Until now, his interactions with women had always been simple. Caster girls threw themselves at him in one of his clubs, hoping for something—a TFP from his winnings, a supernatural favor, another chance after their luck ran dry at one of his gambling tables.

Nox's answer was usually no, except on the rare occasions when he met a girl who just wanted to be with *him*. Sometimes, if he was bored enough and she was attractive enough, he'd give her what she wanted.

But until now that had never included his heart.

This time it was different.

This time, Ridley was the girl and that changed everything.

He finally understood all those stupid love songs and tragic romance movies, because the girl he wanted more than anyone in the Mortal or Supernatural universe wanted him, too. Desperately, fully, completely *wanted* him.

Now Rid was looking at Nox the way she used to look at Link. Maybe in a way she'd never looked at Link. And Nox wanted her. He had always wanted her. That had never changed.

But that also wasn't the point.

If he let this happen, if he let his guard down and surrendered to the feelings and the impulses that had been building up inside him since the day he first met her—if he took anything at all from Ridley, knowing she wasn't herself—then he wasn't man enough to be worthy of her.

So he sat there staring at the metal bars between them.

We have to get out of here.

Nox looked over at the next cell, where she lay resting a few feet above the bed, on what appeared to be an endless gust of wind that never seemed to settle anywhere at all. Her pink-streaked blond hair fanned out beneath her, giving the illusion that she was floating on the surface of a rippling body of water.

Rid caught his eye—and before he said a word, he found her lying next to him, on her side of the row of iron bars. She wasn't dressed in a hospital gown anymore.

Now she was wearing her red leather bodysuit, tight and leaving nothing to the imagination. *Like the Devil's own version of Catwoman*, Nox thought.

"Well?" She reached through the bars, twisting the edge of Nox's jacket. "Feeling any better?"

He let her pull him to the edge of the bars. As she moved her face toward his, he couldn't resist. In some ways, he was only human, after all.

You live among them long enough and it's bound to happen.

Again.

And again.

CHAPTER 22: RIDLEY

Revolution Calling

The moment she kissed Nox, Ridley had a realization. A breakthrough, really. You could even call it an epiphany.

For the first time in her life, Ridley didn't crave sugar. She didn't feel sweet, and she didn't want to be sweet, either.

Not that the latter had ever been her problem.

She was hungry for something much more substantial than sugar. It was time to put the cherry lollipops aside. The power games of her childhood were no longer enough.

This kiss only proves that.

Nox didn't taste sweet. He tasted strong.

Like steel and fire.

Electrical fire.

That was the taste of power.

That's what I want now.

Isn't it?

She had a fleeting thought of Link—of his partly Mortal warmth, his open face, the goofball way he curled his enormous hand around her smaller one, his lanky arm around her slight one. Then she put those thoughts aside.

Link was just another toy from her childhood. She couldn't imagine feeling anything for him now. She remembered feeling something—scattered moments, a rogue look in his eye, a sudden, Linkish laugh—but even those were fading into a distant, hazy blur.

Nox was the only one who understood her—who could give her what she needed.

Besides, how can I inflict myself on a Mortal in this state? What has Silas even done to me? What kind of Caster am I?

I'm nothing that has ever been before.

Silas had made sure of that.

Nox could see it, too, and he wasn't frightened. At least, those weren't the signals he was sending right now.

She pulled him closer, feeling the burn against her lips—when she heard a sound in the corridor and opened her eyes.

"What the—?" Nox pulled away from her as Silas waved his Darkborns into the glorified dungeon containing their prison cells. One of them quickly unlocked the door of Nox's cell.

Silas' thugs flung Nox against the far cell wall before she could say a word. Silas moved into Nox's cell behind them.

"Silas, stop it." Ridley panicked, clutching the bars between them.

"That's exactly why I'm here. To stop it"—he looked at Nox—"from living."

"Don't be ridiculous. You can't kill him," she said, trying to hide the fear rising inside her. "He's on our side now. I promise."

She had no idea what she was saying. Nox had never been on Silas' side—and he never would be—but she was desperate to keep him safe.

"Ridiculous? Listen to your own babble." Silas glanced in her direction and laughed. "I don't care whose side this kid says he's on. He screwed me, and now he's going to pay for it."

"Silas. Listen to yourself. You sound like an angry child." Ridley was the angry one now.

Silas' eyes narrowed. "Yeah? You screwed me, too, so I'd be careful how you talk to me."

Nox stumbled to his feet, moving between them. Even after a beating, his first instinct was to protect her. Ridley appreciated it, but she also knew she wasn't the one who needed protecting at the moment.

"It's okay, Rid. Don't worry about me." Nox gave her a weak smile. "I knew this was coming." He looked at Silas. "Weak men have no mercy. Especially not Ravenwoods."

One of the guards grabbed the back of Nox's neck and slammed his face against the bars.

"No!" Ridley shouted, heat burning through her veins.

Blood gushed from Nox's nose.

Silas shook his head. "You got a real gift for saying the wrong thing at the wrong time, kid."

"Stop! You're hurting him!" Ridley ran to the door of her cell, her fingers curling around the bars. She shook them, but they didn't budge.

I won't let you hurt him. I'll kill every single one of you first.

The moment the thought took shape in Ridley's mind, she realized something new about herself. Her *new* self. It wasn't just a threat. She could actually *do* it.

The delicious cocktail of powers swimming inside her was calling to her—saying: *Don't let them hurt the boy you love.*

The words formed themselves before she could stop them.

Do I love him?

Is that what this is?

Do I want that?

But it didn't matter. Ridley gripped the bars tighter, focusing her wrath—and her power—on the Darkborns dragging Nox out of his cell.

You'll let him go. One way or another.

The walls in the dungeon began to move—at least they looked like they were moving. Ridley knew it was only an illusion, but even she had never seen one that looked so real.

Silas looked around, as if he wasn't sure he could trust his own eyes.

The four walls that formed the cellblock drew in toward the middle of the room.

"What's going on?" the Darkborn holding Nox by the neck called out, her eyes darting around the small space.

Silas smiled. "Ignore it. The Siren's creating an illusion. It's just a reaction to how I juiced her up. For an Illusionist, it's perfectly natural, not all that much different from a tantrum." He turned to Ridley. "Though we might have to find something else to call you after this little display. You aren't exactly a Siren or an Illusionist anymore, are you?"

Ridley didn't answer.

Her mind was elsewhere.

She pictured the walls crushing the Darkborns—and the moment she did, the back wall of Nox's cell burst through the barred doors on that side of the room. The Darkborns threw themselves—along with Nox—toward Ridley's cell, narrowly escaping the falling metal bars. But the wall didn't stop moving. And the ones at either end of the dungeon were coming closer, too, now.

Ridley fixed her violet eyes on Silas. "One more chance, little man."

"Excuse me?" Silas looked at her, raging.

"I said... Let. Him. Go."

You want to let him go, Ridley thought, focusing every ounce of her Power of Persuasion in Silas' direction. *Tell your men now, before I kill you all.*

Silas rubbed his hands over his face, looking confused. He was one of the strongest Blood Incubuses in existence. Ridley knew he wouldn't be that easy to take down, but she didn't care.

"Silas, make her stop," one of the Darkborns called out as the back wall pushed him closer to Ridley's cell—and to being crushed.

"This isn't an illusion!" the other shouted. "I can't breathe."

"Shut the bitch down," called the first.

But Silas didn't. He was too confused to do much of anything. He opened his mouth to say something, and then closed it again without a word.

It was true.

She wasn't just one thing. Not since Silas had given her the transfusions.

Idiot.

He was the one who had set her free without even knowing it.

There was no limit to what she could do—at least, it didn't feel like there was.

Here they'd been, trapped in these little rat cages, when all she had to do was force them open in her mind.

Ridley felt a surge of heat and a wave of dizziness as she summoned whatever power she had left.

Let Nox go, she thought, her eyes drilling into Silas like she was reaching into his mind. *And while you're at it, unlock my cell.*

The Darkborns who weren't holding Nox had their palms flat against the shifting walls now, pressing against them.

Screaming.

"Let the boy go," Silas said.

The Darkborns moved toward Nox, their shocked expressions only fueling Ridley's power—and the incredible high it gave her.

Not enough, she thought.

She closed her eyes again, and the walls shuddered. Plaster fell from the ceiling.

"I said let him go!" Silas shouted, looking even more confused. He seemed even more surprised by the words coming out of his own mouth than his thugs were.

The Darkborns released Nox, and he fell to his knees, in the center of what was slowly turning into a shoe box of a room.

The walls in the room stopped moving all at once.

"Ridley, you can stop." Nox choked out the words. "I'm okay."

I'm not finished yet. I want Silas Ravenwood to know that no one controls me.

Her eyes darted back to Silas. *You want to open my cell, Silas. More than you've ever wanted anything in your pathetic life.*

Silas marched toward Ridley's cell, as if he were a little puppet on a string.

My puppet. My string.

When he reached the door, he held out his hand to one of the guards. "Keys."

The Darkborn dropped them in his palm.

Silas looked back at Ridley.

Do it, she thought. *Do it now.*

The Incubus raised a shaky arm. "Are you sure?"

"Oh, I am." Ridley smiled. "It's about time for the princess to rescue herself from the dungeon. And maybe burn down the castle while she's at it. You know how these things go. It's nothing personal."

Ridley looked at Nox. "The prince is welcome to come." Then she looked back at Silas. "The dragon, not so much." She nodded, and Silas moved the key, slowly, as if he was fighting for control of his own body.

"This is a mistake," he said as the key slid into the lock.

"I like to think of it as more of an upgrade," Ridley said as she pushed the door open and stepped across the threshold. "Ridley 3.0."

CHAPTER 23: LINK

Queen of the Reich

Angelique smiled when Sampson mentioned the meaning of Chloe Boucher's last name, but Link had a completely different reaction.

The Butcher? That can't be good. Like slasher-movie-Stephen-King not good.

"So what's the game plan?" Link asked. "You know, besides you gotta kill 'em all?"

No one laughed, not even Link.

"Any thoughts, ladies?" Angelique asked, addressing Necro and Floyd, the other Dark Casters.

"I might be able to deal with the Incubuses," Floyd said. "But the Darkborns are out of my league."

"They must have a weakness," Liv reasoned, turning to Sam. "We just have to figure out what it is."

He held up his hands. "Don't look at me. If we have one, I don't know what it is."

"Humility?" Necro asked innocently.

"How many Darkborns did you say there were out there?" Angelique asked Floyd.

"I'm not sure. At least two, plus Chloe the Butcher."

Angelique pushed up her sleeves and moved toward the Outer Door. "I love a challenge. Not to mention a butcher."

Link stepped in front of her. "Hold up a minute."

Angelique stared at him with an expression that said *Move it or lose it.*

He took the hint and stepped aside. "Sorry. I just missed the part about what the rest of us are supposed to do."

Angelique pointed her finger at the door, and without a word, it flew open. "Try to stay out of the way." She stalked out of the protection of the Tunnel and into a sea of grass and trees behind the plantation's main house. "I wouldn't want to kill you accidentally."

Link scrambled after her with his friends as the Cataclyst shook out her red curls and cracked her knuckles like a thug getting ready to fight. The bloodlust propelling her reminded him of the only other Cataclyst he'd ever met, and Sarafine had been a complete psycho.

Sampson fell into step next to Link. "She's crazy," he said, keeping his voice low. "And she's going to get herself killed before she makes it into the building."

"I'm not so sure," John said.

"You'll have to pass notes later, children," Angelique said. "We have company."

Two Incubuses emerged from the trees. Neither one was

paying attention, until they spotted Angelique marching toward them. The Incubuses' black eyes narrowed as they zeroed in on what they probably considered their next victim.

This is either gonna be really good or really bad, dependin' on which side you're on, Link thought.

Angelique raised her hand, but Floyd jogged up beside her and pushed her out of the way. "Don't be a ball hog. I'll take care of these two."

Angelique backed off, intrigued.

The trees around the Incubuses began to change, the massive oaks transforming into towering mirrors. Within seconds, they formed a maze, like the House of Mirrors at the Gatlin County Fair. The Incubuses waved their arms in front of them to avoid crashing into one of the huge trunks.

"Nicely played." Angelique glanced at Floyd. "It's about time. I was beginning to think you didn't have a Dark bone in that skinny body of yours."

Floyd frowned, focusing on her illusion. "Never underestimate a girl with a guitar."

Sampson studied the mirrors as everyone walked right by the Incubuses trying to find their way out of the mirrored maze.

"Hopefully, getting past all of Silas' men will be that easy," Necro said, still looking exhausted after what happened to her at the Sultan's Palace.

"Don't count your fried chickens before I've slaughtered them," Angelique called out. "I'm sure there will be plenty to go around. Just remember, Silas is mine." The Cataclyst sounded vicious when she said his name, as if she was growing Darker with every step.

Up ahead, Link caught his first glimpse of what had to be

the labs. The rectangular gray cement building reminded him of an elementary school building—minus the windows—and it looked out of place on the grounds of the Louisiana plantation. But he didn't have time to give it too much thought because three guys were coming straight at them, and judging by their size alone, he was pretty sure they were Darkborns.

"This isn't good." John picked up his pace.

"Darkborns?" Link asked Sam.

His friend nodded. "Yeah. Big ones."

Angelique didn't break stride. In fact, she looked kind of bored. "My turn," she said in a singsong voice, without taking her eyes off her targets. She stopped and a light wind began blowing around her.

John grabbed Liv and Floyd, pulling them back. Sampson stayed next to John, but Link couldn't resist taking a closer look. The way Angelique controlled the air reminded him of those magicians on TV—the ones who made airplanes disappear, doing things that seemed impossible even while you were looking right at them.

The air whipped around the Darkborns, but it didn't slow them down.

Angelique turned things up a notch, sending a gale-force wind right at them.

But the Darkborns kept walking—straight into the wind tunnel. They shielded their eyes from flying leaves and dirt and a wind so strong it blew one Darkborn's jacket off his body.

"Um...Angelique. I think you need to throw a little more Cataclyst mojo at them," Link said. "Don't hold back now."

The Dark Caster flicked her fingers toward him without looking back, and a surge of air sent Link flying. He landed on his butt in the dirt. "When I want your opinion, I'll ask for it," she called out over the wind. "Which will be exactly ten minutes after Hell freezes over."

John grabbed Link by the shirt and yanked him back to his feet.

"Am I nuts or is she a serious bitch?" Link asked.

"She's definitely getting nastier," Liv offered. "Maybe it's being back here. Silas experimented on her, after all."

"Or maybe she really is just a giant bitch," Floyd said.

Before John had a chance to respond, two Incubuses materialized behind them.

"I'll take the big one," John said, Ripping from the spot where he was standing and materializing in front of them.

"I'm good with that," Link answered.

Just don't let me land on my ass in front of the bad guys, Link prayed, Ripping after John.

This time, Link didn't land on his ass. He landed on the Incubus and wrapped his arms around the guy's neck, trapping him in a headlock.

The big Incubus was grappling on the ground with John. "You'd better kill me, kid. Or I'm gonna take a bite outta your girlfriend's neck, and maybe a few other places," the Incubus said, pinning John. "I missed dinner."

Link squeezed the guy's neck harder, cutting off his airway. "Come on, pass out already, Dog Boy."

The Incubus' body finally went limp, and Link let him drop. Just as Link started to Rip his way over to John, he saw Sampson out of the corner of his eye.

Holy crap.

Sam looked scarier than Link had ever seen him—like the feral dogs that lived behind Edgar Nubuck's house back in Gatlin.

When Link materialized again a moment later, Sampson was pounding the hulking Incubus into the dirt with his gigantic fist. A third pack member emerged from the tree line and lunged at Sam from the side, but the Darkborn tossed him a good six feet with one arm.

Link hauled John off the ground. "You okay, man? Anythin' busted?"

"Just my pride." John brushed off his jeans, wincing. "And maybe that rib right there."

Sampson stood up, his black leather pants coated in a fine layer of dirt, and looked at John. "Next time, *I'll* take the big one."

"Deal."

Angelique didn't seem to be having much luck dealing with the Darkborns, either.

"The wind isn't slowing them down," Liv shouted, checking her selenometer from where she stood behind Angelique.

"Then let's see how they deal with something a little more *destructive*." The Cataclyst held her arms out in front of her, palms facing the ground. Then she flipped them over and threw her arms skyward.

The ground in front of her tore open—a crack racing from the tip of Angelique's lace-up boots all the way to the advancing Darkborns. Hunks of earth and rock ripped from the ground and flew into the air, as if guided by her hands.

Angelique's eyes blazed as she smiled. "If Silas had mentioned that I would be able to do all this afterward, I might have actually volunteered."

Link shuddered, hoping she wasn't serious. A power-hungry Cataclyst was like a ticking bomb, something he'd learned from watching Sarafine Duchannes destroy half his town, back when she was still alive.

The Darkborns kept coming, until they reached the enormous fissure and more earth gave way beneath their feet. When they fell in, Angelique flipped her palms over again, and the dirt that had ripped itself from the ground rained back down, pummeling the Darkborns and burying them. She dropped her hands together and dusted off her palms. "Two indestructible Supernaturals down."

Liv pointed at five figures moving toward them. "And five to go."

The Darkborns fanned out, advancing in military-style formation.

This time, the air around Angelique did more than blow. With one flick of her wrist, a tornado touched down in front of the Darkborns. The wind spiraled and twisted, pulling up the trees and bushes in its path.

"Holy crap," Link said, watching.

The Darkborns shielded their eyes, but aside from that, they walked right into the tornado.

John turned to Sampson. "Are all of you that strong?"

Sam nodded. "Pretty much."

"Hmm," Angelique said, unimpressed. "Wind isn't my favorite element. It lacks drama." She whispered something in Latin, and the tornado twisted one last time before it transformed into a vortex of flames. The flames spiraled downward and hit the ground, then spread like they were following trails of gasoline. "That's more like it."

"Get off me!" Floyd screamed.

Link, John, and Sampson spun around. Two Darkborns had

snuck up on them from the side—and one of them had his hand around Floyd's neck.

"Let go of her," Sampson growled, storming toward the guy holding Floyd by the throat. "Now."

"Stay back," the Darkborn said, tightening his grip on Floyd. "Or I'll snap her neck."

Sam froze, and Link turned to Angelique. "We need a little help, Fire Woman."

She glanced at Floyd, then went back to aiming her Cataclyst juice at the Darkborns. "I'm a little busy at the moment, but I'm happy to cremate her body if they kill her."

"Fire can't hurt them," Liv said, moving beside Angelique.

"That's because they've never been touched by my fire," Angelique said, sounding more psychotic by the minute. It reminded Link of the arrogance Sarafine had always shown in the face of a potential threat. He wondered if their powers made all Cataclysts this crazy.

The Darkborns walked through the flames like they had a force field around them, the same way Sampson had repelled the flames the night he saved Link and Rid at Sirene. Another Darkborn stood in the center of the flames, smoke billowing up around her. From this distance, Link couldn't see much except for her platinum-blond hair. But the woman could only be one person.

Chloe the Butcher.

Angelique cocked her head to the side, studying the blond Darkborn coming her way. "It's about time. I was getting bored."

"I thought Cataclysts were dangerous," Chloe called out as she strode through the blaze in high-heeled boots. She was pulling someone along beside her, her hand clamped around a girl's neck. "I'm disappointed. This is rather pedestrian, in terms of power."

Link's heart leaped until a curtain of black hair swung over the girl's shoulder.

Calm down. It's not Rid.

Chloe jerked the girl's limp body upright, still holding the back of her neck. The girl looked around Link's age, younger than Angelique. "Maybe Silas should've picked your Empath friend instead of you."

The girl's eyes fluttered open, her black hair knotted and singed around her ash-streaked face. "Gigi?" she rasped, looking at Angelique. "Help me."

"Lucia." Angelique stepped back, clearly thrown by the sight of her friend. She regained her composure, tearing her eyes away from the girl and turning them back on Chloe. "Leave her alone. Or are you afraid to pick on someone who can fight back?"

"Not at all." Chloe smiled, sliding her free hand under Lucia's chin, while her other one remained clamped around the back of the Empath's neck. In one swift movement, Chloe jerked her hands in opposite directions, breaking the girl's neck.

Liv and Necro gasped as Lucia's body dropped in the dirt, her dark, lifeless eyes open as if she were staring at Angelique.

Chloe dusted off her hands casually. "I was never planning to fight her, *Gigi*. I just wanted you to watch her die. Consider it one last gift before you die."

Angelique's eyes changed from gold to bright yellow, like a comic book sun. "I'm going to burn the skin off your bones."

"You made a mistake coming back here, Cataclyst. But I'll

enjoy adding your skull to my collection. You can keep your skin." Chloe was only a few yards away now.

Angelique raised her arms skyward and began to chant. "From the mouth of the Dark Fire, bring me the heat of flame, the power of a nova, and the heat of a thousand burns. Give your Darkest daughter the power to control any fire."

It sounded like a whole lot of Caster mumbo jumbo to Link, but *something* was happening, even if Link couldn't figure out exactly what.

The Darkborns stopped moving. Every one of them—at exactly the same time.

They looked at one another, exchanging confused and questioning glances. And they weren't the only ones.

"What are you doing?" Chloe shouted at them. "I didn't tell you to stop!"

None of them moved or responded in any way, which made Link feel like he'd entered the Twilight Zone. Chloe opened her mouth to yell at them again, but her expression changed from anger to confusion before a single word left her lips. She was still coming, which was more than anyone could say about the rest of her Darkborns, but her movements were sluggish, like she was wading through swamp mud. The other Darkborns stood frozen in place, watching as Chloe pushed forward.

Chloe's eyes met Angelique's. "What are you doing, Caster? Is this one of your spells?" Chloe hissed.

"Wouldn't you love to know? Unfortunately, I'm not in a sharing mood," Angelique said, but judging by the expression on her face, she didn't have any idea how she was controlling them, either.

"Get up!" Chloe screamed at her lackeys. A few of the more

determined Darkborns struggled to sit up or stand, but none of them could move. "We are the most powerful Supernaturals that have ever walked the earth—born from the Dark Fire itself. Do not let *her* control you."

The comment must've annoyed Angelique, because she closed her hands, then flung open her fingers again. The Darkborns' bodies flew backward, some falling into the flames while others rolled into them across the ash-covered grass.

Angelique held up her hands and wiggled her fingers, as if she still couldn't believe she was the cause of all this. "Well, that's new."

Sampson stared in shock. "No one can control a Darkborn."

"Except me," the Cataclyst said.

The Darkborns surrounding Floyd looked stunned, too. They were whispering to one another and backing away—taking her right along with them.

"Angelique!" Link pointed.

The Cataclyst closed her hand like she was the one strangling Floyd. Then she opened it again slowly, and the hand around Floyd's neck opened along with hers.

Sampson threw his body forward to lunge for Floyd, but he was moving more slowly, too. But John still had his speed, and he caught Floyd's arm, yanking her away from the Darkborns, who didn't seem like they could move when Angelique aimed her fingers—and whatever power she was using—at them.

Sampson winced. "Would you mind aiming your tractor beam *away* from me?"

Angelique turned her wrist enough to allow Sam to step out of her path.

"She's controlling their bodies," Necro said. "Like they're puppets."

"You're all my puppets," Angelique purred. "Don't feel left out. You're equally pointless to me."

"Well, one a your puppets is headed this way." Link nodded in Chloe's direction.

Chloe the Butcher was still trudging toward them, even though she wasn't moving much faster than Ethan's Great-Aunt Mercy, who was around a hundred years old by Link's calculations.

"The Dark Fire," Liv whispered to herself. "That has to be it."

"What's going on in that head of yours?" Necro asked, leaning over Liv's journal.

"I think I know why she can control them."

Angelique raised an eyebrow and looked at Liv. "Do tell."

Sampson waited anxiously for Liv's answer. He looked like Superman after he opened a box and realized it was full of kryptonite.

"She's not controlling the Darkborns," Liv explained. "She's controlling fire—the Dark Fire that's part of them."

Angelique smiled. "Clever girl. You might be worth keeping around."

"You're saying she can control our bodies because we were created by the Dark Fire?" Sam asked.

Necro looked up from the journal. "Exactly."

It was all the information Angelique needed. She focused her gaze and her fingers at Chloe, opening and closing her hand like she was crushing a beer can.

Chloe's knees buckled, and she cried out in pain. The Darkborn writhed on the ground, the flames rising up behind her. "I'm not afraid of you, Cataclyst." She choked out the words. "Silas *made* you, and he can destroy you."

“Just like *I* can destroy you.” The Dark Caster’s eyes narrowed. “You shouldn’t have killed Lucia.”

“Enough with the threats. If you were going to kill me, you would’ve done it already,” Chloe said as her cheek hit the dirt.

Angelique laughed. “Don’t be silly. It’s never too late for murder.”

CHAPTER 24: NOX

Pull Me Under

Silas backed away from Ridley slowly, his confused expression replaced by a sadistic smile.

Seeing her standing outside the cell *should've* worried him, but Silas was taking something else away from all this—something Nox hadn't figured out yet.

The Darkborns practically tripped over themselves trying to get away, and Nox couldn't blame them. He'd never seen an illusion that realistic, one that actually made you *feel* like the walls were closing in on you.

Or one that actually *made* the walls close in on you.

Rid wasn't just an Illusionist anymore.

Part Siren. Part Shifter. Part Illusionist.

He wasn't sure what else, but Silas hadn't held back and it was a game changer. A new game for a New Order, with a new Ravenwood dealing a new deck.

Whatever Silas had done to Rid had amped up the normal level of Caster powers.

Silas tipped an imaginary hat to Ridley, who was still standing just outside her cell. "Imagine what you'll be able to do after the next infusion, my dangerous girl." He backed down the hallway, as if still under Rid's influence. "So many different Casters to choose from... Palimpsest, Thaumaturge, Evo, Empath. The possibilities are endless."

The thought of Silas shooting Ridley up with another set of powers made Nox shudder, but the expression on Ridley's face made it clear that she didn't share his revulsion.

With her violet eyes glowing and her lips parted, she looked almost euphoric.

We'll be long gone before Silas gets his hands on you again. And I'll find a way to fix all this.

Nox pulled himself up off the ground and stumbled toward Ridley.

She caught him as he fell against her. Silas' guards had broken at least one of his ribs for sure.

Ridley touched his face. "Did they hurt you, Baby?"

The way she said *Baby*, like he was the only person she could've been talking about, made his heart race.

He nodded, wincing. "I'm okay. But we have to get out of here while we can. Whatever you did to Silas will wear off eventually, and then he'll be back."

She studied his face like she was trying to memorize every detail. "If he comes back, I'll give him another taste of my powers. Trust me, Silas Ravenwood can't hurt us. No one can."

"Maybe that's true, but we don't need to stay down here locked up like animals to prove a point." Nox turned toward the hallway that led away from the cells, her hand curled inside his.

Ridley's fingers slipped from between his. Nox tried to catch them, but when he turned around, he realized it wasn't an accident.

She was standing inside her cell again.

"Rid, no!" He started toward her, moving as fast as he could with his ribs jabbing him.

Nox closed his hand around one of the bars just as she slammed the cell door shut, trapping herself inside.

He let his head fall against the bars. "Why, Rid? We could be on our way somewhere safe. Together."

She reached through the spaces between the bars and took his face in her hands again. "Shh. You worry too much, Nox. Everything is going to be fine. We'll leave as soon as I get my next infusion. I promise. It's just—I think there's more I could get from Silas. Things I might need, if I'm going to take down his organization." She looked more determined than he'd ever seen her. "The whole House of Ravenwood is going down."

Nox's blood ran cold. "What are you talking about? You can't let him do this to you again."

She ran her thumbs along Nox's jawline. "I'm not letting anyone *do* anything to me. I want it, Baby. Don't you understand?"

"You aren't thinking straight. Whatever Silas gave you is messing with your head."

Ridley's lips grazed his, and every nerve in Nox's body burned for her. She let her lips hover just in front of his, then pressed them against the bars, pulling him even closer. This time, she kissed him the way he'd always wanted to kiss her. Like she belonged to him—and he belonged to her.

"Does that feel like I'm not thinking straight?" she murmured against his mouth. "I need this, Nox. The power—it's part of me now, and I need it just like I need you."

"Rid, I don't—"

She found his mouth again, raking her hand through his hair. "Don't you need me?"

He nodded, unwilling to move his mouth away from hers.

"We tried being good, Nox. I know you tried for me," she whispered. "But we aren't cut out for it. I'm not saying we're bad…we're just different. I can do things no other Siren has ever been capable of. And you can see the future. We finally have a chance to be who we are, and to be *together.*"

Rid sounded sincere, but there was no way to know if she was in her right mind.

Does it matter?

Nox tried to tell himself it didn't, but he wasn't sure.

"Are you sure that's what you really want?" Nox couldn't believe he was asking the question.

But I need to know if this is real. If she wants me as much as I want her.

She dragged her lips up to his ear. "Of course I'm sure."

He swallowed hard.

You have to ask her.

Nox reached through the bars and held Ridley by the shoulders, pushing her back so he could look at her. "What about Link?"

Her violet eyes met his without hesitation. "Link who?"

CHAPTER 25: LINK

Diary of a Madman

"This isn't over, Caster," Chloe said, her body still under Angelique's control.

The Cataclyst eyed her coldly. "It certainly looks over to me, and you are horribly tiresome." She flung her fingers open, and the Darkborns' bodies hurtled back again. Angelique aimed strategically, and the Darkborns slammed into the trees behind them.

Chloe's head cracked against a thick trunk, and she collapsed on the ground in a heap. The other Darkborns all suffered the same fate.

"Are they dead?" Link asked, not sure which answer would worry him more.

Angelique strode past the crumpled forms. "One can only hope. At the very least, radically incapacitated."

Maybe she didn't know how to kill a Darkborn any more

than he did. This was the first time he'd ever seen anyone take one down—let alone a whole posse.

"Do you think Silas knows we're here?" Sampson asked as they followed Angelique to the cement building the Darkborns had been guarding.

"I wouldn't be surprised if that sick bastard was watching us right now," John said, anger churning in his eyes.

Link knew coming back to the place where Abraham had experimented on him had to be tough. But John wasn't the kind of guy who complained. He took the punches life threw at him, just like Link.

Still, that didn't make returning to the scene of the crime any easier.

Sampson beat Angelique to the door. "Want me to go in first?" he asked.

She laughed and pushed him aside. "After my demonstration just now, I think we both know I don't need your protection." She patted his cheek as she walked by. "But don't feel bad, Goliath. If I had a purse, I'd let you carry it for me."

"It's Sampson," Sam muttered, looking embarrassed.

Link whacked him on the back. "Don't take it so hard, Sammy Boy. It's nothin' personal. She's just a—"

"Narcissistic egomaniac?" Sampson finished.

"Pretty much," Liv said, following Angelique through the heavy metal door at the side of the building.

"If the shoe fits…" Link shrugged.

"You're talking, but all I hear is blah, blah, blah," Angelique said.

Link wanted to run inside and find Rid, but he waited until everyone else went in, including Lucille, who trotted after Sampson.

Inside, the stark white walls reminded Link of a hospital, minus all the doctors and nurses rushing around. This place was dead silent. At the end of the short hallway, there was a door with some weird strips of plastic hanging in front of it on one side and another long hallway on the other.

Link pointed at the curtain of plastic. "Looks like a car wash."

John looked up at the sign above the doorway: RESTRICTED ACCESS. TRIALS IN PROGRESS. "I'm guessing it isn't." He turned to Angelique. "Which way?"

The Cataclyst nodded toward the long hall. "I wasn't at the top of my game when I followed the old lady out of this dump. But I don't remember seeing a door like that one."

"I think we should go this way," Liv said, separating the car wash flaps.

Angelique noticed the sign above the door as she walked through. "I can't wait to burn this place down."

"Not until we find Rid," Link reminded her.

John rested his forehead against the wall and closed his eyes.

"You okay, man?" Link asked.

"Of course he's not okay," Liv said. "He shouldn't be here. I can't imagine how difficult this must be for him."

"I'm all right. I just need a minute." John took a deep breath. "It was a long time ago, and I'm a different person now."

Link knew it was true, but watching John come face to face with his past wasn't easy. Especially not for Liv, who seemed to feel everything John felt.

Floyd grabbed Link's hand. "Come on. Follow Angelique. They'll catch up." It was a casual gesture, and Floyd was dragging him along more than actually holding his hand in a romantic way. But it still felt wrong now that he was so close to finding

Ridley. Link pushed the flaps aside, using it as an excuse to let go of Floyd's hand.

When Link stepped into the dim room, it took a moment for him to process what he was seeing.

Some kind of weird hospital room, full of glowing machines and fancy medical equipment—and rows of gurneys. But that wasn't the part that made Link's stomach turn.

Every single gurney had a person sleeping on it—at least, Link hoped they were sleeping.

The people lay hooked up to IVs and heart rate monitors, unmoving.

"Are they Mortals?" Floyd asked, skirting past a woman with an oxygen mask strapped over her nose and mouth.

Angelique examined one of the IV bags. "Doubtful. From what I overheard, Silas only used Mortals in the early trials. He hates them too much to waste his time experimenting on them this far into the process. He says they dilute the results."

Liv inspected another bag. "She's right. The bags are labeled with the type of Caster they are attached to." She pointed at a line of black script. "This one's a Sybil."

Sampson read the label on another. "Cypher."

"Diviner," Floyd said, reading the one closest to her. "It's like a Noah's Ark of Casters in here."

John stayed close to the wall, avoiding the bodies laid out like meat on slabs. He was practically hyperventilating. Liv glanced over at him and he nodded at her, encouraging her to keep looking around.

Necro seemed spooked, too, and she stuck close to Liv, who was opening drawers and reading the labels on every vial and container she could find.

Liv opened a drawer and took out a stack of notebooks. "Score."

"Whatcha got there?" Link asked.

She flipped through the pages of tiny handwriting and what looked to Link like math equations. "Notebooks and scientific logs. They must belong to whoever is conducting the experiments."

Link watched one of the blinking monitors, the zigzagged line of the girl's heartbeat stretching across the screen. "Hey, Liv. What's that blue stuff?"

A stream of glowing blue liquid rose from the IV in the girl's arm, filling a clear plastic bag hanging from an IV pole next to her bed. It reminded him of the glow of fireflies lighting up dark summer nights.

Angelique cringed and staggered back, as if she wanted to get as far away from the glowing blue stuff as possible.

"I didn't think Silas could be as sick as Abraham," John said softly. "But he's worse."

Angelique regained her composure, but she didn't get any closer to the IV. "Something I know firsthand."

Floyd walked over to the IV tube. "Is the blue liquid Silas is pumping out of her—"

"Her power," Liv finished, holding up the notebook. "It's all in the lab notes. Silas isn't wasting his time with genetics anymore. Now he's playing God."

Angelique fluttered her fingers. "Then that makes me the woman who is going to destroy Heaven. Burn it down, technically." She paused. "Which is fine with me."

"Let's stop talkin' about burnin' the place down till we find my girlfriend, okay?" Link asked.

Liv walked over to the shelves of metal canisters labeled with Caster powers, like NECROMANCY, DIVINATION, ILLUSION, PALIMPSESTRY. "Can you store power in containers like these? I think he's stockpiling."

John shook his head. "I grew up listening to enough of Abraham and Silas' crazy theories to know that. Power is a living entity, and it can only survive inside a living organism. It's a symbiotic relationship."

Angelique eyed Liv and Link coldly. "I'm sure the two of you are familiar with the terms. Mortals have all sorts of symbiotic relationships. It's not as if you people can survive on your own."

"Us people? You're getting a little personal, aren't you?" Liv sounded offended. "We all want the same thing. To stop Silas and right the incredible wrongs that have been perpetrated here."

John paced in front of the door. "If Silas is siphoning off their powers for his Frankenstein Caster experiments, where are the Casters he's putting them *into*?" *Like he did with Angelique*—that was the part he didn't say.

The Cataclyst shrugged. "I was already part of the Menagerie, so he took me right out of my cell. I don't know about the others before me. And honestly, I don't really care."

Liv looked up from the lab notes. "It says something in here about 'incubation' and 'long-term storage for SD Sample.' "

"Does it mention what kind of methods he's using?" Necro asked.

John peered through the window cut into the door. When he turned around again, he looked sick. "I'm not sure you want to know." He looked right at Link. "But you need to see this, man." He paused, frowning. "You all do."

Link worried that being back in the labs was messing with John's head more than he was letting on. Sure, this place was creepy, but they were in Silas Ravenwood territory, and he was even more twisted than Abraham.

"What kind of freak show does Silas have in there?" Link asked, making his way over to the door. "Vampires and werewolves?"

"Worse." John pushed the door open, and a trail of luminescent light stretched across the floor.

Link gave John a gentle whack on the shoulder as he walked by. "Everything's gonna be okay, dude."

John swallowed hard. "There's nothing okay about this. There never was." Liv slid her hand into his and squeezed it.

Link caught a glimpse of the room out of the corner of his eye.

What the hell?

It was dark inside, illuminated by hundreds of thin filaments hanging from the ceiling like glowing fishing lines. The lines were connected to what looked like magical cocoons spun from the same luminescent filament.

Link heard footsteps behind him, and someone gasped. He probably would've had the same reaction, except he was holding his breath, convinced the slightest sound might snap the magical strings and send the cocoons and their fragile contents crashing to the ground.

Their contents.

Link couldn't wrap his mind around what he was seeing—dozens of men, women, and guys and girls around his age hanging from the ceiling.

Angelique glided past him and walked to the center of the

room, her face tilted toward the human cocoons above her. "You've been busy since I left, haven't you, Silas? It's a regular factory in here."

"A power factory." Liv shuddered.

Floyd stumbled toward Angelique and Necro, who was already walking in the Cataclyst's direction. "What is he doing to them? They look dead."

"They'd probably wish they were if they had any awareness of what Silas was doing to them," Liv said.

"Which is?" Sampson asked, walking up behind Floyd.

Liv stared up at the imprisoned Casters. "Suspended animation."

Link followed John and Liv as they joined the others in the middle of the room, below the sea of bodies. He tried not to imagine one of them falling on him, but it was tough.

"It's all right here in the notes." Liv tapped on the page. "He's using them as incubators until he's ready to drain their powers. Then he moves them into the room we were just in to do the *extraction.*"

"And he has other rooms for the infusions," Angelique said.

"We've got to cut them down," Sampson said as Lucille wove her way between his ankles.

"Only if we want to kill them." Liv was still reading. "According to these notes, it's a Cast—the Dreamless Sleep. If you touch them without breaking the Cast first, they'll die."

"We can't leave them here like this," Floyd said.

"You're right." Sampson walked over to the steel drawers lining one side of the room and started pulling them open and rummaging through the contents one by one. "There has to be a way to help them."

"That's the problem with Mortals," Angelique said. "No sense of self-preservation. You're always so worried about everyone else. You're like Boy Scouts, and just as goofy. No wonder you're always getting yourselves killed." She swatted Liv on the back of the head as she walked by. "It's the way we get you every time. We give you a shiny ball to keep you occupied while we kill your friends...destroy the world...I'm sure you can fill in the blank." She pointed up at the bodies. "Those are the shiny balls. Would you rather stay here and try to break a Cast we know nothing about or find your friend?"

"Shut up," Link said.

"I'm laying out the odds for you, because they're not in your favor. What are you going to do, save the world? That only happens in Mortal movies."

Sam shut a metal drawer a little hard, and Link looked over at him. The Darkborn had a weird look on his face. "I found"—he held up a glass vial—"*something*."

Necro walked over and nudged him. "What kind of something, exactly?"

He handed her the vial. "Isn't that—?"

She nodded.

"What is it?" Liv asked, in the scientist-Keeper tone Link recognized. She took the tiny bottle out of Necro's palm and read the label. "'Infusion: Patient 12.'" Liv turned to Angelique. "This must've been your injection."

Angelique dismissed it with a wave. "Spare me the walk down memory lane. I don't care where it came from. I know where it is now."

"Turn it over, Liv," Necro said quietly.

The Keeper frowned, turning the vial between her fingers.

"Why? Is there—?" She gasped, the color draining from her face. "Oh my god."

"Liv? You okay?" Link asked, already knowing she wasn't and wondering just how bad it was.

"The power infusion Angelique was given... the sample code and the name of the Caster it was extracted from are printed on the back. It says 'SD Sample'—"

Liv's hand was shaking.

" 'Sarafine Duchannes.' "

CHAPTER 26: NOX

Rainbow in the Dark

Nox took a long look at the girl he loved.

He was thinking she needed a twelve-step program.

She was hooked on whatever Silas was pumping into her, which meant she wasn't leaving without her next fix. And that only left him with two choices—keep trying to talk her into leaving or stay here with her until she was ready to go.

Because leaving without her wasn't an option.

I'd let Silas kill me first.

He stared into her violet eyes one more time, squeezing her hand through the bars.

I've officially lost it.

And I know this is wrong.

I know she isn't mine.

But it doesn't matter, as long as I get to look at her and know she's okay—and as long as I get her out of here.

Who was he kidding? Nox was addicted to every single thing about Ridley Duchannes, and they both knew it.

She was his drug.

CHAPTER 27: RIDLEY

Powerslave

I need him.

As she held his hand, Ridley could feel his presence—the energy between them pulsed through her, a different kind of high. One she needed almost as badly as the infusions.

Almost.

When I'm with Nox, I'm more powerful, and I'm more aware of my own power.

Like needs like.

Power needs power.

Maybe it was the TFPs, or something from his Siren mother—she couldn't be sure. All she knew was that being with Nox made her sharper, clearer.

It made her a stronger version of her new self, and that was what she needed right now.

He was what she needed.

Nox's eyes searched hers. "Rid, I think we should leave. I know you want the next infusion, but I have a bad feeling about it. And you're powerful enough already."

She gave him a strange look. "You can never be too powerful. It's like saying you can be too rich or too beautiful. There's never too much."

He bit his lip, which made Ridley want to nibble on it and kiss him again.

And again and again.

What's wrong with me?

When was I ever like this about a boy?

A Caster boy?

Who wasn't Link, she thought, in spite of herself.

Who wasn't mine?

She didn't know if it was right or wrong, and she was starting to doubt if she even knew what was best for her.

I want what I want.

But what does that even mean now?

And who am I to discount the person I was before? All those years?

Even if I know that Nox is the right thing for me now?

She drew a breath.

There wasn't a second when she wasn't evaluating her options. Sooner or later, she'd have to make a decision. But that moment wasn't here yet.

"We'll be out of here soon enough," she reminded him. "You'll see."

She heard footsteps in the hallway. "Shh. Someone's coming."

A moment later, Ridley saw Silas' wing tips.

Ridley moved toward the bars, and Silas actually moved away.

He's afraid of me. She smiled.

"She startled me when she came in," Ridley said. "I didn't mean to hurt her."

Now it was Silas' turn to smile. "Of course you didn't. You haven't adjusted to how powerful you are yet." Silas rose and walked over to Ridley's cell. "It'll come, and if it doesn't, a few people get hurt every now and then."

"Mortals, yes. But Casters? You really are getting cold-hearted in your old age, Silas." Ridley shook her head.

"It's all the same to me. There's what I want and what stands in my way." He shrugged. "As long as you work with me, there's no problem. The moment you don't…" He shrugged again. "Who needs that?"

Ridley caught a glimpse of Nox as he moved closer to the door of his own cell. "You're a piece of crap, you know that, Silas? We both know you don't care about Ridley or anyone else. If she gets hurt from whatever you did—"

"It's okay, Nox." Ridley cut him off. "Silas isn't doing anything without my permission."

Her eyes narrowed, and she trained them on Silas. Snakes slithered up the bars, their tongues darting out of their mouths only inches from the Incubus' neck.

She was beginning to enjoy herself, and that worried her. "Remember who's in control here, Silas, or I'll have to remind you again."

"I'm not the one in the cell," Silas said, stupidly.

Ridley's cell door flung open. Silas flew back into the small square of space that had been her prison, while she stepped out. "Think again."

Silas rolled his eyes, reaching into his pocket and taking

out a cigar. He cut off the end and lit the Barbadian, taking a long pull. When he exhaled a thin stream of smoke, the snakes recoiled. "Of course not, my dear. No one is going to do anything without your consent. So do I have your consent?"

"Excuse me?" Ridley tried to ignore the rush she felt at the thought of whatever Silas was offering.

"It's time for another infusion." He paused. "Unless you don't *want* another one. In which case, I'll move on to a new subject."

"No," Ridley said, louder than she meant to. "I mean, I'm ready." She reached toward him and patted his cheek. "Just behave. That's all I ask. Give me my infusion and I'll be done with you before you know it."

"Like a partnership," he said, trying to manage a smile.

"Exactly," she lied, feeling the power burning in her veins.

Silas unlocked the cell and extended his arm. "Shall we?"

Let the little man put on his little airs.

Or not.

Just get what you want and go.

Ridley eyed his arm and then stepped past it. She wasn't interested in Silas' theatrics. She wanted whatever he had waiting for her in the lab—and nothing else.

"Rid, please don't do this," Nox pleaded, his hand stretched between the bars. "You don't need it."

But I do, she thought. *More than anything.*

And you need me to have it.

I'm more powerful like this, and the one thing we're going to need is power.

But she didn't say that.

She just smiled at him. "It's going to be fine, Baby. You'll see. I'll be back before you know it."

"I love you exactly the way you are," he called out. Within seconds, his face reddened and Ridley knew the words had just slipped out, as words do.

She smiled. "But I don't."

Ridley ignored the way his shoulders sagged and followed Silas down the hallway. "What kind of power am I getting this time?" she asked, her body trembling with anticipation.

Silas dropped the five-hundred-dollar cigar on the floor, only half-smoked. "I thought I'd surprise you."

Ridley relaxed. She loved surprises.

Surprises, and powers that didn't belong to her.

And possibly, for the very first time, Caster boys.

CHAPTER 28: LINK

At War with Satan

Angelique strode across the room and snatched the vial out of Liv's hand. She read the label—the one that said Sarafine Duchannes' Cataclyst powers were running through her veins.

She threw her head back, red curls whipping through the air, and laughed. "Do you have any idea what this means?"

"Yeah. We're screwed," Link muttered to himself.

But Angelique wasn't finished. "Most Casters consider Sarafine Duchannes the Darkest Caster who ever lived. Her powers were legendary."

The last comment appeared to snap Liv right out of the state of shock they all seemed to be sharing. "We're aware of that, you idiot."

John looked at Liv. "How could Silas have saved Sarafine's powers all this time if she's been dead? I thought he was keeping the Casters in those cocoons until he was ready to extract their powers and inject them into someone else. Angelique's only had her powers, what—? Weeks?"

Liv shook her head. "I have no idea how he did it. All I know is that those powers should've died with Sarafine."

Link was still trying to wrap his mind around the fact that some part of Ridley's murderous aunt was inside the Cataclyst standing a few feet away from him. "Ethan saw her die," he said.

Floyd touched his shoulder. "She is dead, right, Liv?"

"Yes." Liv sounded flustered. "Very dead. Ethan was very clear about it." She took a deep breath and looked at Link. "Whatever Silas did, he managed to do it without Sarafine—at least without her being alive."

Now that Link knew the truth, he realized the signs had been there all along.

The way Angelique flexed her fingers before she was about to use them...

And the way she fluttered them exactly as Sarafine had, just before she uncurled them...

The bloodlust, even the smartass comments—they were all things Link remembered about Sarafine Duchannes.

A Caster so Dark she burned her own house down, with her husband and daughter inside.

Lena, the daughter Sarafine tried to kill how many times?

Link had lost count a while ago.

God, what would Lena think of this? Link did not want to ever tell her.

Angelique glanced up at the glowing cocoons. "Well, this certainly has been enlightening, but I've got places to go and people to kill."

"Can you at least tell us where they might be keeping our friends, if they're here?" Sam asked. "You owe us that much."

"Actually, I owe you nothing." Angelique waved her hand casually. "But I'm not heartless. Just unstoppable."

Link headed for the door across the room from the one they'd come in through. He couldn't get away from creepy cocoons or Angelique and her Sarafine blood—or whatever it was—fast enough. The only person who seemed to want out even more was John, who was right on Link's heels, dragging Liv along with him.

The moment they entered the hallway, Angelique strode past them. "This place is bigger than it looks. Silas has private lab rooms, and the cells are in the dungeon."

"There's a dungeon?" Necro cringed.

"That's what we called it," Angelique said before turning back to Link. "If your girlfriend's here, he's probably keeping her there. But I only know the way to the cells and the lab room where he gave me my infusions."

Infusions. Cells. Link had trouble thinking about anything else as they followed Angelique through the gleaming white hallway and down a stone staircase that led underneath the building and into stone tunnels.

"Now I understand why they call it the dungeon," Necro whispered.

"Shh," John said. "I heard something."

Sam nodded. "Me, too. It sounds like a girl's voice."

It was all Link needed to hear. He bolted through the tunnel, his Chucks slapping against the stone floor.

I'm coming, Rid.

Within seconds, he saw the iron bars and rows of cells.

But when he reached the first cell and looked through the bars, his heart sank.

A pretty brunette scrambled away from the cell door and cowered in the corner.

"Hey, I'm not gonna hurt you." He tried to smile, but he couldn't. "I'm not one of Silas' guys. I'm here lookin' for my girlfriend. Her name's Ridley. Maybe you've seen her?"

Necro caught up with him just as a girl in another cell stepped forward.

"We know her," the girl said with a Russian accent. "The new one."

Link darted toward the bars. "Right. That one. Where is she? Is she okay?" He rushed through the tunnel, searching every cell. They were full of girls, but Ridley wasn't one of them.

"I see you found the Menagerie," Angelique said as she caught up with them. Liv, John, Floyd, and Sam were farther behind her, whispering to the terrified imprisoned girls. "Looks like Silas moved everyone."

"Angelique? Is that you?" Another girl approached the bars, craning her neck for a better view.

The Cataclyst walked over to the girl's cage. "Drew. It's nice to see you're still alive."

Relief spread across Drew's features. "I can't believe you came back for us."

The other girls were coming to the doors of their own cells now.

Angelique brought her fingers to her lips like she was trying not to laugh. "I didn't come back for you, Drew—or any of the rest of you," she said, looking around. "I came back for *me*. But it was fun catching up."

Necro stormed over to Angelique, who was reminding Link of Sarafine more and more by the minute. "We can't leave them here like animals."

"Rescuing people wasn't part of the deal, Necromancer." Angelique continued down the tunnel. "I don't need to add hero to my résumé. Again, those are the shiny balls. Not my thing."

Necro looked over at Link. "I'm not leaving without them."

Floyd shouldered her way past Link and stood next to her friend. "Me neither."

"We'll get you out somehow," Link said, staring at the Russian girl behind the bars. "I hate to ask you this, but do you know where Silas is keepin' Ridley? I've gotta find her."

The girl shook her head. "Our cells were all together for a while. Then Silas moved us."

"But they did it at night when it was pitch-black so we couldn't see where they were taking us," the other girl, Drew, added. "I guess Silas doesn't want anyone else escaping."

Link glanced down the tunnel as Angelique moved farther away. He didn't want to leave these girls, but he needed to find Rid. And the Cataclyst knew her way around, at least a little.

"Go." Floyd gave him a shove. "Find Ridley. Necro and I will take care of this."

"I can stay and Rip them out one at a time," John offered.

Necro shook her head. "Link might need you. You and Liv go with him. Sam will help us. We've got this."

Liv shook her head. "But how—?"

"I've picked a few locks before," Floyd said sheepishly. "I know my way around a prison."

Sam grinned. "And I've ripped a few doors off their hinges."

"Floyd and I are Dark Casters, after all," Necro added. "So

you probably shouldn't ask for the details. Now go." She gave Link a hard shove.

In that moment, Link loved her. Necro was a true friend, maybe the truest he'd ever had, besides Ethan. He didn't know how to tell her that, but he hoped she knew.

"Thanks," he said. It wasn't enough, but he didn't know what else to say. Instead, he took off after Angelique.

As Link ducked through a doorway after her, he realized there were worse things than unconscious Casters hanging from the ceiling from magical marionette strings and a Menagerie of girls locked in cages.

At least, there was one thing worse.

Silas Ravenwood.

"Crap." It slipped out right before Link started holding his breath. He didn't want to end up in some kind of hybrid Incubus cocoon.

"You can say that again," John muttered.

Silas' eyes narrowed, and the four Darkborns flanking him—including Chloe the Butcher—didn't look any happier to see them.

Angelique breezed over to the Blood Incubus. "Silas," she purred. "What an unpleasant surprise."

Silas lit a cigar, trying to look half as relaxed as Angelique genuinely seemed. "Can't be much of a surprise if you're breaking into my labs."

"We have a score to settle, and it's not my fault you hired..." The Cataclyst glared at Chloe. "*Ineffective* security."

Chloe lunged at Angelique, her hand closing around the Dark Caster's throat. With the flutter of Angelique's fingers, the Darkborn froze, wincing as her arm retracted involuntarily.

"Now, now," Angelique said. "Unless you want me to make you dance for us, I suggest you control yourself, Ms. Boucher."

Silas' eyes widened. "Chloe told me about your unusual ability. But I never would've believed it."

"Sounds like you lack imagination, Silas." Angelique closed her hand, releasing her hold on the Darkborn. "Although your handiwork on me and your little collection of caterpillars in the lab does make me wonder. It's a shame you won't live to see it through."

"Aren't you the least bit curious?" Silas asked.

Liv held up the book of lab notes. "We know exactly what you're trying to do. Drain Casters of their powers and inject them into other Casters—"

"Trying?" Silas raised an eyebrow. "I'm doing a lot more than trying, you stupid Mortal."

John charged at Silas, but Angelique threw up her arm to stop him.

"Tsk, tsk, Silas is mine, remember?"

The Blood Incubus noticed John for the first time. He'd been so focused on Angelique that he'd barely glanced at the rest of them. Silas pointed a ringed finger at John. "*You*. How dare you set foot on my family's property? We raised you—"

"Raised me?" John snapped. "You experimented on me."

Silas clenched his jaw, his expression murderous. "Actually, we engineered you like the animal you are. Bred you like a dog. And before this night is over, I'm going to put you down like one, too. You'll be sorry you killed my Grandfather Abraham."

"Umm, hello?" Link raised his hand like he was in summer school. "Technically, *I* killed him."

John clapped a hand on Link's shoulder. "We both did. It was a coordinated effort."

"This is all very interesting." Angelique yawned. "And by *interesting*, I mean boring." The wind picked up, blowing her red hair around her head like a fiery halo. "But Silas and I have some unfinished business." She turned to him. "The kind that ends with you lying dead on the floor. So how about a little fire and blood?" She cracked her knuckles, readying her fingers. "That's what you made me for, isn't it?"

"Angelique, I'm hurt." The Incubus held a hand over his chest. "I harvested that sample of Sarafine Duchannes' power a year ago, and I've been saving it all this time. Waiting for the right Caster—someone worthy of such a gift."

"I didn't ask for any gifts from you," she hissed. "Just like I didn't ask to be kidnapped and live in a cell. Or to be forced to use my powers when you rented me out to your disgusting friends in the Syndicate."

Silas dropped the cigar and snuffed it out with his wing tip. "That's where you're wrong. Sarafine's powers *are* a gift. Originally, I took the sample for research purposes, but when I realized how strong her powers were—the fact that a sample from her was equal to a full extraction from the other Dark Casters we drained—I couldn't waste them."

Angelique walked toward him, stopping only a few feet in front of him. "I'll consider it payment for services already rendered. Enough is enough."

"What if I can offer you something more valuable than revenge?" Silas sounded too calm for someone who was about to die, which made Link nervous.

"What's he doing?" Link whispered.

Liv didn't take her eyes off the Incubus. "Making a deal."

But Angelique didn't seem interested. "Nothing is more valuable than revenge."

"How about power?" Silas asked.

"Already have it," she countered. "Thanks to you, I have the power of the most dangerous Cataclyst in history running through my veins. I can even control this new breed of so-called immune Supernaturals. What more could a woman want?"

Silas stepped closer to the Dark Caster who was probably about to kill him. "I can think of a few things. An empire. Powers so potent that no one can touch you, including my other test subjects. Information on the scope of Sarafine Duchannes' powers."

Angelique tilted her head to the side, as if she was considering it.

"Don't listen to him," Link said. "He's just tryin' to save his own sorry ass."

Silas ignored Link, his black eyes locked on Angelique. "Oh, and one more thing." He paused for a moment. "How do you feel about immortality?"

CHAPTER 29: LINK

Bringin' on the Heartbreak

Link had been in enough trouble, enough times, to know he was knee-deep in it.

The moment Silas said the word *immortality*, the game changed.

Angelique's expression shifted, rage and bloodlust replaced by a different type of lust—the kind that involved cheating death.

Who wanted to die?

Who wanted to turn to dust in the earth, to be forgotten by the living?

Even Link understood the appeal.

If Silas isn't lying.

Either way, once Silas planted that seed in her mind, Link and his friends became expendable.

Link leaned closer to Liv and John. "We've gotta get outta here."

Liv nodded and opened her hand so Link could read something she'd written on her palm.

We're dead

"Meet me at the car wash," Link whispered to John, who nodded.

Silas rolled up his sleeves. "Do we have a deal, then?"

Angelique tossed her hair over her shoulder. "I want the details. I didn't see any immortality serum in your lab. Which makes me think you're all talk."

"This isn't the only lab, or the biggest. How do you feel about palm trees? Movie stars and the beach?"

He's talking about Los Angeles.

Angelique pointed at Chloe the Butcher. "Do we have to bring your pet? She's irritating."

Chloe leered.

Liv slipped her hand into John's, and Link inched closer to Lucille.

Silas nodded at Link and his friends. "I don't know. Are you planning to bring yours?"

Angelique glanced over her shoulder, as if she'd forgotten they were still standing there. "Do whatever you want with them."

She walked away.

Link stared, but there was nothing anyone could do to stop her.

Chloe smiled just as John nodded, his hand gripping Liv's. Link scooped up Lucille and Ripped faster than he ever had in his life.

Link and Lucille broke through the darkness and crashed to the floor. Lucille landed on her feet, but Link wasn't as lucky. He rolled over onto his side, his cheek pressed against the concrete. They were back in the hallway, but Link didn't see the door with the plastic car wash flaps.

Crap.

A moment later, John and Liv appeared.

"I was worried you weren't going to make it," John said. "The car wash is back that way."

Lucille strolled past him without so much as a look and took off, like she had a Sheer chasing her.

"Where the hell is she goin'?" Link shook his head. All he wanted to do was find Ridley and get out of this place. When they turned the corner, Link noticed another stone staircase leading down. "This has to lead back down to the dungeon."

When they reached the base of the steps, Link caught a glimpse of another row of barred doors at the end of the passage.

Rid?

He bolted toward the cell door without considering who else might be on the other side—Darkborns, Incubuses, or golden-eyed Casters. The one person he didn't expect to see was the guy staring back at him.

Lennox Gates.

"What are you doing here, Link?" Nox actually sounded concerned. Concerned, and a whole lot of things Link didn't have time to decode now.

But Link was speechless.

Did I really come all this way to rescue this fancy-pants rich boy?

Link looked around. All he could think about was finding Ridley, which meant actually speaking to Nox. He walked over to Nox's cell. "Where's Rid? Have you seen her?"

Come on. Say yes. Please say yes.

Nox cleared his throat. "About Ridley..."

John and Liv walked over, and John rested a hand on Link's shoulder.

"What about her?" Link could barely choke out the words. "Is she alive?"

"Yeah, sorry. I didn't mean for you to think she was gone." Nox scrubbed his hands over his face. He seemed to be having a hard time saying whatever it was he was trying to tell Link.

"Is she okay?" Liv asked finally.

"Silas took her a while ago. Said he was taking her to one of the private lab rooms." Nox looked like he wanted to throw up.

"Why would he take her there?" Link grabbed the bars, wishing he could rip the door off like Sampson. Deep down, he already knew what Nox was going to say.

Nox stared at the floor. "It's one of the places he conducts his—"

"Experiments," Link finished.

Nox nodded. "Rid's been through a lot. She's...changed. I don't know how to explain it better than that." He looked at Link. "I didn't do this, and I didn't ask for this. You need to know that."

Why is he telling me this? Link wondered. *Why doesn't he just shut up?*

John's eyes darted toward the staircase. "Someone's coming."

Link braced himself. After what Nox had just told him, he was ready to kill someone.

A moment later, Lucille trotted into the tunnel, with Necro, Floyd, and Sam behind her.

"Nox!" Floyd rushed to the cell the moment she saw him. "Are you okay?"

Liv looked behind Sam. "Where are the girls?"

"Headed far away from here," Necro said, smiling proudly at Sampson. "Sam helped a little."

"How did you get them out so fast?" Liv asked.

"We ran into this old lady who knew Nox," Necro explained. "She said she helped him find his way here. Mrs. Blackwell—?"

"Blackburn," Nox said.

"I guess she'd been trying to find a way to help them, but she couldn't open the cells." Sam shrugged. "Since we covered that part, she told us to come help you."

"She's an old friend," Nox said sadly. "I owe her everything."

Link didn't have to ask how Necro, Floyd, and Sam had found them, not when they'd walked in behind Lucille. He had noticed that she had scampered off after they Ripped.

Necro looked around. "Where's Ridley?"

Link looked at Nox. "You tell them."

"Silas injected her with an Illusionist's powers and I don't even know what else." Nox shook his head and looked at Link. "And it changed her."

"Changed her *how*?" Link waited for the rich boy to answer him, but someone else did first.

"For the better, if I do say so myself. Think of it as a makeover."

Link spun around.

Ridley walked toward them. Everything about her seemed different and yet the same. From the sultriness in her voice to the calculating expression on her face, it was all her but more pronounced. Like Ridley was more...just more, somehow.

But one thing was definitely different.

Her eyes.

The gold Dark Caster eyes he'd stared into so many times were a violent purple now.

It doesn't matter. It's still Rid, and she's okay.

Link moved toward her, encircling her in his arms. It was so good to be near her.

She was warm and full of life, and love—

But when he pulled back and looked at her again, she seemed different.

She's been through so much. It's a miracle she's alive.

"I thought you were dead, Rid. You don't know how happy I am to see you." He noticed the strange way she was looking at him, like she was scared. But he ignored it and slung his arm around her neck anyway. Ridley recoiled like he'd tossed a pot of boiling water all over her.

"What's that smell?" She covered her nose and mouth, angling her body away from him. "It's like you dragged a rotting body in here."

Link sniffed under his arm.

Maybe she's messing with me.

But the way she was holding her arm out to push him away definitely didn't make it seem like that.

"I don't know," Link said. "We were around a buncha Sheers in this house in New Orleans where they were murdered. Can you smell dead people now? That's kinda cool, I guess."

The thought gave Link the creeps, but he didn't want to make her feel bad.

Liv walked toward them slowly, watching Ridley as she moved closer. When Liv was a few feet from Link, Ridley gagged and stumbled away from them.

"You smell even worse than he does. Don't come any closer. Please." Ridley braced herself against the wall with one arm and dry-heaved.

Liv froze. "Oh my gosh."

"What?" Link knew he was missing something important.

Liv backed away and tugged Link's sleeve, giving Ridley some space.

"John," Liv said, waving him over. "Can you and Sampson come over here?"

Sampson and John walked over and stood next to Liv and Link.

"What's going on?" John asked.

Liv nodded in Ridley's direction. "Keep walking."

Sampson and John exchanged a confused look and did as Liv asked.

Ridley had caught her breath by now, and she didn't react at all as the hybrid and the Darkborn approached. "Am I under arrest?" she teased.

"Want to tell us what we're doing?" John looked back at Liv.

"Testing a theory," she said quietly.

"What kind of theory?" Link asked. "What the hell's goin' on, Liv? Why can't we get near Rid without makin' her want to puke?"

Liv looked away. "I think it's because we're both Mortal—at least, part Mortal."

Link's stomach twisted into a knot, and for a second, he thought *he* might puke. "That can't be right." He shook his head. "Tell her she's wrong, Rid."

Ridley kept her distance and tossed her pink-streaked blond hair over her shoulder casually. "Makes sense to me."

The way she said it was almost like she didn't care.

"But what about us, Rid? How are we gonna fix it?" Link swallowed hard, a sinking feeling settling inside him.

She looked troubled, avoiding his eyes. "We aren't. It was good while it lasted, Hot Rod. But things are different now."

"Rid, we can figure this out. Maybe there's some kinda antidote or somethin'." Link knew he was begging, but he didn't care.

Everyone turned away like they were watching a car crash.

"You don't get it, Shrinky Dink. I'm not the same person."

"Then who are you?" Link was hurt and confused, but he wanted to understand. He hadn't come all this way for nothing.

Ridley looked away. "To be honest, I feel like throwing up. I need some air."

Link shook his head. "I don't know what Silas did to you, but deep down, you're still the same girl."

"Hardly," she said. "I don't know what I am. Not anymore." She had never spoken more honestly in her life.

Link ran his hand through his spiky hair. "I know who you are. You're the girl who gives me a hard time and won't let me call her *Babe*. The girl who lives to torture my mom, but who's always there for the people she cares about."

Ridley shrugged. "What kind of torture are we talking about? You know, so I can picture it."

She smiled at him, but she wasn't with him. Not really.

Link reached into his pocket and took out something he'd been saving.

A cherry lollipop.

He held it between them.

"The girl who loves cherry lollipops." He took a deep breath. "And me."

Link realized she probably couldn't stand to get close enough to take it from him, so he laid it on the floor and backed away.

Ridley walked toward it slowly, her eyes darting between him and the lollipop. When she finally reached the red and white wrapper, she stopped.

She's gonna pick it up.

Link's heart swelled.

Ridley stared at him—and then at Nox, who wasn't saying a word. In fact, it looked like he'd rather be anywhere in the world other than where they were right now.

But it was time.

"Rid. Just tell me. Do you love me?" Link asked.

Ridley said nothing.

He swallowed.

"Do you love me? Even a little?" It was the same question Link had asked her on the highway, when they were trying to get away from New York City.

Before the accident.

Ridley looked him in the eye and stepped on the lollipop, crushing it under her platform shoe. "I don't know. I don't think so. Not anymore." She leaned closer, dropping her voice to almost a whisper. "There's nothing sweet about me anymore, Shrinky Dink."

"What?" He couldn't believe what he was hearing.

"I don't want to be sweet. That girl is gone. She's dead. Silas Ravenwood killed her."

In that one moment, Link's world imploded. Every dream he'd ever had—everything he'd ever cared about—since the day he met Ridley Duchannes died.

As John Ripped the rest of them out of the labs and away from Silas and Angelique and New Orleans, Link felt like part of him died, too.

The sweetest part.

But Link refused to leave.

He'd Rip himself out of there when he was ready. For now, all he could do was sit alone in the prison cell where Ridley Duchannes had destroyed him.

Link stared at the prison bars, the plaster ceiling, and the frail little bed.

How can I blame her? Who knows what they did to her in here?

Then something caught his eye.

Letters, scratched into the nightstand.

LINK

She wrote my name.

That was when he realized Rid hadn't forgotten him.

She had been stolen from him, and he'd do anything to get her back.

Because Ridley Duchannes is my *girl.*

Nothing could ever make him forget about her, and he swore that someday she'd remember him the same way. It wasn't a promise.

It was a Binding, even stronger than the ring he was wearing around his finger.

When he held up his hand and looked at it, the ring glowed green for the very first time since he saw her.

This was his vow.

Even if she would be the last to know it.

CHAPTER 30: NOX

Heaven and Hell

Nox stood across from Ridley, staring into those hypnotic violet eyes—speechless. They were still standing outside the cells.

Rid had refused to leave with Link, and from what Nox could tell, she'd seemed physically repulsed by the Mortal part of him.

Something he can't change.

Ever.

"What's wrong, Baby?" She hooked her fingers through Nox's belt loops.

"What kind of power did Silas give you this time, Rid?"

Her eyes sparkled at the mention of the infusion, and Nox felt sick. The look in her eyes reminded him of the Chemist and the Shine.

Rid nuzzled close to his ear. "It's a surprise." Her lips grazed his, and he couldn't think about anything else but her. "You like my surprises, don't you?"

"I love everything about you, Rid."

He spoke words she expected to hear, even though he felt miserable saying them. Because they were the truth.

Even now. Always.

Nox deepened the kiss and lost himself in her.

"I hate to interrupt," a voice said from behind them, and Nox almost jumped out of his skin.

He turned around. "Mrs. Blackburn? What are you doing here?"

"The right thing," she said. "Something I should've done for your mother all those years ago."

"Nox, who is this lady?" Rid asked.

"She works for Silas, and she worked for Abraham before him—I've known her since I was a kid."

Ridley only nodded.

"We don't have time for introductions," Mrs. Blackburn said. "I need to get you two out of here. Silas is heading to his lab in LA with one of the other Casters he experimented on." She shook her head. "He said he could make her immortal."

Ridley's head snapped up when she heard the word. "Are you positive that's what he said?"

Mrs. Blackburn frowned. "I may be old, but I'm not deaf."

Rid's eyes lit up, and Nox's spirits sank.

Immortality?

She looked mesmerized.

Nox grabbed her hand. "Come on, Rid. You said we could leave after... you know, it was finished."

Ridley gave him a quick kiss, a viper curling around her neck. "I'm done here."

"How are we going to get past Silas' guards?" Nox asked the old Caster.

"We aren't." The cook headed down the hallway, with Nox and Ridley on her heels. "I'm taking you through the Tunnel that leads to the house. Leave the same way you came, and you'll end up at the Mile."

"Thank you," Nox said.

"I owe it to you. You, and your mother."

"There's a Tunnel that leads into the house?" Rid asked. "Are you sure?"

"Of course I'm sure. Who do you think cooks all the meals for Silas' research staff?"

Mrs. Blackburn led them to her secret Tunnel like she promised, and when they reached the Outer Door inside Silas' house, she gave Nox a quick hug. "You know it's your job to get that girl right again, don't you?" she whispered.

He nodded.

It's all I think about.

It's the only thing that matters.

Whether or not it means she stays with me.

Ridley and Nox didn't stop again until they were safely out of Silas' house and in the Tunnels. It was the first time he felt like they actually had a chance.

He pulled Ridley against him. "So where do you want to go?"

She tilted her head, as if she was deciding. "I'm thinking LA."

Nox felt like someone had punched him in the gut.

LA.

The place where Silas has a bigger lab, and she can get a bigger fix.

"You heard Mrs. Blackburn. Silas is going to LA. We should stay as far away from there as we can."

Ridley rolled her eyes. "Oh, please. It's a *huge* city, with a serious music scene. You can open another club—the kind with no address, where people have to know someone to get an invite."

"I don't want to go to LA, Rid. Pick anywhere else." He needed to stand his ground, but it felt like he was already sinking in quicksand.

Ridley moved closer, her violet eyes searching his. "I want to be with you, Nox. Don't you get that? This is our chance." Her expression hardened. "But *I'm* going to LA. Are you coming with me or not?"

Nox thought about his mom—how disappointed she'd be if she knew about all the bad decisions he'd made—and all the terrible things he'd done.

All the things I'll end up doing if I go to LA. Not to mention potentially messing with Silas Ravenwood and Ridley's psycho Cataclyst aunt.

Ridley was offering him love, gift-wrapped in an addiction he couldn't begin to understand. But for the first time in his life, Nox had a chance to start over. Disappear and do the right things—be a better man.

A man I can be proud of.

There was only one problem. Ridley wasn't the only one with an addiction. Nox couldn't live without her any more than he could survive without oxygen.

So he made a decision that would change everything. He

stopped worrying about being a better man and focused on being the man Ridley Duchannes loved—the one she wanted to run away with to LA. The one who'd lured a Siren and her clueless boyfriend to New York without thinking twice. Guilt was a sucker's emotion.

Who cares where we go? As long as I have her.

Nox took Rid's hand, lacing his fingers between hers. "When do we leave?"

She smiled and pushed up on her toes to kiss him.

Nox felt a snake wrapping itself around their wrists.

Binding them together.

AFTER

Ridley

Here's the thing.

There are certain times when a girl hates herself.

You know that.

When she teases a guy she has no interest in being with.

When she pretends to be stupider than she is, or more innocent, or whatever it is the boy she loves wants her to be.

When she has to tell her boyfriend about all the boys she's kissed or loved before him.

When she sees that look in his eyes—the look that says he thought he was the only one, that he had always been the only one.

It's all pretty dull, but it's life.

So here's what I want you to know:

I'm *not* that girl.

I think I've been perfectly clear about that.

I will always disappoint you.

You, and everyone else.

That's the girl I am.

The one people whisper about.

The scandal.

The problem.

I'm fine with that.

But know this—and I don't know if you're listening, and I don't know if you care—there was a boy named Wesley Lincoln, once.

And I loved him, with my whole heart, and maybe even part of my soul. I imagined a future with houses and children and all sorts of things I had no right imagining.

He gave me a ring once, and I pretended it meant something different than it did.

But that life isn't for me.

I know that now.

I'm not that girl.

I didn't deserve him, and I never will.

I deserve lots of things—the destruction of men and boys—the cataclysm of worlds—the end of the New Order, possibly. The heart of a certain Dark Caster.

But I want you to know, just between us, that I lost something.

That there was something I wanted.

Even if it was something I knew I could never have.

There was a boy, an ordinary boy, and he was my heart.

Now I have no heart.

That's my story.

I hope yours ends differently, but I doubt it will.

Acknowledgments

Team Dangerous Creatures is a talented and dedicated group that has worked tirelessly to continue Link and Ridley's story in *Dangerous Deception.* This book would not be in your hands today without them.

Our agents, Jodi Reamer (and everyone at Writers House, on behalf of Kami) and Sarah Burnes (and everyone at the Gernert Company, on behalf of Margie), have supported us from the moment we dreamed up the Dangerous Creatures novels.

Our editors, Erin Stein (for Kami) and Kate Sullivan and Pam Gruber (for Margie), as well as our former editor, Julie Scheina, are brilliant and dangerous creatures themselves. We believe that all four of you have Caster powers.

The publishing, sales, editorial, marketing, publicity, school and library services, digital, art, and managing editorial teams at Little, Brown Books for Young Readers have worked tirelessly on behalf of Casters everywhere. Ridley and Link thank you.

SallyAnne McCartin and Jacqui Daniels of McCartin-Daniels PR brought energy and creativity to the world of Dangerous Creatures. Thank you for joining the party.

Our behind the scenes team and assistants, Erin Gross, Chloe Palka, Nicole Robertson, Victoria Hill, Zelda Wengrod, Emma Peterson, and Rachel Lindee, have done everything from typing and research to keeping us on track (and offline) to cheerleading; and our Latin translator, May Peterson, makes sure the Casts actually mean what we think they do.

Our reader, writer, teacher, librarian, bookseller, journalist, and social media friends have been with us, and have stayed with us, since the beginning—and we are so grateful.

But the love and support of our families make everything in our lives possible. We love you more than we can ever express.

Alex, Nick & Stella and Lewis, Emma, May & Kate: We'll save all our best songs for you.

You truly are Beautiful Creatures.

XO,

Kami & Margie

Read on for a taster of *Beautiful Creatures* and discover where Ridley and Link's story began . . .

⟡ BEFORE ⟡

The Middle of Nowhere

There were only two kinds of people in our town. "The stupid and the stuck," my father had affectionately classified our neighbors. "The ones who are bound to stay or too dumb to go. Everyone else finds a way out." There was no question which one he was, but I'd never had the courage to ask why. My father was a writer, and we lived in Gatlin, South Carolina, because the Wates always had, since my great-great-great-great-granddad, Ellis Wate, fought and died on the other side of the Santee River during the Civil War.

Only folks down here didn't call it the Civil War. Everyone under the age of sixty called it the War Between the States, while everyone over sixty called it the War of Northern Aggression, as if somehow the North had baited the South into war over a bad bale of cotton. Everyone, that is, except my family. We called it the Civil War.

Just another reason I couldn't wait to get out of here.

Gatlin wasn't like the small towns you saw in the movies, unless it was a movie from about fifty years ago. We were too far from Charleston to have a Starbucks or a McDonald's. All we had was a Dar-ee Keen, since the Gentrys were too cheap to buy all new letters when they bought the Dairy King. The library still had a card catalog, the high school still had chalkboards, and our community pool was Lake Moultrie, warm brown water and all. You could see a movie at the Cineplex about the same time it came out on DVD, but you had to hitch a ride over to Summerville, by the community college. The shops were on Main, the good houses were on River, and everyone else lived south of Route 9, where the pavement disintegrated into chunky concrete stubble—terrible for walking, but perfect for throwing at angry possums, the meanest animals alive. You never saw that in the movies.

Gatlin wasn't a complicated place; Gatlin was Gatlin. The neighbors kept watch from their porches in the unbearable heat, sweltering in plain sight. But there was no point. Nothing ever changed. Tomorrow would be the first day of school, my sophomore year at Stonewall Jackson High, and I already knew everything that was going to happen—where I would sit, who I would talk to, the jokes, the girls, who would park where.

There were no surprises in Gatlin County. We were pretty much the epicenter of the middle of nowhere.

At least, that's what I thought, when I closed my battered copy of *Slaughterhouse-Five*, clicked off my iPod, and turned out the light on the last night of summer.

Turns out, I couldn't have been more wrong.

There was a curse.

There was a girl.

And in the end, there was a grave.

I never even saw it coming.

02.9

Dream On

Falling.

I was free falling, tumbling through the air.

"Ethan!"

She called to me, and just the sound of her voice made my heart race.

"Help me!"

She was falling, too. I stretched out my arm, trying to catch her. I reached out, but all I caught was air. There was no ground beneath my feet, and I was clawing at mud. We touched fingertips and I saw green sparks in the darkness.

Then she slipped through my fingers, and all I could feel was loss.

Lemons and rosemary. I could smell her, even then.

But I couldn't catch her.

And I couldn't live without her.

I sat up with a jerk, trying to catch my breath.

"Ethan Wate! Wake up! I won't have you bein' late on the first day a school." I could hear Amma's voice calling from downstairs.

My eyes focused on a patch of dim light in the darkness. I could hear the distant drum of the rain against our old plantation shutters. It must be raining. It must be morning. I must be in my room.

My room was hot and damp, from the rain. Why was my window open?

My head was throbbing. I fell back down on the bed, and the dream receded as it always did. I was safe in my room, in our ancient house, in the same creaking mahogany bed where six generations of Wates had probably slept before me, where people didn't fall through black holes made of mud, and nothing ever actually happened.

I stared up at my plaster ceiling, painted the color of the sky to keep the carpenter bees from nesting. What was wrong with me?

I'd been having the dream for months now. Even though I couldn't remember all of it, the part I remembered was always the same. The girl was falling. I was falling. I had to hold on, but I couldn't. If I let go, something terrible would happen to her. But that's the thing. I couldn't let go. I couldn't lose her. It was like I was in love with her, even though I didn't know her. Kind of like love *before* first sight.

Which seemed crazy because she was just a girl in a dream. I didn't even know what she looked like. I had been having the dream for months, but in all that time I had never seen her face, or I couldn't remember it. All I knew was that I had the same sick feeling inside every time I lost her. She slipped through my fingers, and my stomach dropped right out of me—the way you feel when you're on a roller coaster and the car takes a big drop.

Butterflies in your stomach. That was such a crappy metaphor. More like killer bees.

Maybe I was losing it, or maybe I just needed a shower. My earphones were still around my neck, and when I glanced down at my iPod, I saw a song I didn't recognize.

Sixteen Moons.

What was that? I clicked on it. The melody was haunting. I couldn't place the voice, but I felt like I'd heard it before.

> *Sixteen moons, sixteen years*
> *Sixteen of your deepest fears*
> *Sixteen times you dreamed my tears*
> *Falling, falling through the years . . .*

It was moody, creepy—almost hypnotic.

"Ethan Lawson Wate!" I could hear Amma calling up over the music.

I switched it off and sat up in bed, yanking back the covers. My sheets felt like they were full of sand, but I knew better.

It was dirt. And my fingernails were caked with black mud, just like the last time I had the dream.

I crumpled up the sheet, pushing it down in the hamper under yesterday's sweaty practice jersey. I got in the shower and tried to forget about it as I scrubbed my hands, and the last black bits of my dream disappeared down the drain. If I didn't think about it, it wasn't happening. That was my approach to most things the past few months.

But not when it came to her. I couldn't help it. I always thought about her. I kept coming back to that same dream, even though I couldn't explain it. So that was my secret, all there was to tell. I was sixteen years old, I was falling in love with a girl who didn't exist, and I was slowly losing my mind.

No matter how hard I scrubbed, I couldn't get my heart to stop pounding. And over the smell of the Ivory soap and the Stop & Shop shampoo, I could still smell it. Just barely, but I knew it was there.

Lemons and rosemary.

I came downstairs to the reassuring sameness of everything. At the breakfast table, Amma slid the same old blue and white china plate—Dragonware, my mom had called it—of fried eggs, bacon, buttered toast, and grits in front of me. Amma was our housekeeper, more like my grandmother, except she was smarter and more ornery than my real grandmother. Amma had practically raised me, and she felt it was her personal mission to grow me another foot or so, even though I was already 6'2". This morning I was strangely starving, like I hadn't eaten in a week. I shoveled an egg and two pieces of bacon off my plate, feeling better already. I grinned at her with my mouth full.

"Don't hold out on me, Amma. It's the first day of school." She slammed a giant glass of OJ and a bigger one of milk—whole milk, the only kind we drink around here—in front of me.

"We out of chocolate milk?" I drank chocolate milk the way some people drank Coke or coffee. Even in the morning, I was always looking for my next sugar fix.

"A. C. C. L. I. M. A. T. E." Amma had a crossword for everything, the bigger the better, and liked to use them. The way she spelled the words out on you letter by letter, it felt like she was paddling you in the head, every time. "As in, get used to it. And don't you think about settin' one foot out that door till you drink the milk I gave you."

"Yes, ma'am."

"I see you dressed up." I hadn't. I was wearing jeans and a faded T-shirt, like I did most days. They all said different things; today it was *Harley Davidson.* And the same black Chuck Taylors I'd had going on three years now.

"I thought you were gonna cut that hair." She said it like a scolding, but I recognized it for what it really was: plain old affection.

"When did I say that?"

"Don't you know the eyes are the windows to the soul?"

"Maybe I don't want anyone to have a window into mine."

Amma punished me with another plate of bacon. She was barely five feet tall and probably even older than the Dragonware, though every birthday she insisted she was turning fifty-three. But Amma was anything but a mild-mannered old lady. She was the absolute authority in my house.

"Well, don't think you're goin' out in this weather with wet hair. I don't like how this storm feels. Like somethin' bad's been kicked up into the wind, and there's no stoppin' a day like that. It has a will a its own."

I rolled my eyes. Amma had her own way of thinking about things. When she was in one of these moods, my mom used to call it going dark—religion and superstition all mixed up, like it can only be in the South. When Amma went dark, it was just better to stay out of her way. Just like it was better to leave her charms on the windowsills and the dolls she made in the drawers where she put them.

I scooped up another forkful of egg and finished the breakfast of champions—eggs, freezer jam, and bacon, all smashed into a toast sandwich. As I shoved it into my mouth, I glanced down the hallway out of habit. My dad's study door was already shut. My dad wrote at night and slept on the old sofa in his study all day. It had been like that since my mom died last April. He might as well be a vampire; that's what my Aunt Caroline had said after she stayed with us that spring. I had probably missed my chance to see him until tomorrow. There was no opening that door once it was closed.

I heard a honk from the street. Link. I grabbed my ratty black backpack and ran out the door into the rain. It could have been seven at night as easily as seven in the morning, that's how dark the sky was. The weather had been weird for a few days now.

Link's car, the Beater, was in the street, motor sputtering, music blasting. I'd ridden to school with Link every day since kindergarten, when we became best friends after he gave me half his Twinkie on the bus. I only found out later it had fallen on the floor. Even though we had both gotten our licenses this summer, Link was the one with the car, if you could call it that.

At least the Beater's engine was drowning out the storm.

Amma stood on the porch, her arms crossed disapprovingly. "Don't you play that loud music here, Wesley Jefferson Lincoln. Don't think I won't call your mamma and tell her what you were doin' in the basement all summer when you were nine years old."

Link winced. Not many people called him by his real name, except his mother and Amma. "Yes, ma'am." The screen door slammed. He laughed, spinning his tires on the wet asphalt as we pulled away from the curb. Like we were making a getaway, which was pretty much how he always drove. Except we never got away.

"What did you do in my basement when you were nine years old?"

"What didn't I do in your basement when I was nine years old?" Link turned down the music, which was good, because it was terrible and he was about to ask me how I liked it, like he did every day. The tragedy of his band, Who Shot Lincoln, was that none of them could actually play an instrument or sing. But all he could talk about was playing the drums and moving to New York after graduation and record deals that would probably never happen. And by probably, I mean he was more likely to sink a three-pointer, blindfolded and drunk, from the parking lot of the gym.

Link wasn't about to go to college, but he still had one up on me. He knew what he wanted to do, even if it was a long shot. All I had was a whole shoebox full of college brochures I couldn't show my dad. I didn't care which colleges they were, as long as they were at least a thousand miles from Gatlin.

I didn't want to end up like my dad, living in the same house, in the same small town I'd grown up in, with the same people who had never dreamed their way out of here.

On either side of us, dripping old Victorians lined the street, almost the same as the day they were built over a hundred years ago. My street was called Cotton Bend because these old houses used to back up to miles and miles of plantation cotton fields. Now they just backed up to Route 9, which was about the only thing that had changed around here.

I grabbed a stale doughnut from the box on the floor of the car. "Did you upload a weird song onto my iPod last night?"

"What song? What do you think a this one?" Link turned up his latest demo track.

"I think it needs work. Like all your other songs." It was the same thing I said every day, more or less.

"Yeah, well, your face will need some work after I give you a good beatin'." It was the same thing he said every day, more or less.

I flipped through my playlist. "The song, I think it was called something like *Sixteen Moons*."

"Don't know what you're talkin' about." It wasn't there. The song was gone, but I had just listened to it this morning. And I knew I hadn't imagined it because it was still stuck in my head.

"If you wanna hear a song, I'll play you a new one." Link looked down to cue the track.

"Hey, man, keep your eyes on the road."

But he didn't look up, and out of the corner of my eye, I saw a strange car pass in front of us. . . .

For a second, the sounds of the road and the rain and Link dissolved into silence, and it was like everything was moving in slow motion. I couldn't drag my eyes away from the car. It was just a feeling, not anything I could describe. And then it slid past us, turning the other way.

I didn't recognize the car. I had never seen it before. You can't imagine how impossible that is, because I knew every single car in town. There were no tourists this time of year. They wouldn't take the chance during hurricane season.

This car was long and black, like a hearse. Actually, I was pretty sure it was a hearse.

Maybe it was an omen. Maybe this year was going to be worse than I thought.

"Here it is. 'Black Bandanna.' This song's gonna make me a star."

By the time he looked up, the car was gone.